Praise for *The Placebo Effect*

"This novel heats up and never stops."   *—The Globe and Mail*

"The success of his epic novel *Shanghai*, which was published in 2008, demonstrated that Rotenberg could break away from convention without loosening his hold on the imagination of his readers. Rotenberg blends the best of [his previous] books in his latest effort, *The Placebo Effect*."   *—National Post*

"*The Placebo Effect* . . . is a thoughtful, challenging novel masquerading as a . . . thriller."   *—Quill & Quire*

"A moody speculative-fiction thriller."   *—The Winnipeg Free Press*

Praise for *Shanghai*

"*Shanghai* is heart pounding and brutal. It puts you right into the thick of the city, its people, its passions."   —Jurgen Gothe, *NUVO* magazine

"Rotenberg's Shanghai . . . is a place full of effective, unexpected entertainment.   *—Publishers Weekly*

"*Shanghai* is jam-packed with story and adventure."   *—Maclean's*

A MURDER
OF CROWS

Second Book of the Junction Chronicles

DAVID ROTENBERG

A TOUCHSTONE BOOK
Published by Simon & Schuster
New York   London   Toronto   Sydney   New Delhi

 ★ Touchstone
A Division of Simon & Schuster, Inc.
1230 Avenue of the Americas
New York, NY 10020

This book is a work of fiction. Names, characters, places, and incidents either are products of the author's imagination or are used fictitiously. Any resemblance to actual events or locales or persons, living or dead, is entirely coincidental.

First Touchstone hardcover edition February 2013

TOUCHSTONE and colophon are registered trademarks of Simon & Schuster, Inc.

For information about special discounts for bulk purchases, please contact Simon & Schuster Special Sales at 1-800-268-3216 or customerservice@simonandschuster.ca.

Manufactured in the United States of America

10 9 8 7 6 5 4 3 2 1

ISBN 978-1-4391-7013-7
ISBN 978-1-4391-7265-0 (ebook)

I'd like to thank three doctors who are helping me through some pretty trying times:

Dr. Laurence Klotz, who goes the extra yard for me
Dr. Kasra Khorasani, who helps me keep my mind from going into overdrive
Dr. Ken Lipinski, who offers consultation and words of wisdom whenever I ask
To the three of you, this one's here because of your help.

And as always there would be no books without Susan, Joey and Beth.

The gods themselves cannot recall their gifts.

—Alfred, Lord Tennyson

For fear of nightmares
Humanity will abandon dreaming.
Just watch 'em.

—graffiti on Canal Street subway wall circa 1979

1

THOUGHTS AT T MINUS 12 DAYS, 4 HOURS AND 16 SECONDS

This is a foolish country. And this town with its obsessively symmetrical old church is ridiculous.

These people believe they will live forever. They hide death behind walls and bury it in places with names like Pleasant Valley and Peaceful Rest. We in the East know that death is neither pleasant nor restful.

Perhaps we spend too much time thinking about our deaths—but death is real. It is the only certainty. And to refuse to confront a certainty is a foolishness. A foolishness that all these Americans will be forced to abandon when we force them to understand that Judgement awaits everyone—everyone.

Look at all these kids and their parents. Look at them. So self-satisfied. So convinced they are special—the chosen ones. And they all love America. Well, why not? America is going to make most of these privileged kids rich. While backed by their military might this horror of a country makes the rest of the world its slaves. And these science profs up there on the stage invented much of the military prowess of this country while these students all around me are preparing to take their places.

All are soldiers of the oppressor.

But there will be justice—even here, on this pampered campus in upper New York State there will be justice. It will come. As surely as putting potassium permanganate together with glycerin will cause a massive explosion—it will come.

2

A BOUNTY OF GIFTS—BEFORE

LEONARD HARRISON, HEAD OF THE NSA, A TOMMY LEE JONES without the snark—or the smile—was hiding something.

He's always hiding something, Special Agent Yslan Hicks thought, but she wasn't going to be drawn into guessing what the hell it was. So she leaned back in her chair—and waited.

Finally he reached into his briefcase and pulled out her latest report and dropped it on her desk.

"Something wrong with it?" she asked.

"No. It's perfect—like all your work—perfect . . . as far as it goes."

"Meaning what?" Then she quickly added, "sir."

"Meaning that you've accurately stated what we know about the synaesthetes we've been tracking."

She nodded for him to complete his thought.

He didn't.

So she prompted, "Yes?"

"But we don't know very much do we, Special Agent Hicks? After six years of tracking and investigating and spending millions of dollars, what do we really know?"

"Names, addresses, abilities—"

"And which ones are of no use to us."

"Yes. Silly synaesthetes."

"Knowing the smell of colours hardly helps us keep the homeland safe."

"We agreed on that long ago and removed them from our database."

"Leaving us with . . . our special synaesthetes."

Yslan thought about that for a second, then said, "If they actually are synaesthetes."

"Agreed. But we had to call them something."

"Why not just call them what they are—gifted. Call them the Gifted."

"Semantics." He was suddenly angry. He was bright, diligent and incredibly detailed in his analysis, but when those qualities failed to solve a problem he seemed to somehow fall and his anger bloomed. As it did now. "Go through them one at a time for me," he said, pointing at the file.

"It's all—"

"I know it's all in there, but I want to hear it in your own words."

He leaned against the window, the Lincoln Memorial over his shoulder, and Special Agent Yslan Hicks began to speak about what had become her life's work—her special synaesthetes—the Gifted.

3

A VAGARY OF VEGAS—T EQUALS 1 MONTH PLUS

DECKER ROBERTS WAS NOT A HAPPY CAMPER.

If his son, Seth, wasn't sick and might need extra cash he'd never have taken this job. This was not the final vetting of an executive for a high-ranking position or the interviewing of a potential buyer for a company. No.

This was clearly personal.

Personal to the creepy, middle-aged casino exec with the polio limp who had hired him—and besides, Las Vegas wasn't his favourite American town.

He took off the headphones and looked at the exec, then looked at the svelte Eastern European woman being questioned on the other side of the one-way mirror.

"Put them headphones back on," the man ordered.

"I'm not some cheap detective for hire—unlike Jake Geddes, I don't do divorce work."

"Who?"

"Never mind."

"Hey, this is business. Besides, she ain't my wife."

No, Decker thought, *she's more important to you than most wives are to their husbands. She's your heart's desire—the one. The one you were willing to give up everything for. Or at least so you thought.*

Decker glanced at the printout that was slowly scrolling onto the table. Somewhere in the vast casino complex someone else was listening to the interrogation and committing it to paper. "Do me a favour."

"Wha's that?"

"Flip the printout to the front page."

The casino exec did.

"See where she says her name and when and where she was born?"

"Yeah."

"Underline where she was born."

"Why?"

Decker put the headphones back on their hook and said, "Because it's the only truth she's told in the entire interview."

"You kidding!"

"No. Where she's born—that's it."

"And all the rest?"

"Equivocation, prevarication, paltering or just plain old-fashion lying—I can't tell you which."

"Why?"

Decker heard it. The man wasn't asking why he couldn't tell the difference; he'd leapt all the way to "why" his love had deceived him. But Decker sidestepped the man's real question and answered, "Because I only know when someone's telling the truth or at least the truth as she believes it. That's what you pay me for."

The casino exec ran his hand through the few strands of hair that he'd carefully manoeuvred to cover his liver-spotted scalp, then moved to the console and flipped a toggle. For a moment Decker wondered why a casino would have a room set up like this—then he stopped his mind from going there. It was none of his business.

The casino exec flicked the toggle a second time.

Decker saw the interrogator on the other side of the one-way mirror put his hand to his left ear.

After a pause the exec leaned into the console and said, "Ask her directly if she met with that reporter guy."

Decker put the headphones back on, felt the cold approach and something metal in his hand—then the slime of blood between his fingers.

The interrogator asked, "Have you ever met with Charles Lipinski?"

"No. Never," the woman answered.

Squiggles crossed Decker's retinal screen.

The exec shot Decker a look.

Decker shook his head.

The exec leaned in and flipped the toggle twice then said, "Ask her what the fucking day of the week is."

The interrogator gave a quizzical look then asked, "What day of the week is it?"

"What kind of dumb—"

"What day of the week is it?"

"Wednesday, March sixteenth, 2011."

The exec looked at Decker.

Perfect squares crossed his retinal screen. He nodded.

"Now ask her what she had for breakfast."

"Coffee—I only have coffee in the morning."

Squiggles. Decker shook his head.

"Fuck!" the exec shouted.

"Ask her to give the interrogator her name in her native language," Decker said.

"Why?"

"Maybe her accent is confusing me."

Leaning into the mic on the console the exec said, "Have her say her name in Romanian."

Question, answer, squiggles—not the truth.

Decker looked more closely at the man at the console—fortyish, a sedentary man's gut, that pronounced limp, probably never was handsome even as a child, and that would put him in some way outside, alone, ostracized. The man was pacing now, clearly not just hurt, frightened. It occurred to Decker that this man ran the casino but didn't own it. Money—big money—owned it. "Did she have access to a lot of the casino's secrets?" he asked. He wanted to add "and your secrets" but didn't.

"All of them," the man said and seemed to deflate as if his bones had turned to mush. Decker thought he might fall and smash his head on the edge of the console.

"Then I'm afraid you're going to have to consider that those secrets are not secrets any longer."

The man was staring through the one-way mirror—at his love.

"*Everything* she said was a lie?"

"Except where she was born."

"Not even when she was born was the truth?"

"I wouldn't hold that against her," Decker said, putting aside the
headphones again. "Do you have my money? My work's done here."

Without taking his eyes from the woman the exec pointed to a
thick envelope on the table.

Decker picked it up, quickly riffled through the bills and took
one last look at the casino exec. He wanted to ask, "What's going to
happen to her?" then thought the better of it. After all, this was Las
Vegas. As Hunter S. Thompson so accurately put it, it's the kind of
place that "the whole hep world would be doing on Saturday night if
the Nazis had won the war."

4

AN ISLAND OF HICKS—T EQUALS 1 MONTH PLUS

AS NSA SPECIAL AGENT YSLAN HICKS PUT ASIDE THE FILE FOLDER with the information on Martin Armistaad, who was still in Leavenworth Penitentiary, she allowed her fingers to trace Decker Roberts' name on the thick file on her desk. She felt her eyes drawn to the wall of her office where a print of a black on black Rothko painting hung. She stared at it. The colours began to pulse and she recalled where she'd first seen the painting: in the Rothko Chapel, in Houston, thirteen months ago.

She'd been sitting on the bench in the very centre of the nine Rothko canvasses, where they had videotaped Decker Roberts after his fruitless search for his son, Seth.

In the video it was clear that Roberts entered the chapel terribly agitated. Every move betrayed his deep distress. He had walked up close to the large painting on the south wall then slowly turned a full circle and a half, ending facing the huge canvas on the north wall. Then he sat on the bench where Yslan sat and somehow his agitation—after only a minute or two—ceased and he remained perfectly still for the better part of a half hour, after which he got to his feet and walked calmly out of the chapel and headed back to his Toronto home in the Junction. Once there he picked up his life where he'd left off before his confrontation with the head of Yolles Pharmaceuticals in that old Pittsburgh synagogue.

It had surprised Yslan when Roberts moved in with Eddie—Crazy

Eddie—who had so profoundly betrayed him. But she thought she understood it better after watching the tape of Decker's acting exercise, the Betrayal Game.

She looked back at the massive darkness of the print on her wall and thought, *Maybe all this—this abstract expressionist stuff—was all just one big hoax.*

Three months ago she'd been called in to watch the interrogation of a trickster who'd gotten himself in trouble passing stolen strip bonds. She couldn't have cared less about the theft, but this guy, Mike Cranston, had for a few years been the toast of the New York City art scene and his canvasses—large white things with diagonal slashes of crimson—had at one time sold for in excess of a hundred thousand dollars. That all ended when, in a drunken stupor, he'd confessed to a fellow party guest that he didn't know shit about art—"Just copied what was popular and made it bigger." His line "The real ones commit suicide, the smart ones just sit on their shoulders and make money," made headlines in the *New York Times* Arts section—the party guest had been a reporter for that paper.

For a while Cranston was actually made into a hero by the Fox News folks. They called him the Robin Hood of modern art, fooling the intellectual elite. He had his fifteen minutes of fame seven or eight times over.

But there he sat in the interrogation room, ravaged by some inner torment, the skin on his arms and face seemingly alive with angry red blotches that he tore at with his ragged fingernails.

She watched closely as the lead cop presented the evidence against him. Cranston didn't request a lawyer or deny any of the charges. And when they put a confession in front of him, he went to sign it—then stopped.

"One request."

"Maybe."

"Let me keep the painting in my room."

Yslan quickly went through the police photos of his shabby tenement room. In the sixteenth photo she saw it: hung to one side of the entry door a perfect, reduced in size, copy of the massive Rothko painting on the north wall of the chapel in Houston that bears the great artist's name. It was the same print that now hung on her office wall.

She stared at the print again.

Decker Roberts believed in art. And somehow she thought that understanding the art he believed in would allow her to understand him—and his gift.

But the more she looked, the more bewildered she became.

"Bewildered," she said softly.

She thought about the word. She knew it came from the Anglo-Saxon fear of the danger in the woods. To be confused was to be lost in the woods—bewildered. She sensed that she was in the woods when it came to knowing her special synaesthetes, but she also sensed that she had to go deeper into the woods to really understand them. *Deeper into the woods! What does that even mean?* she asked herself. But she ignored her own question because she sensed that there was a profound secret in the woods—in bewilderment. And after her time with Decker Roberts she'd begun to believe in her intuition, that which she sensed.

Her private line buzzed and she picked up.

"We lost him."

She was suddenly on her feet. She held the phone away from her face until she had her anger under control then asked, "How?"

"Don't know. We've got watchers on the front and back of their house."

"And no one left?"

"For fourteen hours, no one came or went. Lights on and off but it's probably a variable timer."

"But you saw no one leave?"

"No. No one left."

"But now they're gone? Both gone? You're sure?"

"Yeah, we've been inside. They're gone. "

Yslan grabbed her coat. "Wait for me. Don't do anything else till I get there."

The sharp beep of a cell phone turned her to the door.

"Lost someone, Special Agent Hicks?" Leonard Harrison was standing in the door of her office, his eyes fastened to his BlackBerry. "One of your Gifted perhaps?"

"*Our* Gifted . . . sir." This last she added quickly.

"Decker Roberts?"

Yslan nodded. She wanted to ask how he knew—but she knew how. One of her two assistants up in the Junction—guys Decker Roberts had named Mr. T and Ted Knight—had clearly called Harrison before he called her. Shit!

"Well, what are you waiting for, Special Agent?"

Yslan leaned forward to pick up her briefcase. Leonard Harrison watched every move, every arch, and muscle contraction—all of it.

Then Yslan felt Harrison's gaze move past her to the west wall of her office where she'd hung the Rothko print. "Sir?"

His phone gave off a quick sequence of beeps, the digital equivalent of dashes and dots, paused for a three count, then gave a single high-pitched tone.

Harrison's phone had been switched over to high encryption. He hit the accept button.

She knew that he had accepted a countdown to some operation or other. She'd seen him do this very thing several times before, but never had she seen him smile as he set his watch to the countdown timer. He mumbled just loud enough for her to hear, "One for the good guys."

"Sir?"

"All you need to know is that it's T equals plus a month and counting," he said, then without any further explanation, turned and left her office.

So that's what he had been hiding, she thought.

She knew better than to ask her boss for clarification. T plus a month and counting to something that's one for the good guys was all she was going to know about that operation. She closed the door behind him and turned back to the Rothko print. Only thirteen months ago she'd have scoffed at the idea that she'd buy a piece of abstract expressionist art. But that was before she'd kidnapped Decker Roberts from that restaurant in New York City and interrogated him for three days.

Before she'd accompanied him to the Junction.

5

MORE VAGARIES OF VEGAS—
T EQUALS 1 MONTH PLUS

THE DRY HOT AIR OF LAS VEGAS HIT DECKER LIKE A STEAMROLLER. He shielded his eyes by pulling down his Djuma Game Reserve baseball cap. He never wore sunglasses because he valued the accuracy of his sight too much to allow a coloured lens between what was out there and what he saw.

He flipped open the new cell phone Eddie had insisted that he buy and called Eddie, who picked up on the first ring. "You asked me to call when I finished. I never do that—why this time?"

"Because you rented a suite at the Bellagio."

"I did?"

"You did—well, your credit card did. Can't have you staying in the Paris of the Desert all by your lonesome—too sad."

"Really?"

"Yep."

"So you're in Vegas?"

"Across the street, genius."

Decker looked across Fremont, and there was Eddie, waving like he'd found a long-lost friend.

Taking his life in his hands, Decker crossed the six lanes of traffic to Eddie. "Which way?"

"To our hotel?"

"Yeah."

Eddie pointed. Decker moved.

"We're going to walk? Nobody in Vegas walks."

"I walk."

"So I see," Eddie said, catching up by using the strange hop/hobble he'd had to adopt since he snapped his Achilles tendon all those years ago on the Ledbury Park playing field.

"How'd you find me, Eddie?"

"Remember me? The one who sets up gigs for you?"

"Right. Were you followed, Eddie?"

"No."

"How'd you manage that?"

"Same as you."

"You left through the old steam tunnels?"

"First to the generator station, then a cab to Hamilton Airport—nobody serious watches Hamilton Airport. Used my new passport."

"Who are you this time?"

"Roberto Clemente, humanitarian, Hall of Famer—"

"And dead—and Puerto Rican."

"Really?"

"Would I lie to you?"

"Do tell."

Despite himself, Decker smiled and said, "Welcome to Las Vegas."

"Thanks—this is my kind of town," Eddie said, pulling out a pair of wraparound yellow sunglasses as he tipped his hat to two young women—clearly hookers. "And a very fine day to you too, ladies." The women ignored Eddie. "You know it's raining in the Junction."

"No kidding."

"It's sunny here, you may have noticed."

"It's always sunny in Las Vegas."

"Now why's that?"

"Cause God has a weird sense of humour."

"Why do you hate Las Vegas?"

"I don't—hate it, that is."

"But you don't like it."

"Well I don't like Dupont Avenue either, but—"

"Nah, nah, nah there's something here that annoys you. Let me guess—the relentless pursuit of money, the greed—"

"No. I actually like the energy those things give this place."

"The lack of class, then. Fat ladies in shorts, smoking as they plug the one-armed bandits while their half-naked no-neck monsters terrorize the help?"

"The visual is none too pleasing, but that's not it."

"Well, what pray tell is it?"

Decker thought for a second then said, "It's wildness without restraint to give it form."

Eddie stopped and turned Decker to him. "Run that by me again."

"Well come on, Eddie, you sense the wildness here."

"For sure."

"It's unleashed—money and greed have unleashed it."

"But that's not what pisses you off about Las Vegas? The wildness?"

"No, it's not. It's the lost potential. There's no sternness here forcing that wildness into any form."

"You already said that, but I still don't see what you're getting at."

"Do you remember *Fanny and Alexander*?"

"*Fanny and Alexander;* in Swedish; *Fanny och Alexander,* 1982, written and directed by Ingmar Bergman. Originally conceived as a four-part miniseries for TV. A one-hundred-eighty-eight-minute version was released as a movie. The TV version has since been released as a film; both the long and the short version have been shown in theatres around the mundo. Supposedly Bergman's last film, but it wasn't."

"Plot, Eddie—do you remember the plot?"

"Boy wants to be a writer. His father dies. His mother marries a prick of a pastor who makes the kid's life hell. Mother finally leaves the pastor and marries kindly merchant. Very Dickens that—who else believes that merchants are kindly, I mean really?"

"Eddie—the plot."

"Right. Once at the merchant's place the boy begins to write, roll credits, *finita la musica*."

"Good, Eddie, but you missed something."

"Me, the great raconteur, missed something? Enlighten me."

"At the end of the film the boy finally sits down to write, but he feels a cold gust of wind. He turns and sees—"

"The mean pastor."

"And what does the mean pastor say to him?"

" 'Never forget me—you must never forget me.' "

"And the pastor's right, Eddie. The freedom—the wildness—that boy feels living with the kindly merchant doesn't make art. It—the wildness— makes art only when constrained by the pastor's sternness."

"Art? You think Las Vegas should be about art?"

Then Decker found himself laughing—the absurdity of it simply overtook him. Talking art philosophy on the streets of Las Vegas— what was he thinking! He dug into his pocket and pulled out the USB key that had the data from his casino truth-telling session and held it out to Eddie. "Take it and hide it for me, Eddie, and don't tell me where you hid it."

"Another dangerous one?"

"Yeah—a lover betrayed."

"Yikes."

"If Seth weren't so sick I'd have walked out of that thing on the second question, the cash be damned. But Seth might need the money—right, Eddie? Seth might need it, right?"

Eddie looked away then back to Decker. "Okay. Ask."

"About my son? You'll answer questions about Seth?"

"He swore me to secrecy but he's sick now, so ask away."

"Do you know where he is?"

"No."

Decker knew that even if he wanted to "truth-tell" Eddie, it wouldn't work. He cared about Eddie. It never worked on people he cared about.

"Honestly?"

"Honestly, Decker, he never told me and when I'd ask he'd duck the question."

"Did he cash the twenty-thousand-dollar bank draft I gave you for him?"

"Not yet."

"But he got it."

"Yes, Canada Post did a fine job getting it to him."

"So you do know an address, dammit, Eddie."

"I don't. He gave me a generic Victoria, BC, postbox."

"When did you hear from him last?"

"A while after you tried to find him out there."

"And?"

"Not sure you want to hear this, Decker."

"Fuck, tell me!"

"He said to tell you to keep away from him. That bad things happen to people you get close to. Then something about a dead boy in ice that he said you'd understand."

6

A DREAM OF SETH'S—T EQUALS 1 MONTH PLUS

SETH WAS FLYING IN HIS DREAM.

He saw the huge glass structure in the far distance and turned toward it. The faster he flew the farther away it seemed to get. But it was always there, beckoning him onward to go deeper into the dream. It was his favourite dream, and he was urging himself forward when suddenly he felt himself falling and crashed into waking as the vomit lurched from his mouth and splattered on the rocky Vancouver Island beach.

He'd had his BCG treatment less than an hour ago. Usually it took longer for him to get sick. His urologist had lowered the dosage when Seth told him of his reaction to the treatment for his bladder cancer, but he also warned Seth that they couldn't lower it much more or it wouldn't have any protective effect. Then he'd said the words that Seth had dreaded hearing since he first began to pee blood just over two years ago: "We may be near the end of the benefits that BCG can offer you."

"If that's so, what's next?" he'd asked.

The doctor hesitated then said, "Surgery."

"Remove my bladder?"

"Yes . . . and your prostate."

"I'm only twenty-one years old."

"You have cancer, Seth, cancer."

He retched again, just missing his boot.

"Thanks, Dad. Thanks a lot." He swore as he wiped his mouth

with his sleeve then shouted at the surf, "Stop feeling fucking sorry for yourself and fucking do something. Do something!"

When he began his research, references to a Wellness Dream Clinic kept popping up on the sidebar of his Gmail account. And almost every time he opened a bladder cancer site there was a link to that clinic prominently displayed.

Five full days of research on the Web and phone calls and time in the reference library and he'd called Eddie.

"Twenty thousand dollars—that's a lot of money, Seth."

"Yeah," he'd said.

"Gonna tell me why all of a sudden you need so much money?"

"No, Eddie, I'm not going to tell you."

After a moment Eddie said, "I'll get it for you."

"Thanks, Eddie," he'd said, then asked, "How're you doing?"

"Great."

Seth cared about Eddie, and despite the fact that he couldn't see him he knew, beyond knowing, without closing his eyes, that Eddie had not told him the truth.

He walked down to the water's edge. The surfers in their thick wet suits waited on their boards for a wave—something to carry them. They rose and fell with the swell. *Like a heartbeat,* Seth thought. *No,* he corrected himself, *like a dream.*

He knelt and plunged his hands into the freezing cold Pacific and tossed the salty water into his mouth. Better the bitterness of the ocean than the taste of death—his inheritance from his dad for his "gift."

And there he stayed for more than an hour, as the tide slowly crept around his feet, then his knees.

Then he saw them, darting in the shallows—crimson torpedoes, salmon, salmon heading toward the mouth of the river.

He marvelled at the power of life in the fish, returning—after years at sea returning home. He got to his feet and ran to his car, gunned it back up the logging road, then took the first fork north and ground to a stop. He threw open the door and plunged into the bush. Ignoring the branches tearing at his pants and face and arms he forced his way through the brush until he got to the river . . . and there they were—hundreds and hundreds of them fighting the fierce current, moving, no, fighting upstream toward the making of new life and the giving up of their own.

He made his way upstream watching the fish battling to gain every inch, leaping over rock dams and fallen trees, moving, always moving upstream toward the completion of their dream.

Four or five hundred yards farther upstream he saw the first of the carcasses floating back downstream. Around the bend there were hundreds more on the sandy shore—those who didn't make it, those not chosen to complete the dream. *Chosen,* he thought. *Some are chosen.*

A fish jumped high out of the water in a vain effort to leap a log, the fading sunlight glistening off its back, and Seth thought for a moment that the creature had turned toward him as if pleading for help. But there was no help here. There was the challenge and the dream—that was all.

Three fish jumped in unison; one cleared a fallen tree branch while the two others slapped back into the water. One then began to float back down the stream.

On the far bank Seth saw the bush in motion and knew there would be bears. Shortly two females and a cub emerged and waded into the river, quickly emerging with wriggling fish in their mouths. Those not chosen were a God-given banquet for these black bears and the grizzlies who were yet to come.

Seth watched, then felt the weakness come upon him again. Vomit flew from his mouth and splatted in the fast-moving water.

Then he was falling, his knees weak, his world in motion. And before he blacked out from the pain there was a single thought in his head: *The black bears eat those not chosen—but the chosen move on. The chosen, those who could enter the dream.*

Then his own dream took hold of him and he was once again flying, soaring to worlds unknown, to beauty beyond comprehension. As the vision ebbed and left him cold and shivering in the shallow water he begged to dream again, and again, and again.

7

AN APPROACH OF GRADUATIONS—
T EQUALS 1 MONTH PLUS

THE GRADUATION TENT ROSE SLOWLY FROM THE GROUND WITH each pull on the dozens of ropes attached to the tall poles. From a tarplike cover that hid the rented plank flooring and the raised platform stage for the professors, it lifted like a huge, slowly waking white albatross and took the assigned form dictated by the twenty stanchions.

Tears clouded Grover Cleveland Rabinowitz's eyes as he watched the tent assume its predestined form. He would graduate in three weeks and have to leave Ancaster College—a place he thought of as home—a place of science for scientists like him.

He loved Ancaster College.

As the south end of the tent began to obscure the college's famous eighteenth-century church steeple, Grover Cleveland worked out the algorithm that would have permitted the tent to encompass the beautiful symmetry of the steeple in its midst.

While Grover was busy with his mathematical twitterings, Professor Neil Frost watched the damned thing take shape, and all he could think of was that it was going to be hotter than hell in there but if he didn't attend the ceremony he'd be docked his final paycheck. Just more bullshit from this bullshit place.

Even more bullshit than usual. And moving on—always moving on and leaving him behind. Every year the students seemed to get younger while he felt five years older. These ungrateful, self-satisfied, spoiled . . . but not for long, not for long.

A crowd had gathered and cheered as the thing rose.

But in the crowd there was someone who was not concerned about the tent rising. No. He was concerned that as it rose it didn't reveal two carefully chosen hiding spots.

The thing rose; the hiding spots stayed hidden.

8

*A BEGINNING OF BETRAYALS—
EIGHTEEN MONTHS EARLIER*

CRAZY EDDIE SAT ON A BED IN THE LAS VEGAS HOTEL ROOM AND switched the NPR South by Southwest podcast on his iPod from Pree, who reminded him of Rickie Lee Jones, to Broken Bells, then to Edward Sharpe and the Magnetic Zeros. He fast-forwarded their concert to the group's song "Home" and as the two lead singers began to whistle to each other, he put his daughter's photo on his chest and fought off the tears. But when they sang, "Home, home is wherever I'm with you," he could fight no more and the tears came in waves of anguish and anger and profound regret.

He rocked the picture gently in his hand as if the motion would animate the girl trapped within the boundaries of the frame. But Crazy Eddie's daughter did not move. Her eyes did not find either purchase or clarity—just the madness he'd sensed in her so long ago.

"She needs help. Let's do whatever is best for her. Please think about her like I do," he'd pleaded with his common-law wife way back when they had lived together in Portland, Oregon.

"She needs to be away from you. Why the fuck do you think your friends call you Crazy Eddie? Because you're nuts and she's terrified of you. Terrified, you hear me?"

In an effort to calm her he had agreed. "Maybe. Maybe she is frightened of me, but can't you see that she's just on a different path?"

"I see that she's off her rocker."

"Don't say that. Look, maybe you're right. Sure, this is all my fault, I'm a brute."

He had no idea she was wearing a wire.

And his wife had used those ambiguous words in court to insinu-ate that he had molested his daughter—a vicious lie that he did not have the money to contest.

The last time Eddie had been allowed to see Marina was two sum-mers ago. He'd forgotten how cold an August morning in Portland could be. But as he sat and waited for the court appointed and su-pervised visit with his daughter he did his best to count his blessings.

After a long wait—no doubt to make it clear to him that he was an imposition on the system—the court-appointed supervisor, a heavy-set woman dressed in a thick twill suit, opened the door and ushered in Marina.

The girl stood for a moment in the doorway not knowing what to do.

The woman took a seat against the far wall and stared at Eddie, challenging him with her every breath.

Marina stood quietly and looked at the floor. Eddie rose from his chair; his leg brace gave an uncharacteristic clack. The girl's face snapped up. "What's that?" she demanded.

She'd already forgotten.

Eddie pulled up his pant leg to show the old gizmo that lifted the front of his foot as he walked, preventing him from tripping on his down-pointed toes. "An old football injury," he said.

Marina's face instantly brightened. "You play for the Seahawks, don't you, Daddy?"

Such naïveté from a teenager shocked Eddie; the word "daddy" pierced his heart.

"It's not good to lie to the girl," the court-appointed supervisor said.

"I never lie to my daughter—"

"Then why does she think—"

"Do you have to be here?" Eddie demanded.

The woman folded her arms across her ample bosom and nodded once, her disgust with what she thought Eddie had done to this poor girl openly on display.

"Marina, I played football with my friends when I was in high school back in Toronto, never for the Seahawks."

"Too bad," the girl said, "I like the Seahawks. I tried to get Mom to buy me a Seahawks jersey . . ."

"What number, Marina? What number would you like on the jersey?"

"Fourteen. I like number fourteen."

"I'll send it to you. I promise."

The girl beamed, then without evident segue her face fell and a profound anger filled it. "Did someone hurt you?"

"I tore my Achilles tendon. No one did it to me. It just happened—sometimes things just happen."

"Like me being stupid." It was a statement, not a question.

Eddie approached her, aware that he was not allowed to touch her like in some idiotic table dancing club—*You can look but no touching,* he thought. He threw the thought from his head. What was wrong with him? Maybe they were right.

"Are you okay, Daddy?"

The word "daddy" brought him back from the dark places. "Who said you were stupid, Marina?"

The girl looked away.

The supervisor looked grim.

"Marina, who said you were stupid?"

"Everyone."

"But who specifically said you were stupid?" Images of watching Seth's hockey games came to Eddie. Of a father grabbing his son by the cage on his helmet and shaking it so hard that the boy's head thumped against the sides, then the father screaming through the cage's bars into the boy's soul, "You're fucking stupid, how could you do that? Stupid, fucking stupid."

"Who did this, Marina?" he asked even more gently.

Marina brought her shoulders together as if to protect her centre, then pulled down hard with her clasped hands.

"Marina?"

"Mommy's boyfriends. All of Mommy's boyfriends."

That was the exact moment that Eddie had decided to return the phone calls from the lawyer in New York—the ones that suggested that for a "favour" he'd help Eddie get back his daughter. The lawyer's name was Ira Charendoff and he had offices in Patchin Place in New York City, and all Eddie had to do was give him information about Decker Roberts. And he'd done the favour—the favours—and betrayed his friend.

9

A FRIENDSHIP OF EDDIE'S—
T EQUALS 1 MONTH PLUS

LATER THAT NIGHT WHEN DECKER CAME BACK TO THEIR HOTEL
suite with beer and other necessities, Eddie was squatting on the
floor of the living room intent on the screen of his laptop. On the
rug beside him was a clipping from a newspaper of a man in a
suit being arrested by FBI agents. Beside the photo were pages of
printouts with the word "PROMPTOR" circled in red Magic Marker.

Eddie looked up from his computer.

"More PROMPTOR investigations?" Decker asked.

"Yeah. The feds hate PROMPTOR—so it's worth investigating."

"Remind me again why the Feds hate PROMPTOR."

"Again? I don't believe I 'reminded' you before."

"Okay, so tell me for the first time why they hate PROMPTOR."

"Because, my Luddite friend, PROMPTOR provides an Internet
user with complete anonymity. So if you wanted to go online and
look for video of Gretzky's 1993 winner against the Leafs—"

"He high-sticked Gilmour. He should have been in the box for five
not—"

"True, but that's not my point. If you wanted to watch it over and
over again and *didn't* want anyone to know that you were wasting
your time reliving Leaf infamy, you could keep your secret obsession
from the world by using PROMPTOR."

"Cause PROMPTOR would hide my identity."

"Yeah, and where you signed in, where your computer is, what
your real URL address is, and all the little cookies and snitches that

the CIA and other delightful security services are forever seeding on your computer."

"And how does PROMPTOR do this?"

"You don't want the full technical explanation, but think of it this way. If you are on PROMPTOR there are thousands of PROMPTOR volunteers who receive data from your computer and each strips off one layer of identity then passes it to another volunteer, until your identity is completely lost in land digitalis."

"Not hard to understand why the feds hate it."

"Not even a little hard to understand."

Eddie closed his laptop then hit a remote and the demanding jazz explorations of a young Havana pianist poured from Eddie's iPod dock in the corner of the room.

Decker tried to put the mise-en-scène together but couldn't find any semblant order in what was in front of him: Eddie and PROMP-TOR; Eddie and newspaper clippings; and Eddie and this Cuban jazz pianist.

Finally he said, "Didn't know you liked him."

A concerned look crossed Eddie's face.

"What?" Decker asked.

"Okay. This Cuban kid is just a kid, right?"

Decker nodded and gave the international signal for "So?"

"Well, you can hear him muscling the piano. Working hard. Banging the thing. Pushing it."

"Pushing it to what?"

Eddie looked hard at Decker and said, "To . . . to . . . to . . . to I don't know what. Fuck." He punched the remote and the speakers went silent. He picked up his newspaper article on PROMPTOR and his laptop then hop/hobbled out of the room, taking the Whippets Decker had brought with him.

Decker retrieved the remote and pressed play. He listened as the young Cuban demanded the piano give up its secrets. He pounded on the keys and banged on the instrument's sides and top, evidently believing the keys were not enough to contain his dreams.

He hoped the young man would avoid the trap he'd heard other jazz musicians speak about. Most tellingly he remembered hearing an old jazz musician say, "When you stretch the notes of a chord so far apart sometimes you lose the music. And sometimes you can't find your way back—to the music. Unfortunately, heroin shows you the way."

Heroin shows you the way—the way, Decker thought. *The path.*

Crazy Eddie reentered, his mouth full of marshmallow cookies. "Who exactly decided that a crowd of geese was a gaggle?"

Decker looked up and heard the movement of subtext beneath the surface of Eddie's words—in acting terms the Z behind the Y that leads to the line reading. He said, "Say what?"

"Don't do that. You heard what I said."

"Well, Eddie, I don't know the answer to that extremely interesting question."

"Don't do that either—that 'I'm smarter than the world' thing you like to do."

"Okay. Sorry." He saw Eddie's face grimace. "I guess someone came up with the name gaggle and others picked it up and it became part of the language."

"It got accepted?"

The word "accepted" hit the air with a thump.

Decker was slow to respond but finally said, "Yeah."

"How does that work?"

Decker heard it even more clearly—Eddie's desire to bridge the huge chasm between them. But it was too early, too fast, so Decker said, "I really don't know."

"And it doesn't bother you?"

"Not particularly."

"Language is important."

"Okay, I agree with that."

"Then how can you not give a shit how words get accepted into the language? I mean, who invented the word 'deplane'? We don't 'onplane' so why should we 'deplane'? I mean, who made up that word?"

"Some airline guy?"

"So why can't you and I invent words—" Eddie stopped midsentence.

It was clear to Decker that Eddie wanted him to see where this was going and save him having to spell it out. But Decker remained silent.

Eddie finally continued his thought. "Why can't we send invented words out into the ether and see if they stick?"

Decker still refused to play along. He said, "Okay, if that's what's on tap for a Saturday night in an expensive hotel suite in Las Vegas, sure. You start."

"So if there's a gaggle of geese, how's about a PROMPTOR of lawyers?"

Decker couldn't believe he'd gone right there—right to Ira Charendoff. Slowly he asked, "Because lawyers are hidden in life like PROMPTOR allows you to hide your identity on the Net?"

"No, not that."

Decker knew that Eddie wanted to talk about his dealings with the lawyer Charendoff to get back his daughter. Those dealings had led directly to his betrayal of Decker—and they both knew it. But there was something else here. Something he couldn't put together with the words. Something to do with PROMPTOR and Charendoff—but what?

"How's about an ambivalence of lawyers?"

"Because we turn to them for help but are never sure exactly what they want?"

"Yeah, that."

Decker looked at his friend and finally asked what had been on his mind since this afternoon. "Why are you really here in Vegas, Eddie?"

Eddie reached into his coat pocket and held out a set of airline tickets.

"More truth-telling jaunts?"

"No. Travel. Faraway travel. Time for you to disappear for a bit—while I get serious about Charendoff."

"Using PROMPTOR?"

"Maybe. Not sure about that yet. But it's safer if you skedaddle."

"Make like a bread truck and haul buns?"

"Who said that?"

Special Agent Yslan Hicks, Decker thought, but he said, "Some southerner."

"Fine," Eddie said, then shoved the airline tickets at Decker.

"And if I don't want to go?"

"I beat the crap out of you and throw you to your NSA friend."

"What about my classes at the Lab? I'm midsession with those actors."

"Actually, you cancelled your classes due to a family emergency." He turned his phone to show Decker a copy of an e-mail message he'd just sent his seventy students.

"Fine. I guess. Any suggestion as to where I should go?"

"South Africa would be good."

"Why there?"

"Because they have very little broadband and the ANC government is particularly anti-American. At least it will make it difficult for the NSA to track you."

"But they can still—"

"Sure. But once you leave Cape Town they'll have real problems following you. You wanna go back to Kruger?"

"No." Memories of the trouble with his son Seth up in the national park still haunted Decker. Seth had been only a boy but so angry at Decker's response to his mother's death that he destroyed an entire resort bar in the middle of the night. It had started the disastrous relationship he now had with his son.

"I know you've got a standing offer to direct at the University of Cape Town. It's time for you to direct again."

Decker hesitated.

"Do it. You're a better man when you direct."

"Nice of you to say."

"Besides, it's all set up," Eddie continued.

"What?"

"Yeah. I contacted them for you last week."

Around the time when I first found the clippings about PROMPTOR all over the house, Decker thought.

"So what are you going to direct?"

Decker had two one-act plays that interested him. The first by a wild Irishman who'd lived for a bit in Newfoundland named Ken Campbell. The second, only really good for pros, was a miracle of a Pinter satire called *Love and Pain and the Dwarf in the Garden* written by a guy who had been at the Yale School of Drama with Decker but seemed to have fallen off the face of the earth. A shame. The man was a real talent.

Eddie held out a thin volume and flipped it to him. "Why not direct this?"

It was his copy of *Love and Pain and the Dwarf in the Garden.*

Decker stared at Eddie. "How did—"

"You're not all that mysterious, Decker. I caught you reading it last week, then I found it in the bathroom—potty reading, is it?" Before Decker could respond he asked, "You've done it before?"

"Yeah, as a student at Yale."

"And you kept the script."

"Yeah."

"You don't throw out scripts you've directed."

Decker wondered why these were statements, not questions, but answered, "No. Never. Why?"

"Nothing. Look, I've made a few notes in the margins."

Decker took a peek at Eddie's first note. *You have to make this truthful—not necessarily real, truthful. And it has to be art—Art with a capital A. Go to YouTube and search Paul Simon–Toronto–Duncan–Rayna to see what I mean.* Decker agreed with the first part of the note. He knew the difference between the two. As to the reference to a YouTube video, he suspected it was just another example of Crazy Eddie being Crazy Eddie.

Eddie turned to go to his bedroom, and as he made his awkward hopping exit he said, "Don't say I never gave you anything."

"Are you going back to the Junction?"

"Not just now."

"Later?"

"Eventually we all go back to the Junction—and you know it. Get some sleep—your flight leaves early tomorrow."

Decker stared at his friend's retreating figure and wondered what Eddie meant by "eventually we all go back to the Junction." Then he wondered what a group of Eddies would be called. Maybe an eddy of Eddies—more likely a chaos of Eddies or perhaps a friendship of Eddies. Decker didn't know.

Eddie came back in from the bedroom. "And then there's this." He tossed a brand new BlackBerry-like phone to Decker.

"What's this, some new gadget?"

"Actually it's old, Decker, but new to the likes of you."

Taking the thing, Decker asked, "Can you get HBO on this?"

"Very funny. Tap the screen and take a look."

Decker tapped the screen and blanched. "Fuck, that's our living room."

"Yeah, and that ain't you and me in our living room."

Decker swore. "Mr. T and Ted Knight."

"Big black man, prissy white-haired guy—good call. They work for that NSA chick you told me about?"

"Yeah."

"And they were the ones watching our house?"

"That'd be my guess." Decker hesitated then asked, "Do you have a feed in my room?"

Eddie took the phone and tapped the side twice and said, "You never told me she was cute—in an Americanisher schweinhundisch sorta way."

"What?" Decker said, grabbing the phone.

Decker watched as, on the small screen, NSA Special Agent Yslan Hicks opened the drawers of his dresser—then pulled out the latest version of his book on acting.

On Professional Acting
A Guide Book for Professional Actors to Their Art Form

by
Decker Roberts
(c) Decker Roberts, 2007, 2008, 2009, 2010, 2011

1. A Word of Introduction to This Book

I began teaching professional actors between directing jobs in regional theatre when I was trying to stop smoking—hence no more work in bars. I taught in my Manhattan apartment three nights a week—my wife was very patient. In my second year of teaching I was contacted by a young man from Yonkers. He asked if I would set up a class for him and some of his friends.

That first night four of them showed up—three men and a woman, a dark-eyed girl who clearly was not one of the group. One of their sisters perhaps—I'm afraid I never found out.

That initial class we talked a little about the art of acting. How emotion without form was self-indulgence but form without emotional content was recitation, not acting. We did a bit of improvisation and I showed them something new I'd worked out—how actors need to think backward. A person says X so they must be thinking Y and they think Y because of Z that happened to them in the past. Find the Z (what happened to them) and that will give you Y (their thinking), which tells you how the character says X (the line).

Because the girl decided that she wanted to "just watch," I suggested the three young men prepare something from David Mamet's *American Buffalo* for the following week.

We parted and I watched them from my brownstone window as they walked toward the Lexington Avenue subway, the girl on the other side of the street from the boys.

The following week my Yonkers actors announced that they were ready to show me *American Buffalo*. I said sure, assuming that they had put a few pages of the play on its feet. They started into the play—from the top. They did the whole play, cover to cover, without a break, although they did manage to break the mirror over the mantelpiece, a lamp, and a windowpane. When they were finished my eyes were drawn to the silent girl in the corner who had "just watched." I trembled when I saw the anger on her face and agreed with Hamlet when he said, "There are more things in heaven and earth, Horatio, than are dreamt of in your philosophy."

"So what do you think, Coach?" one of the boys asked.

What I thought was that feelings of exclusion can be terribly destructive and that hunger was an essential part of being a professional actor. These three young aggressive men barged their way into the profession. The fourth—the girl—I never saw her after that second class, although years later I read about her rampage in the *Times*.

That was one of the few times in my life that I taught beginners. I still don't teach beginners, and this book is not intended for novice actors, although if you have enough hunger you'll be able to find your own way of using the ideas and methods in these pages.

Like most good ideas, the concepts in this book are easy to learn but may take a lifetime to master. Nothing of any value can be put on a three-by-five index card—except the thought that nothing of any value can be put on a three-by-five index card.

The actor's territory is the human heart. It is an uncharted land sometimes defended by terrifying dragons, but it also contains great glories, the very roots of music and profound human truths.

To the hungry actor the heart is the only land worthy of investigation.

This book, *On Professional Acting,* attempts to give the actor a compass and a few points of entry into that divine territory. It is a voyage that, for an artist, lasts a lifetime.

NSA Special Agent Yslan Hicks reread the introductory chapter then quickly checked the newly added Hamlet citation. There it was: the central truth of her work with her "special synaesthetes," the Gifted. Work that she was beginning to feel was leading her to truths never dreamt of in her or anyone else's philosophy.

She shot off a priority e-mail to the publisher reminding them of the agreement they'd signed with the NSA not to publish Decker Roberts' book.

Then she opened her now very large file on Decker Roberts and cross-referenced the changes he'd made in this edition with the hundreds and hundreds of speeches that they'd recorded from his teaching at his Toronto studio, Pro Actors Lab. Everything matched up with previous references except the reference to outsiders.

She accessed the NSA's data banks through her BlackBerry and within twenty seconds had a name—and a hideous crime—committed by the girl who just wanted to watch.

11

A SEARCHING OF DECKER—
T EQUALS 1 MONTH PLUS

"WHAT'S THAT YOU'RE READING, BOSS?"

It was Mr. T at the door of Decker's bedroom.

Yslan didn't like that he'd crept up on her. She turned on him. "So how the hell did he get out of here without you seeing him—him and that Crazy Eddie?"

"Through the tunnel."

"What tunnel?" Then she remembered the steam tunnels that ran beneath much of the Junction. It was how Decker had managed to get out of his other house seventeen months ago when it was torched.

Mr. T was generating an explanation of why they lost Roberts, but she put up her hand, stopping him. "Get me addresses for his three contacts here. Get them for me now."

TRISH

Trish Spence, the TV documentary producer whom Decker Roberts was working for, strode out of the CBC building on Front Street in downtown Toronto. Her six-foot two-inch frame allowed her to cover a lot of ground, and she was clearly angry, so she was walking even faster than usual.

"Ms. Spence," a voice with a southern accent commanded her to stop. She turned toward the source of the voice—a five-foot six-inch blonde with almost translucent blue eyes leaning against a lamp post, taking in the scene. "I'm sorry, Ms. Spence, I didn't mean to startle you."

"You didn't."

A lie, Yslan thought as she crossed to the taller woman. "How's *At the Junction* going?"

"Are you a fan?"

"Hey, I wouldn't miss an episode."

"Great," Trish said, then turned to go.

Yslan reached out and touched Trish's bare forearm. Trish's entire body recoiled as she spun to look at Yslan. Of late she'd begun to hate being touched. It was a new thing—but she really hated to be touched.

"So how's your show going?" Yslan asked a second time.

"They don't like dead people."

"Excuse me. I thought TV folks loved dead people."

"Not CBC."

"Sorry to hear that. Look, my name's Yslan Hicks, I'm a friend of Decker Roberts."

Trish took a closer look at the woman and said, "I doubt that."

"Why's that?"

"I don't believe Decker Roberts has any real friends, that's why. So who are you and what do you want?"

"I just need to find Mr. Roberts."

"Why?"

"Where is he, Ms. Spence?"

"I don't think we have anything to talk about, Ms. Hicks," Trish said and turned to go. Over her shoulder she threw back, "If that's even your real name."

THEO

"You've been down that aisle three times already, lady, so I assume you're not really here looking for a book. Besides, I can't imagine early Chinese gay literature is really of much interest to you."

Yslan turned to face the small dusty man and said, "I'm sorry, Theo, I'm looking for Decker Roberts."

"And you didn't know how to just come over to me and ask."

"Right."

"So?"

"Well, I'm looking for Decker Roberts."

"Yeah. She told me."

"Trish Spence?"

"Yeah, she called, warned me that you were an American spy or something."

"Can we leave it at 'or something'?"

"Maybe."

"Fine. Do you do the research with Decker Roberts for the CBC documentary *At the Junction*?"

"You know I do."

"Right. Can I ask you about Decker Roberts?"

"You can ask."

"When did you see him last?"

"Ten, twelve days ago."

"Where?"

"Here."

"What was he doing?"

"It's a bookstore—you may have noticed that."

"And you haven't seen or heard from him since?"

Theo shook his head no and pointed toward the door. "That's the way out."

Yslan headed toward the exit then turned back. "What did he buy?"

"Guess."

"A book."

"Good guess, lady."

"Which one?"

Theo turned away.

"Come on, Theo, what book did he buy?"

Theo stopped, spat something of an unknown colour onto the old wood floor and said, "Hunter S. Thompson. *Fear and Loathing in Las Vegas*. Now get your pretty little ass out of my dirty old bookshop."

LEENA

"Something wrong with the pastrami sandwich?" Leena asked as she reached across the table and picked up an empty water glass.

"No," Yslan answered. "No, it's good. A little dry maybe."

"You the one who asked for it extra lean, no?"

"Yeah—cholesterol, you know."

"I wouldn't know," Leena said. She picked up a used pickle dish from the table and was about to leave. "Want some butter for that?"

"Is that allowed in this restaurant?"

"Yeah, we don't keep strict kosher, but I don't think I'm going to get you any butter."

"Can I ask why?"

"You're the one they warned me about."

"Who?"

"Trish Spence warned me about your eyes. And Theo warned me about your ass. Being warned about pale blue eyes I get—about a tight small ass, I've got no clue."

"So you've been warned."

"I have." Yslan watched confusion cross Leena's face. She saw the remains of an injury she'd received in a car crash when she was Decker Roberts' high school girlfriend some twenty-four years ago.

"Is Decker in trouble?"

"I don't know, but if I can't find him I can't protect him."

"Protect him from what?"

"Himself mostly."

Leena nodded as a deep sorrow washed across her features. "I tried to do that for a while."

"But he didn't go along with it?"

"No. Decker Roberts lives his life in tightly contained boxes. He's not into sharing. He . . ." She couldn't find the words so Yslan supplied them: "Doesn't play well with others."

Leena's look turned hard. "Yeah. That. You finished with that sandwich?"

"Yes, thanks. Does he like Las Vegas?"

Leena stared at Yslan. "He loathes it."

"And fears it?"

"Sure—fears and loathes Las Vegas."

YSLAN

It was already late afternoon when Yslan contacted the NSA office in Las Vegas. Shortly thereafter she learned that she couldn't get a flight to Las Vegas until tomorrow morning.

After swearing at the airline schedules she told Mr. T and Ted Knight she'd meet them at the airport at 5:30 the next morning and drove off. She didn't want them with her when she drove her rental car past the hotel on Lakeshore that she and Decker had stayed in only fourteen months ago. She got out of the car in the parking lot and stared at the building. She couldn't get over the idea that something had happened in there—something important.

She saw the security guard at the hotel looking at her with that look security guards have right before they approach.

She turned and got back in her car.

By late twilight she found herself walking along Bloor Street West. It was more alive now than when she was last here. Maybe it was because it had been winter back then and it was spring now—but she doubted that was all there was to it.

She walked north then west along Annette Street, passing by the many houses of worship. She stopped in front of one that had been converted into expensive condos. There was another church down the way that was undergoing the same fate.

Why does this bother me? she asked herself. *A church is just a building.* But she didn't believe it. She used to believe that—but not since she'd met Decker Roberts.

She turned onto the street where Decker Roberts used to live and passed by the remains of Roberts' house, its blackened beams still in plain sight, mocking the very idea that a home was a sanctuary—let alone a man's castle.

An hour later she used her key picks to open the door of Roberts' acting studio on Stafford Street around the corner from what looked to her like the world's largest state fair—but they didn't have states up here. Did they have state fairs? She didn't know.

She'd been in Roberts' acting studio once before right after she'd forced him to acknowledge that his friend Crazy Eddie had betrayed him to a lawyer in New York City named Charendoff.

At that time she'd perused the place, made sure that their hidden cameras and mics were still working properly, then commented on a review in the local paper for his television documentary *At the Junction,* saw his sixth-grade report card tacked to his office wall with the teacher's comment *Does not play well with others* circled in red. Back then her two assistants, Mr. T and Ted Knight, kept on asking her what exactly she was looking for. She didn't know then. She didn't know now, but she sensed that she was closer to knowing— closer to knowing Mr. Decker Roberts who did not play well with others and both feared and loathed Las Vegas and, oh yes, was the only human being she knew who had the gift of knowing beyond knowing when someone was telling the truth.

EMERSON REMI

Emerson Remi saw the lights in the Pro Actors Lab studio blink on and was surprised. Wasn't there a note on its website that Decker Roberts had to leave town on a family matter?

Yes, there was.

So who was in the acting studio at this hour of the night?

He stepped further back into the shadows and waited. Since he'd first met Decker Roberts, he'd become good at waiting.

And when Yslan Hicks, a former lover of his, stepped out the front door at 72 Stafford Street, Emerson Remi—Princeton graduate, grandson of an Irish witch—smiled. "So he's given her the slip," he whispered to the night air. "Good. Very good, Mr. Roberts. My brother in arms is on the loose—a wild thing—like myself."

12

AN ADVANCE OF AFRICAN TRIPS—
T EQUALS 1 MONTH PLUS

TWO DAYS LATER DECKER WAS SITTING IN THE HEATHROW departure lounge in B concourse because his flight to Johannesburg had been delayed by a British Air strike when he heard, "Will Mr. Decker Roberts please report to security to receive an important message."

Decker picked up the security phone and wasn't even a little surprised to hear the southern stylings of Special Agent Yslan Hicks.

"You know who this is?"

"Jodie Foster?"

"Very funny."

"Ah, not Jodie Foster, Clarice Starling."

"When did you become such a smartass?"

Decker didn't respond. He'd stopped answering open-ended questions a long time ago.

"Fine. You have a ticket waiting for you to JFK, it leaves gate twenty-nine in thirty-six minutes."

"First class?"

"The U.S. government doesn't do first class. Be on that plane, Mr. Roberts. Someone will meet you at JFK."

"Why?"

"I don't like you travelling to foreign lands—"

"Without reporting in first?"

"That was the deal, so get your ass on that plane. By the by, how'd you like Las Vegas?"

After a moment he responded, "Not much."

"Too much fear and loathing?"

"Maybe . . . sure. Question?"

"Maybe."

"When did *you* become such a smartass?"

The question floored Yslan—when the fuck *had* she become such a smartass? She always was annoyed with people who had a quip for every circumstance. Who talked like, well, like smartasses on TV.

Decker hung up the phone and looked around him. No doubt someone was watching him. He'd known he was being watched for some time now. But an airport was a good place to lose a tail—and that's exactly what Decker believed he'd done.

Three hours later he handed over a fake passport to the air hostess at Gatwick. She smiled at him as she said, "Enjoy you flight, Mr. Rose."

Gatwick to Amsterdam. Amsterdam to Cape Town.

He had promised Eddie that he would lose himself in Africa for a while, and that's just what the fuck he was going to do. And direct a play—he hadn't directed a play in a while and was surprised how much he was looking forward to it. The very thought of directing again had released two wonderfully random ideas in his head.

Four months back while he'd prepped a Canadian/Somali singer for a film audition, the musician had mentioned that most Somali men have committed their family histories to memory in verse. The poems often ran to several hundred stanzas and traced their exact lineage back to the first Somali. He had recited his. The buzzing cadence and the rhymes of the poems were unique and clearly present in the man's music. *They are the "path" of his music,* he thought. *A path backwards.*

The other idea that intrigued Decker was the Australian aboriginal use of song lines, intricate memorized songs that described in great detail all the twists and turns of long land journeys, some in excess of a thousand miles with as many as seven hundred exact references such as "at the bend in the river, find the fallen rock with the cleft in its side—turn toward the rising sun at the rock. That is the track to follow. But do not drink from the water of the river there."

A path forward, Decker thought, and somehow he knew that he personally stood at the meeting point of the two paths—one forward, one back.

13

A MURDER OF CROWS—
T MINUS 12 DAYS, 4 HOURS AND 8 SECONDS

THOUGHTS: We look like crows—all of us in our black gowns and the profs up there in theirs. We look like a flock of fucking crows. No, that's not the right collective noun. Not a flock of crows, but a murder of crows—yeah. A murder of crows. Good phrase that—a murder of crows. Gotta love that—a murder of crows.

How does that joke go? Yeah, there's this Taliban suicide prevention hotline and a kid calls up in the middle of the night and claims he's thinking terrible thoughts—that he's seriously considering killing himself. "Please help me," he says.

The guy on the helpline says, "Sure. Can you drive a truck?"

14

A SINGULARITY OF TURD—
T EQUALS 1 MONTH PLUS

AS GROVER CLEVELAND RABINOWITZ EMERGED FROM THE FOURTH stall on the third-floor men's room of Lyndon Baines Johnson Dormitory at Ancaster College, he noticed that the turdlet had returned.

He'd first seen it almost five months ago. Then it disappeared and re-appeared periodically thereafter. This time it had been gone for almost a week but now it was back—a desiccated thing, no more than an inch long, sitting on top of the floor drain almost directly across from the janitors' cleanup sign-in sheet, upon which the dates and times were all carefully printed but the signatures were completely illegible.

He closed his bathrobe and nudged the thing with the side of his flip-flop. If it wasn't the same one that had been there before then it was its twin sister—to Grover Cleveland Rabinowitz all turds (and turdlets) were female.

Grover noted that it didn't stink—no smell whatsoever. The others hadn't stunk either. It had been dried somehow, maybe microwaved. He went through the physics of microwaving in his head—a gross process as far as he was concerned—but yeah, this dried turdlet could definitely have been microwaved, or sun-dried, but that was hard to do in the spring rainy season here in upper New York State.

It never occurred to him to question who could have placed the thing on the drain outside the fourth stall of the men's washroom on the third floor of Lyndon Baines Johnson Dorm, let alone why the individual who did this would have done such a thing.

He was a "how" man—not a "who," let alone a "why" man. "How" was the scientist's question.

And Grover Cleveland Rabinowitz was a scientist.

So he'd carefully noted the days the turdlet had appeared, disappeared then reappeared in a file he kept beside his computer that also contained his thesis on how to dry human fecal material.

It would prove to be a vital clue as to why and even who had planted the bombs that would in a month kill more than two hundred people. It was also the only thing that a heartbroken Mr. and Mrs. Rabinowitz didn't bother taking home from their dead child's room in Lyndon Baines Johnson Dormitory at Ancaster College—the world's most famous institution of higher learning in sciences, maths and applied engineering.

15

A DIFFERENTIAL OF TOWN AND GOWN—
T EQUALS 1 MONTH PLUS

THE ANCASTER COLLEGE CAMPUS OVERLOOKED A SMALL, formerly industrial town in the dead centre of which was its famous eighteenth-century church built by the founders of the college in a pristine symmetry they believed reflected the seriousness of their god.

There was an overpriced inn named after the college, naturally enough, then cheap outlying motels. The inn had an adequate to good restaurant, and the rest of the two-street town had the college's elaborate bookstore, a very fancy candy shop and of course a Whole Foods grocery.

The college was self-contained—the students never carried money, as every establishment in the town took Caster Cards. There was a small movie theatre that showed first-run flicks for five bucks and held pay-what-you-can Sundays and Mondays, but then Ancaster College brought in bands as famous as Arcade Fire and speakers as exclusive as the Dalai Lama—all for free. The students accessed a bar that served the under-aged with watered-down beer. The cops knew, the college knew—everyone knew. All agreed that it was the best way to handle the inevitability that the smartest science students in the world needed a place to blow off steam, no matter what their age.

Some of the faculty lived in college-owned properties on the outskirts of town, but the really famous (and wealthy) professors all flew into the tiny airport for their classes then returned through the same airport to their real residences in New York or Chicago or Boston.

But on the other side of the hill, across the thruway, lived the townies in an enclave of their own, Stoney River—America's version of South Africa's townships.

And in the midst of that side growth to the college was the basement apartment of one of the college's many janitors, but this apartment had a microwave oven that had been used to desiccate several pieces of human fecal material—stuff that the young janitor called shit.

16

AN EXTREMIS OF PROFESSORS—
T EQUALS 1 MONTH PLUS

AS ASSISTANT PROFESSOR NEIL FROST ROCKED BACK IN HIS wooden office chair he plunked his socked and sandaled feet on his desk and stared at the stack of exam booklets that awaited his attention.

He had a terrible urge to fail them all just to show them how unfair the real world was.

Without opening a single booklet he knew that more than 95 percent of them would be perfect or darn near perfect.

These kids had been working at being perfect since they could walk—maybe before they could walk.

The other 5 percent would have some obvious errors since their authors would have been too drunk to notice that they'd skipped some questions—maybe even puked on the booklet so that they couldn't see the question.

At Ancaster College, even on the freshman level where he was relegated to teach, there were few mistakes made on exams no matter how hard professors made the questions, because Ancaster College rejected more than seven thousand applicants every year coming from the very best prep schools in the United States, Europe, Asia, the Middle East and Latin America. Any less than the very best were cordially invited to not apply. The college accepted fewer than three hundred new students into each freshman class. Three hundred of the very brightest maths, science and computer students in the world.

He poked at the pile of exam booklets with the edge of his tattered sandal and wasn't unhappy to see the booklets slide off his desk into the wastepaper basket.

If only I could just leave them there, he thought. Then he remembered his meagre salary, his diffident supposed colleagues, and finally his overdue rent, and he picked up the topmost of the booklets—naturally from a Bengali or maybe it was a Pakistani, who could tell the difference or cared to, Ibrahim Mohammed something or other—and began to read.

By noon he'd finished marking 17 of the 291 exams and was ready for a diversion, so he flicked on his video of the last committee hearing where a busty student named Marcia had complained about the "unwarranted attentions"—he just loved that euphemism, "unwarranted attentions"—of one of Ancaster College's janitors.

He fast-forwarded the tape to the part where he told her, "Look, Ms. Lavin, even the cat is allowed to watch the king."

Her perplexed look so pleased him that he replayed the section, several times.

But he knew that he owed Ms. Marcia Lavin.

Without this bitch's complaint he'd never have met the young janitor who microwaved human shit—Mr. Walter Jones, Esq.

He turned to the window and stared at the neatly manicured campus and remembered when the idea first came into his head.

Popped in—God given, actually.

He was adjusting his girth in his theatre seat at the Brooklyn Academy of Music as the lights were going down. They evidently made theatre seats narrower now than they used to. Must be so they can stuff more seats into the theatre, even though the prices they charged were outrageous. He couldn't believe it when they told him it was $140 a seat to see the RSC!

But as the play began, he found it glorious to hear Shakespeare spoken by his countrymen. And *Julius Caesar* had always been a favourite of his.

He'd played Cassius in college and had for a while considered a career on the stage, but he'd been rejected by RADA, the Central

School and the Old Vic—no doubt Jews were in charge of those places then. No doubt. Then there were those ahead of him: Ralph Fiennes, Kenneth Branagh, Timothy Dalton, et al. *They put me in the shadows, and now they're famous and rich and have women for the choosing.*

His reverie was broken by a familiar speech about brilliance hidden beneath the shadow of Caesar.

Know how you feel brother. You tell 'em.

And what did he do to ol' Caesar—ate two—is what he did!

Ate two—why stop at two?

How's about six or sixty or six hundred? In for a penny . . .

Ouch—the damned seat pinched him!

Show them all. All of them.

A smile crept over his face. *Yeah, time to get back at every one of them who put him in shadow, who rejected his brilliance. Who refused him admission to their damned club. Well, I'll grant you all admission—admission to hell.*

And as he watched the third act he thought of how simple it was to make an explosive device—kid's stuff really. But where to put it? That was the question: where to put it?

Then he saw the mob gathering onstage to hear Anthony's speech over Caesar's dead body—and he knew. A mob gathered to listen. *Oh, yes. Universities have such gatherings once a year. We surely do.*

He ran the three necessities for a crime in his head:

Motive: in spades

Means: you bet

Opportunity: he'd have to work on that. Bombs need to be planted. And what would a professor be doing digging in the ground or lifting platforms. No, he'd need an assist with that.

Then he remembered the janitor who had given "unwarranted attentions" to bouncy Marcia and smiled . . . and to his surprise he felt comfortable in his theatre seat. He had lots of room; it fit just fine.

17

A VOID OF CARING—
T EQUALS 1 MONTH PLUS

WALTER APPLIED THE HOT WAX TO HIS CHEST AND GASPED. THE smell almost made him puke. He counted to twenty then ripped the wax off—with his body hair. He hated body hair.

He waited for his breathing to slow down then he applied more hot wax to his upper thigh. This time although he gasped he also smiled—because things were going along just fine. Better than things had ever gone for him. And soon, so soon . . .

He peeled off the hot wax, then pried open a can of soup and put it on the hot plate. "Dinner," he said aloud to the emptiness of his basement apartment. That used to piss him off—him eating soup out of the can while those students had the choice of more than ten different things to eat at their dining halls. *And people like me to clean up after them,* he thought.

But that didn't bother him now.

Cause this will show her and that snot-nosed professor who thought he was just so fucking clever. Well, Mr. Professor, nobody uses me. I use them. And you, Mr. Bigshot, you don't get it. Or the rest of them who think they're so much smarter—so much better—than me.

He put on an oven mitt and picked up the can of bubbling soup and took a long swallow. It was hot—and it burned—but Walter Jones didn't care. Not a bit.

18

A DREAM OF SOUTH AFRICA AND NAMIBIA— T EQUALS 1 MONTH PLUS TO T MINUS 21 DAYS

DECKER TAUGHT IN THE MORNINGS AT THE UNIVERSITY OF CAPE Town, a school that religiously followed his teaching methods and had even produced two PhD theses based on his unique approaches to acting.

More importantly, the school was now producing some of the finest young actors in the English-speaking world. The students were bright, ambitious and talented. But almost every white student eventually approached Decker about the possibility of working in Canada, since they realised that the sins of their parents were being visited upon them in a fairly draconian fashion. To be blunt, South Africa's affirmative action policy was unapologetically driving many whites from the country. NGO hypocrites always defended affirmative action with the blather of "Yeah but would the whites rather be in their position or in the position of the blacks?"

Only those who don't have to suffer the brunt of discrimination would talk this way. It's the talk of the self-righteous who stand to lose nothing themselves.

Decker felt it was wrong to visit the sins of the parents on their children—period, full stop.

In the afternoons he rehearsed the two short plays and was excited by what he found in the pieces and by the raw talent of some of the students.

Several professional actors (almost all of whom were University of Cape Town Drama grads) sat in on his classes and rehearsals. At first the university had objected, but Decker had insisted that the pros be permitted to audit his classes. Shortly he organised evening classes for the pros—well, actually, for a specific pro, an extraordinary creature named Tinnery who had shown up to watch his third class.

She was a graceful Afrikaans beauty—strong of body, strong of heart, and strong of head—and she was talent that walked and talked.

Decker turned in profile to the attentive actors and pointed at his nose. "Your nose is attached directly to an ancient part of your brain. Modern man doesn't use his nose much except to steer clear of cesspools and the like. But modern man is only the end product of all the creatures who have come before him. And those men and women used their noses, and the knowledge that they gained is still stored in our brains.

"The human brain consists of three parts. Up here the frontal lobes, which in fact make us human. The frontal lobes control the middle section—the mammal portion of the brain—which in turn controls the most ancient part of our brains, the reptilian part.

"When we sleep it's the frontal lobes that sleep. That's why we have nightmares. With the frontal lobes resting the other two parts of the brain tell us what they saw that day—somewhat different than what the frontal lobes saw.

"Have you ever been in the middle of a nightmare and suddenly you pop up and say, 'That's enough, you're scaring me?'

"Well, who exactly are you talking to?

"Your frontal lobes are talking to the reptilian part of the brain. You may have seen an indifferent casting director that afternoon. But your reptilian self saw a huge cobra, its hood wide open, ready to strike. A nightmare.

"And the reptilian part of your brain understands smell.

"Scent helps merchants sell things. Popcorn hasn't tasted good in a hundred years—but the smell of it still prompts you to buy it.

"Same for burgers and other foods.

"But smell is also an extraordinary tool for the actor. It's the most accurate key for recalling an event, a person, a place or most importantly a state of being." As he spoke he felt an odd resistance. In his mind? He thought so. Then the thought came clean. We apparently only use between 12 and 13 percent of our mind's capacity. What's the rest for? Evolution never creates gratuitously. Backup systems sure, but not excess. Useless limbs fall off. Things without function disappear. Still there's a full 87 to 88 percent of the brain that is never used. Why? Then he thought of the Rothko Chapel—of the paintings there. Were these visions drawn from the other 87 percent? Visions of the rest? Perhaps portals to the rest. A path to the rest?

"Can you go over the keying thing again?" Tinnery asked.

Her question brought him back to the present. "Okay. So I used to work for a theatre in Indianapolis, Indiana, for a fabulous director named Tom Haas. And because I was the only Canadian director he knew, he found it fun to always offer me really American American plays.

"Well, he wanted me to direct the one Eugene O'Neill fun play, *Ah, Wilderness!*, which centres on a fifteen-year-old boy getting his first kiss on the dock from a sixteen-year-old girl in the moonlight at the end of a long summer.

"So he sent me his offer on this fabulous rice paper stationery that they always used. I think the company was a sponsor of the theatre. And in the offer was a request for me to come to Indianapolis and audition this real fifteen-year-old boy for the lead.

"Well, I trusted Tom, so I hopped on an airplane and headed out. And sure enough the boy was blond, blue eyed, had good shoulders and could repeat well enough, so I agreed.

"Then Tom wanted me to cast a real sixteen-year-old girl from Indiana, but I refused, telling him that I would go back to New York and get what we, at the time, openly referred to as a midget. A twenty- or thirty-year-old actress who was small enough to get away with playing teenagers on the stage. Every director I knew had a few midgets he used. And I had a few so I got in touch with one of them and in two weeks she and twelve other New York actors piled onto a plane and we headed out to Indiana.

"Well, that first night as we sat around the table to read the play it became obvious that this fifteen-year-old boy from Indiana was really quite struck by this thirty-one-year-old—and very sexually active—actress from New York City.

"So much so that every time we rehearsed the scene on the dock leading up to the kiss we would stop just before the kiss and jump to after the kiss.

"We did it for weeks.

"Then one day the scene was on its feet and the stage manager came in and put one of those beautiful pieces of rice paper on the table in front of me.

"It said, 'Your father called.'

"Well, it was before long distance was cheap and my father never called so I was emotionally out of the room when I heard the actress shout, 'Decker, Decker!'

"And I looked up and they had done the kiss—and the boy had fainted dead away in her arms, and she was holding him.

"Well, it was an interesting moment for me. It was the very first time in my life that I realised that I was no longer young. That I would never again feel the glory that boy felt kissing that girl. And I can get that incredibly complex left-handed primary state of being by just saying the words 'rice paper.'

"The rice paper had nothing to do with the event. But the rice paper was the tactile key to open the door to the event." He paused. *The portal, the path to the event,* he thought.

"Did the rice paper have a smell to it?" Tinnery asked.

Decker just smiled and told her to get her scene partner. "Time to act."

And even as he directed her through her first scene, the two of them had connected. Although she played lover/lover to her scene partner (professional actors reduce all relationships to those within a family unit: father/son, older sister/younger sister, etc. The only exception is lover/lover in opposition to husband/wife) she was clearly in lover/lover with him. And that night she knocked at his Garden Centre apartment door and without preamble and very little talk she'd bedded him, her strong back arching to the heavens to find her joy.

Looking back on it, it was one of the happiest times of his life. But Decker knew that there was always a price for happiness, and it came on his sixth day of rehearsal—his third day with Tinnery—in the guise of four large men in suits who identified themselves as working for the ANC—"And if you wish to continue to work in our beautiful country, you will come with us."

The room was frigid. This April was unseasonably cold. Northwesterlies whipped through the city—and there was no central heating.

Decker pulled his sweater more tightly around him and cupped his hands over the earphones and leaned closer to the one-way mirror. He wished he could see the entire room but the far corner was obscured.

On the other side of the glass it seemed that a team of middle-aged ANC interrogators were questioning a young Zulu who sat very still in his chair, his hands in his lap. Decker knew from the questions that he was some sort of ANC youth leader who the interrogators believed had overstepped his authority.

"Why were no minutes taken at the Pretoria meeting?"

"There were minutes taken."

"Where are they?"

"I don't know."

"What exactly did you say about South Africa's white population at the meeting in Pretoria last Wednesday?" the lead interrogator asked.

The younger man answered in a language that Decker didn't know. He lifted one earpiece and looked to the translator at his side.

"He wants the questions asked in Xhosa, not English." Then she added, "The language of the oppressor."

Decker nodded, pointed to the computer screen in front of him and returned the earpiece to his ear.

He heard the interrogator snap a question in what he assumed was Xhosa and looked to the computer screen in front of him, where his translator typed the questions and responses in English: *"Did you lead the meeting in Pretoria last Wednesday?"*

"Yes."

"And was the position of the ANC vis-à-vis the rights of whites discussed?"

"No."

Decker closed his eyes and sensed the presence of the cold above him. He moved his head up into the clear air and felt something metal in his hand and the slime of blood between his fingers. From either side of his retinal screen squiggling lines entered the field—not a truth.

Decker noted it on the pad in front of him.

"No?" the interrogator demanded. *"Then what was discussed?"*

"The future of our movement. The future of our country."

Decker closed his eyes again—two perfect squares slowly moved across his retinal screen. A truth—or at least a truth as far as this man was concerned.

Decker shifted in his chair. He wasn't comfortable working for a government—any government.

If it hadn't been for Tinnery he would have told them to fuck themselves, packed his bags and left. But there was Tinnery, so he'd agreed and here he was in this cold room with the female interpreter at his side and a clearly angry young ANC political activist being interrogated on the other side of a one-way mirror.

Older ANC interrogators—younger ANC party leader. Was there a civil war brewing in Nelson Mandela's party? The great leader was weak, dying—this might be part of the inevitable power struggle to follow his death, he thought.

The interrogation circled back to some basics about the young man's activities—all of which Decker knew the young man answered honestly.

"Was that the truth?" the interpreter demanded.

Decker nodded. His talent was very narrow. He knew when someone was telling the truth—period.

Then a man, clearly the leader of the interrogators, stepped forward. From Decker's vantage point he couldn't see into the corner of the room—where the older man had evidently been standing.

"So you don't like white people," the old man said.

"I like white people," the young man answered.

The interpreter looked at Decker. Decker saw two parallel lines on his retinal screen and nodded. It was a truth. Of course it was a truth—he likes white people who stay in England or Holland or America. Stupid question.

"But not all white people?"

"Do you like all white people?" the young man demanded.

"No," the old man said.

"Neither do I," the young man said.

Decker watched the old man consider his next question, and when he finally spoke, Decker realised that the old man had sympathy for the younger man's position. It was then that Decker noticed for the first time that the young man's legs were shackled to the chair upon which he sat, and there was a small puddle at his feet—urine.

"Did you say at the meeting that any real South African would rise up and drive the whites from this country?"

"Xhosa, please."

"Did you say at the meeting that any real South African would rise up and drive the whites from our country?"

"No."

Cold, metal, slime—a single corkscrew line crossed his retinal screen. The interpreter looked at him, and it finally occurred to Decker that this woman was not just an interpreter, she was also an interrogator—perhaps the head interrogator.

"So, Mr. Roberts?"

Decker took a deep breath then said, "It's not a truth."

"So a lie?"

"I can tell when someone is telling the truth. His last answer was not a truth."

"Fine," she said and rose. She touched a button on the console, and a drapery silently slid across the one-way mirror. The last Decker saw of the young man was a look of terror on his face as a large man who had also been kept from Decker's view moved toward him. "Thank you, Mr. Roberts. You've been very helpful."

Decker rose and found his legs wobbly. She was holding the door

open for him and as he passed her she said, "I look forward to seeing your play."

He fought the desire to just pick up and leave. But then he saw
Tinnery watching him rehearse, and all thoughts of leaving—left.

Every afternoon she watched him rehearse.

Every evening she outdid her acting partner in his class.

Every night she guided him to a place without a name.

But he already knew that they were good lovers—fuck that, great
lovers—but not very good mates.

They both lived in shells, in a profound isolation that they were
willing to leave to physically find each other but were unwilling to
leave to entwine their thoughts or beings.

She had been the first to acknowledge their divide. "Tell me about
your wife."

"She died a long time back."

"Did you love her?"

"Not enough," he said, thinking that Crazy Eddie had loved her
more than he had—and she had loved Eddie much more than she
had ever loved him.

"Not enough? Evasive, Decker, evasive."

"So?"

"So don't be."

He said nothing in response to that.

"Did she love you?"

"In the beginning."

"And at the end?"

"No."

"No. As simple as that—just no."

"No. Not simple. She loved my friend."

"And that hurt?"

"No."

That surprised her. She looked closely at him. "When you make
love to me are you thinking of me?"

Decker looked away.

"Don't do that," she snapped.

Decker looked back at her.

"When I touch you are you feeling my fingers, hearing me in your ear, sensing my tongue—are you even there, Decker?"

Decker didn't answer.

"And what about your son?"

He wanted to say "He hates me" but didn't say anything.

She nodded slowly. "Not going down that path—not going to open that door?"

Before he could stop himself he said, "Not to you."

She straightened as if he'd hit her, then said, "It's not men or women you're looking for, are you Decker? It's something outside of humanity that you want. But that's all there is—men and women. Those are the choices, Decker—there's nothing else."

For the briefest moment he thought of the young Cuban pianist searching for the secret outside of the eighty-eight keys of the piano.

"You're wrong," he managed, but he wasn't sure.

"No. I'm not wrong, Decker. I'm not. It's you who's wrong, who's full of shit." And then she was there, ripping his clothes and snarling in his ear, "Fuck me, Decker—come on, find me and fuck me, Decker."

And for a brief moment he tried—to find her. To find this extraordinarily alive woman—full woman—reaching across space and time and culture and language and the cosmos to him to bring him out of himself to get him all the way to her. To leave his search for a path and land—land here with her.

But as she arched her back in what should have been pleasure, a fury crossed her face and she cursed his name then leapt from him naked and spat on the ground and stomped on the spittle with her heel, rubbing it deep into the clay floor—an ancient curse that even modern men felt in their hearts.

A week later his shows opened to middling response. He hopped a twenty-hour bus ride to Windhoek, Namibia, rented a car there and drove to a desert resort called Mowani—God's breath in Swahili.

There amongst the desert mountains he found a moment of respite. As he stood on the rocks of Mowani and watched the sun go down, the quiet of the high desert—and the elongating shadows on the remarkable rock formations—called him to peace, to lay down his burden. The desert night was coming on quickly, and the high temperatures of the day were already a thing of the past.

Then he saw her approach—Inshakha. He had no idea how she knew he was there. He had not seen her since his first visit to Mowani four years earlier.

"Do you know your stars yet, Decker Roberts?" Inshakha asked.

"You were a good teacher but I—"

"Am a bad student," she said. She pointed to the east horizon. "Venus," she said, "the first heavenly object to appear in the southern sky. And you can always tell the day of the month by its distance to the moon. As the moon is new Venus is above it; as it ages, Venus is beneath it."

"And you can see the hidden part of the moon all day long."

"Can you not see it in Canada?"

"Not usually during the day."

"Here in Namibia, if the moon can be seen at night it can always be seen in the day. It must be frightening for you to lose the moon."

Decker looked at her incredibly refined features.

"More stars—those two." She pointed in the opposite direction from Venus to two bright stars that had appeared shortly after Venus rose.

"I see them. What are they?"

"You mean their names?"

"Yes."

"I have no idea. Names are not important. They point to the important thing."

"And what is that?"

"The Southern Cross is what your missionaries taught us to call it." She pointed to a pattern of four stars. Decker thought they looked more like a kite than a cross, but then again . . .

"What do your people call that pattern of four stars?"

She smiled but hid her eyes from him. He did not press the issue. "And that?" she said, pointing to the low horizon opposite the moon. Suddenly as if from nowhere a distinct pattern of stars appeared. "What does it look like, Decker? What animal?"

Decker looked again and it was clear. "A scorpion."

"Yes. With its tail raised. See its tail? Now follow it to its body and then its head. It is one of the most perfect of the constellations. And one of the few that we and the Europeans called by the same name."

"Scorpio."

"Yes. Do you see its body?"

"Yes."

"Count three stars from the end of the tail. See the red star—the one that pulses?"

"Yes."

"It is exactly where the heart is on a scorpion. A red heart that pulses."

Decker looked and felt his own heart beat in rhythm to the pulse of the red star of Scorpio's heart.

Then he looked at her and she was smiling. Nodding. Finally she said, "Yes, Decker, you are like the scorpion—crafty and potentially dangerous. And like the scorpion you have a strong heart, a heart that beats heavy in your chest."

Decker looked away from her as if she had suddenly seen into him.

"Why did you come back to Namibia, Decker? Try not to lie— you're a very bad liar."

"To allow my friend to get back his daughter."

She nodded her beautiful head slowly and said, "That is what you made yourself believe. But you came here to hide."

"No."

"Yes. But they have found you." She indicated two men across the way. "I have a cabin for us in Etosha—you'll like it there. It's by the watering hole, and every day the animals from miles around come to drink. Your scorpion's heart is beating, but it needs time in Namibia to strengthen."

19

A CROSSING OF BORDERS—T MINUS 16 DAYS

SETH WAITED HIS TURN IN LINE FOR U.S. IMMIGRATION. HE DID HIS best not to turn on his heel and flee. He knew why he was heading to the United States, but he couldn't completely get over his antipathy to America.

The immigration officer signalled him to come forward. He stepped onto the electronic pad and offered his palm for the hand scan.

"Passport," the man said.

Seth gave him his passport.

"Put your hand down. You're a Canadian, no need for a scan." Then under his breath, clearly for the benefit of the immigration officer in the next booth, he said, "Don't ask me why."

The guy in the next booth chortled.

The immigration officer opened Seth's passport and slid it through the digital reader. As he did, a ding sounded in the Junction, and Eddie turned in his swivel chair and reached for his computer.

"What's the reason for your visit, son?" the immigration officer asked—no, demanded.

Seth took out the treatment regime that had been sent to him by the San Francisco Wellness Dream Clinic. The immigration officer read the document quickly and then asked, "You have an address for this . . . clinic?"

Seth pointed at the address on the bottom of the document, and the immigration officer typed it into his computer. Then he stopped. His cursor was hopping around his screen. "Hey," he called to the next booth. "Your computer okay?" After receiving an affirmative he turned back to his screen—and his cursor had stopped hopping.

Back at home in the Junction, Eddie copied down the address, made a second check to be sure that it had been Seth's passport that had dinged his computer, then found the address on Google Earth. As he did he said aloud, "What're you up to, Seth?"

20

A DRUNKENNESS OF COPS:
GARRETH SENIOR—T MINUS 16 DAYS

THE RETIRED TORONTO HOMICIDE COP WAS SITTING IN THE living room of his home in Seaside, Florida—the house that a drug dealer's money paid for—watching the news on Fox when he got the call from his son, who was a detective on the Toronto police force.

Seaside, Florida, is the crème de la crème of planned communities—rich planned communities. Every house was designed by the central design team. All the houses are named and had the names of the owners proudly displayed on brass plaques hanging from their front picket fences. Several had an added sign that said Be Nice or Go Away.

It was Garreth Senior's gift to himself after forty-plus years of honourable service on the Toronto Police Service—most in homicide. Honourable that is until the day—almost four years ago now.

He had awoken that day thinking about Decker Roberts. He remembered having a beer with his soft-boiled eggs. And another with his toast. But still, Decker Roberts' image was with him, and the image of that little girl who bled to death in the snow. By noon when he stumbled on the Vietnamese drug dealers he was rollicking drunk and it seemed like destiny that he appeared at the exact moment when the money was changing hands.

He'd never been so scared in his life. He'd also never seen so much of what his father would have called cash money. He was on autopilot—the booze was in control. No, fuck that—Decker Roberts was in control. The money was in his hands before he knew it. Then it was in the safe beneath his bed. Then in the Bahamas bank—now in his Seaside house.

The phone was ringing. For a moment he couldn't identify the source of the sound—was he having a fire, or was it the damned carbon monoxide alarm? Then he remembered—it was his phone. It rang so seldom.

"We found his son, Dad."

"Decker Roberts' son?"

"Yeah."

"Where?"

"He just crossed the border at Blaine, Washington."

"And Mr. Roberts Senior?"

"We're not sure. Last we knew he was out of the country—somewhere in Africa."

"Well, perhaps the boy knows his father's whereabouts." The idea hung out there for Garreth Junior to comment on, but he didn't. "Do we know where the young Mr. Roberts is heading?"

"Dad?"

"Come on, Son! If you tracked him to the border you know where he's going."

Garreth Junior sighed then gave him the address of the Wellness Dream Clinic just north of San Francisco.

"Wacko California stuff?"

"Sounds like it to me, Dad. You going to check this out?"

Garreth Senior thought of an old film—*Hud* or *Hush* or something else beginning with an H that was about a killing in one of those weird-assed places—then asked, "Do you really want to know?"

"No. Actually I don't."

"Fine, then we never spoke. One more thing."

"What?"

"What's the young Mr. Roberts' name?"

"Seth. Seth Roberts."

"Book of Seth," Garreth Senior said.

"What?"

"Nothing."

"Okay." He drew a long breath then asked, "How are you, Dad?"

Better, now, he thought, but said, "The same. I'm the same."

"Hey, you know I'm worried about you."

"Are you, now?"

"Yeah. This thing with this Roberts has become an obsession with you. You know?"

Garreth Senior hung up the phone.

He stepped out onto his screened-in porch and felt the thick warm night.

Decker Roberts.

So Decker Roberts had produced a child. A devil's seed.

He'd met Decker Roberts almost forty years ago. It had been a raw January day outside a fancy house in the Glencairn district of Toronto, before the big synagogue was built and the area became an enclave of Orthodox Jews. When WASP Toronto was still fighting a defensive action against encroachment of Jews of any sort. Decker Roberts was four or five years old. And cold. And frightened. And very possibly responsible for the death of a six-year-old girl.

Garreth added a bit of sugar to his bourbon and swirled the dark liquid in the highball glass. Bourbon was a newish delight for him; adding sugar was something his southern neighbours had taught him. He had tried the mint sprigs they also added to their bourbon but disliked the way it covered the slow smokiness of the liquor. Besides, he couldn't get over the feeling that if you added mint you should also add a tiny umbrella and probably a cookie.

No.

Alcohol was a grown-up's pleasure and he wanted to keep it that way.

He tilted the fine liquid into his mouth and savoured it on his tongue. As long as he was tasting it he wasn't drinking just to get drunk—or so he told himself.

Palmetto bugs slapped into the veranda's screens. Beyond them, fireflies flicked into and out of existence. He metaphorically peered into his own darkness.

Garreth swallowed his drink in one long gulp, passed by the TV that flickered light across his hardwood floors and headed into his basement, where he kept the files of his unsolved cases, knowing that the one on top had the underlined name of Decker Roberts on it.

A PLOTTING OF CRAZY EDDIES— T MINUS 16 DAYS

EDDIE ROLLED A BOMBER THICKER THAN HIS THUMB AND INHALED deeply.

The Trojan he'd embedded in the new lease he'd e-mailed to Ira Charendoff, Patchin Place Lawyer, was doing its nastiness and had sent him Charendoff's e-mail contact list, which of course included the man's daughter's address.

Eddie looked at the photograph of the Charendoff girl he'd downloaded from the Paris newspaper's website, then at the photo of the dead boy almost encased in the ice of Stanstead's little river. He turned over several possibilities in his mind, then he reminded himself that the sinner was the father, not the daughter, and how very wrong that Old Testament crap was about visiting the sins of the father on his children.

He fired off a quick e-mail to the daughter and waited for the unsubscribe reply. It came in seconds with a request to remove her from his e-mail list—she did not wish to receive any more correspondence from Iowa Baptist Ministries for Justice and Peace in Moldova.

Good, Eddie thought. *Just wanted to make sure that was you.*

He looked at the photo of the dead Stanstead boy a second time, then replaced the photo of the daughter with one of her father—the sinner.

He pulled out his checklist. *(1) Get Decker safely away—done.* He checked his GPS mapping program, and there he was. Good. *(2)*

Find Marina in Portland—in process. (3) Attack Charendoff—to be executed.

Eddie opened his STUXNET file and added the few new ideas he'd been able to piece together from his recent explorations into the covert world of cyberwarfare. Eddie, like almost every other computer maven in the world, was pretty sure that STUXNET was an Israeli viral attack on Iran's nuclear industry.

Unlike some he believed there were good viral attacks and bad viral attacks.

On a whim he opened his WikiLeaks folder from his computer desktop and reread the news coverage closely. Mr. Assange had got himself in a passel of trouble. But that wasn't really a concern of Eddie's. He had no idea if Mr. Assange was a force for good or evil in the world. Jury was out on that as far as he was concerned, but the American government was clearly anxious to nail his snotty little ass to the wall—which led him back to the PROMPTOR anonymity system.

He reduced the WikiLeaks file and opened his PROMPTOR file. There he quickly scanned the few scraps he'd been able to put together on the founder of PROMPTOR—and, once again, on the American government's interest in silencing him. Two people "of interest" to the American government—the head of PROMPTOR and Mr. Assange.

Eddie thought about that—"people of interest to the American government."

Now if he could get the authorities to take the same kind of interest in Lawyer Charendoff in New York City . . .

He enlarged the article on the second arrest of the head of PROMPTOR and read it slowly, highlighting the claim that the guy made that he was not the real head of/or programmer of PROMPTOR.

"But what if I could make the authorities believe that Lawyer Charendoff was that guy—the head of/programmer of PROMPTOR?" Eddie swivelled in his chair. How sweet to have a man—fuck, a lawyer—like Charendoff hounded by a government that he thought was there to protect him and his property.

"So PROMPTOR is the weapon," he said aloud. "Time to get up close and personal with the world of PROMPTOR."

He hit three keys and entered a sixteen-letter password corresponding to the correct algorithm generated from the date, then pressed enter. Hundreds of seemingly delighted clicks announced that every library computer in the entire metropolitan area was at his beck and call. He pressed two more keys and several thousand more clicks followed: all of the computers at York University and the University of Toronto awaited his bidding. *Good,* he thought. *I'll need the computing power to begin this little exercise.*

He called up his own PROMPTOR program and sent himself a message—"Hey you, it's me, don't disappear up your own asshole!"—and waited for it to bounce through hundreds, perhaps thousands of volunteers' computers, each of which removed a bit of his identity then passed it on. A ding announced his e-mail's return. It showed absolutely no clue as to his identity as the sender.

Then he sent a second e-mail to himself from one of his other accounts. Its dinged return was speedier, but it gave out all the information about who he was and where he was writing from.

He reduced both to half a page and aligned them side by side, then took a deep drag, sat back and studied the two e-mails as he thought about Marina and what he'd need to make the U.S. government think that Ira Charendoff was the mastermind behind PROMPTOR. If he could do that he'd then offer Charendoff a way off the hook—he'd have the leverage he needed to get Ira Charendoff off his fat lawyer's ass and have him arrange for Marina's return.

22

A TENTATIVENESS OF APPROACH—
T MINUS 14 DAYS

TAKING HIS FATHER'S $20,000 BANK DRAFT FROM HIS WALLET AT the San Francisco Wellness Dream Clinic was one of the hardest things Seth had ever done. It surprised him. Shit, no—it shocked him what he was feeling—the intense guilt as he considered handing over the check to the pert blond receptionist.

But he had done his research and knew he needed to move beyond the temporary pause in his cancer that BCG treatments offered.

The past few times he'd been cystoed he'd read the growing concern on the doctors' faces. The last time he hadn't even seen his own doctor—another physician, a British lady, had treated him like, well, like nothing more than a body for the growth of a disease. She'd clucked when she saw the cancerous growths on his bladder wall and even said to the attending nurse, "What is that bladder still doing in him?"

There's something infinitely obscene about two women hovering over a naked man with a tube shoved up his penis and treating him like a piece of diseased meat. At times it felt like the Canadian medical system didn't really treat him. The disease they treated; him they sometimes ignored and he was getting the eerie feeling that he was running up against some sort of protocol in the system. Yeah, his bladder grew tumours, but they were surface tumours that could be lasered out, either under local or general anaesthetic. He'd had both done. But he was getting the distinct impression that the system had a maximum number of times they were willing to do this before they went to the more final solution of removing his bladder—something that in all likelihood would profoundly change his life.

Yes, Ms. Palin, there are no death panels in the Canadian medical system, but all systems have limitations, and those limitations force the system to prioritize. There is never enough money and/or expertise to manage everything, so in Canada diseases are triaged. America does the same thing, but they use money as the determinant—just another form of triage where the poor are last on the list.

So he'd gone in search of an actual cure, found an experimental option in Northern California and requested the fee—$20,000—from Eddie, who got it from his father.

And now Seth was fingering the $20,000 bank draft.

As he did, he was watched on a closed-circuit monitor by a tall, slender man with long grey hair.

Seth handed over his $20,000 and entered the corridor leading to the clinic, unaware that the heavy steel door closed silently behind him, and bolted shut.

23

A CRASH OF RHINOS—T MINUS 12 DAYS

SOMEONE WAS BANGING ON THE METAL DOORS OF THE women's restroom stalls.

Then shouting, "Hicks! Hicks! Get the fuck out here!" It was Harrison—in the women's restroom. What the fuck was Harrison doing in the women's restroom?

As Yslan stepped out of the stall she saw Harrison pacing and muttering to himself. No, not muttering—cursing. Now he was yelling.

"Did you find what's his name?" he demanded.

"Decker Roberts? Yeah. We've tracked him to South Africa and we're on him now."

Harrison laughed, turned to the sink and stared into the mirror.

"Something's funny, sir?"

"No. Nothing's funny. Nothing's funny anymore."

The finality of his statement stunned her.

Then he smashed the mirror with his fist.

Glass tinkled off the porcelain sink and to the floor; blood blossomed from his fist.

And she knew.

It had happened—shit, it had happened again.

She stood perfectly still and said only one word. "Where?"

24

A FURY OF BLASTS—T MINUS 12 DAYS

TWO HOURS LATER YSLAN AND HARRISON ARRIVED AT ANCASTER College. The campus was beautiful in the early spring light. Mature oak and maple trees were in bud and seemed to leap up the mountain upon which the famous college housed its vast lab complexes and state of the art research facilities.

They noted that if you looked up the hill the upper New York State idyll was on view and complete—an elite college for the best and brightest science and math students in the country, perhaps in the world.

But when they lowered their gaze to the base of the mountain they saw a scene reminiscent of a war zone. Two buildings teetered ominously just north of the blast site. The late eighteenth century Calvinist church was no longer a model of perfect symmetry as its iconic steeple, which embossed every piece of the college's stationery, listed far to one side. And almost half a square mile of pavement had evidently been shot into the air. Some of it was now embedded several feet deep in the earth at angles that seemed to defy the laws of physics.

In the epicentre was the huge crater. It was now surrounded by police tape and so many armed and body-armoured soldiers that this could easily be mistaken for a street in Tripoli rather than a quiet upper New York State town that prided itself on its college, its green approach to the environment and its massive U.S. military contracts.

Yslan and Harrison badged their way through the cordon of soldiers and cops until they stood on the very edge of the gash in the earth. The gaping hole before them was still populated by the remains of hundreds of human beings and the obscenely twisted flimsy folding chairs upon which they had been seated only four hours earlier—some of which seemed to be bowing down in prayer to some as of yet unnamed underworld god of vengeance.

From the few still-standing poles the remnants of the huge graduation tent flapped with obscene gaiety in the fresh spring wind.

Yslan was surprised by the overall quiet of the place. She looked skyward at the bright sun, which seemed to be mocking them all. Then her eyes were drawn by some motion down in the pit. At first she thought it was a large stone rolling down the east wall of the blast site, but she was wrong. When she understood what it was that had drawn her eye, her gorge rose. The head bounced, then came to rest on the blast floor, a single eye open—staring, or at least seemingly staring—right at her.

Yslan looked away and tried to concentrate on the preliminary forensic reports that she'd just been given.

There'd been two devices. Why techs insisted on calling bombs devices was beyond Yslan's understanding or concern.

The fucking things blew up—period.

But the devices—bombs—and the hundreds of pounds of scrap metal that had surrounded them were placed perfectly to cause maximum damage. The first blast instantly killed forty-three of the finest maths and science professors in the western world. The second immolated the entire summa cum laude and cum laude graduating class—amongst them seventy-two degrees in advanced electrical/ civil engineering, thirty-nine in computer science, twenty-two in nuclear physics and twenty-one in chemical engineering.

She put aside the report and knelt as she had done that September day long ago when the locusts had come and in one afternoon eaten their entire tobacco crop. She had been only a kid but she knew that the disaster visited from the skies had irrevocably changed her life. For a moment she heard the locusts all around her—in her hair, up her shirt, in her nostrils. She shook her head. *Here!* she commanded herself. *Stay here and find out what the fuck happened here.*

25

A COLLECTION OF CLUES—
T MINUS 12 DAYS

HARRISON AND YSLAN STARED AT THE PHOTOS OF THE BLAST SITE
lined up on the desk in the provost's office. To one side stood a
terribly thin man, the Provost himself, clearly anxious not to be in the
same room as the two NSA agents.

Of the photos there were only two of the faculty on the stage—all of
whom were now dead. One shot was from so far away that they could
barely distinguish male from female. The other was from the side of the
stage so that only a few of the faculty members' faces could be seen.

"Wasn't there a seating plan or something for the faculty?" Harrison demanded of the provost.

"They were all such free spirits, you couldn't tell them anything,
like where to sit." The man's voice was a cross between a whine and
whimper. "Why is this important; they're all dead." This last word
came out more as a breath than a word.

Yslan looked to Harrison. Both knew the provost's question was
reasonable, but until they had real forensic evidence to work with,
identifying the victims was at least a place to start.

Yslan had already established the provost's whereabouts at the
time of the blasts. He was puking his guts out, evidently frightened
at having to read aloud all the foreign-sounding names of the graduates. The students had refused to give their names in phonetics,
stating in an open letter published in the school newspaper, "It's
time you learned how to pronounce our fucking names!" A janitor
who had cleanup duties in the restroom had confirmed his alibi.

"So all we really have to identify the professors who were victims is this?" Harrison said, pointing to the list of attending faculty members and the two photos.

"And the inquiries from families missing loved ones," Yslan added.

"In the hours to come there'll be a lot more of those. Have we asked for dental matches?"

"Yeah, but it could be some time before we get any."

"I can identify some of them from their gowns and tassels," piped up the provost, suddenly alive and confident—lecturing. "You see, in determining your academic regalia colors, all PhD degrees use PhD blue, which is dark blue. For example, a doctorate in psychology would include in your academic hood colors the color gold—of course we don't have any psychology degrees here since we're a science college—however a PhD in psychology, if we had one, would use dark blue. If you have multiple degrees, like Professor Zhang Fang or Professor Charles David—well, almost all of them have more than one degree—the rule is that you use only one hood and only one degree or discipline color. You use the hood and color that represents your highest-ranking degree, with doctoral as highest, master's as second highest, bachelor's as third highest. If you have two different degrees at the same highest ranking, you generally use the most recently awarded degree as your hood.

"If you have an unlisted degree, there is no official color and it is dependent on the individual college or university to determine the color to be used for your hood. Typically, the most similar degree on the official chart is chosen. For example, if your degree is in an advanced computer science field, usually the school chooses science gold for the degree color. Clear?"

"Yeah, perfectly," Yslan said quickly, fearing he would continue. She already felt a familiar weariness in her bones that she remembered all too well from lectures delivered by other self-satisfied professors.

Then much to Yslan's surprise, using the academic colours, the provost named more than half of the professors in the photos.

"What about the students?" Harrison asked. "Surely they were sitting in alphabetical order, weren't they?"

"Some were, yes. Some had already left for jobs. Some were too drunk to attend. Most refused to take any more orders and sat wherever they wanted."

"Swell," Yslan said. " 'Anarchist Geniuses Blown to Bits'—good headline."

"Hicks!" Harrison's voice was as ragged as she'd ever heard it. "Get it through your head what happened here. More than eighty percent of the brains behind this country's present defence systems and as much as fifty percent of the defence network's future brains were obliterated today. This is the single most serious blow to the safety of this country—ever."

Mr. T stuck his head in the office. "Forensics are ready, sir."

"Send them in," Harrison said, then turned to the provost. "Do you mind?"

The provost was about to say that this was his office, then looked at Harrison and decided he didn't really need his office for the foreseeable future. He made his way out as six forensics techs shoved their way past him.

As they flipped open their laptops, Harrison turned to Yslan and said, "Recheck the provost's alibi. He wasn't on the stage when the fucking thing blew up. I want to know why."

"He's a suspect?"

"He's alive when the rest are dead—so yeah, he's a suspect."

"I'll send for the janitor who saw him in the men's room."

The techs began to spout figures.

Harrison put up his hand for them to stop. "When you boys talk numbers it usually means you don't have dick."

The head tech looked up and eyed Harrison. Yslan noted that there was clearly no love lost here. "Two huge blasts, one just seconds after the other. Shards of metal—"

"What kind of metal shards?"

The tech reached into his briefcase and pulled out a clear plastic evidence bag. Inside it was a piece of steel plate maybe six inches by four inches with razor-sharp edges. It clanked as it hit the desktop.

"And you found—"

"Hundreds and hundreds of them."

Harrison picked up the evidence bag. It was heavier than he thought it would be.

"So it wasn't a suicide bomber?"

"Not unless there were two of them and they were both world-class weight lifters."

"So the bombs were planted before the ceremony?"

"Yep."

"Anything more?"

"Not yet."

"When?"

The head tech shrugged.

"We need more," Harrison said, then added, "Quickly."

The forensic guys closed their laptops and headed out.

The white-haired agent that Decker Roberts had named Ted Knight stepped into the room, and Harrison turned to him. "I want names of dissidents within a two-hundred-mile radius and the addresses and names of anyone who's been in a mosque in the entire state—include Pennsylvania, New Hampshire and fucking Vermont, too."

"Already done," Ted Knight said, handing over a lengthy printout.

"How many men—"

"We have forty."

Turning to Yslan, Harrison said, "Get them a hundred more and every Arabic speaker we have. And get our photo geniuses to work on those pictures. Once they're worked up show them to the provost, show them to the grieving families, show them to the goddamned janitor. I want names put to those faces and exactly who sat where."

26

WALTER JONES WAITED PATIENTLY IN THE PROVOST'S OUTER office. He'd only been there once before and then it was to clean up after a party of some sort. And of course the place had been empty then. After five or six these admin offices were all empty. Now, however, it was a hub of activity as what Walter assumed were federal officers came and left the provost's inner office like bees reporting back to the hive then being sent out on new missions.

Walter had been told to be there at six thirty, and he'd arrived a few minutes early, but it was now almost eight o'clock and he had the evening shift. When a large black man came out of the inner office, Walter gathered his courage and said, "My name is Walter Jones. I was told to be here at six thirty."

The black man looked at his watch and mumbled an apology and went back in the office. Five minutes later an attractive woman opened the office door. Walter caught a brief glimpse inside. It reminded him of a war room scene from a World War II movie. He liked World War II movies.

The attractive woman introduced herself. Walter missed the first name, but got the second—Hicks.

"Sorry to make you wait, Mr. Jones."

Walter shrugged and said, "That's okay."

A marine entered, and the woman talked to him in a hushed voice, then turned back to Walter.

"Look, I just need to know one thing."

"Okay."

"Did you see the provost in the men's room shortly before the graduation?" She paused. "Before the bombs."

"Yes," he said.

She smiled and turned toward the office. Then turned back to Walter. "What was he doing?"

Walter wasn't going to tell her that the guy was reciting over and over again to the mirror "We can do this, yes we can, yes we can do this" while he was popping Ativan like it was PEZ. Which he was. But Walter shrugged again and said, "It's a men's room."

This Hicks person smiled, turned and reentered the provost's inner office.

That's it? Walter thought. *That's the entire investigation?* Walter tried not to smile, but he wanted to. Oh, how he wanted to.

27

A MASS OF MEDIA—T MINUS 12 DAYS
TO T MINUS 8 DAYS

THE MEDIA COVERAGE INTENSIFIED AS IDENTIFIED BODY PARTS were slowly released to grieving family members. A memorial was planned to be held in ten days' time. The president himself was going to deliver the eulogy. His imminent presence caused yet more delays as agents had to be pulled from interrogations into protection planning. And all the nation howled for revenge—and the president's office applied pressure to Harrison, that he promptly passed on to Yslan and the interrogators.

But nothing moved.

Upper New York State is cut off from much of the nation. It is a backwater, and those left there are sometimes an angry lot. The place had always been a breeding ground for alternative religions. Joseph Smith found the sacred Book of Mormon just up the road at what the locals call the East Jesus exit of the thruway. The area was also populated by hundreds of radical nuts, dissident nuts and nuts and berries of every variety. And each and every one of these mouth breathers seemed to hold some grudge against the military, the country's foreign policy, Washington or "the lack of godliness in the nation." No doubt someone up here celebrated Sugar Plum Tuesday with the sacrifice of a goat.

Put beside these guys, the mosque folks seemed downright rational—although it was clear they were also terrified and not fully cooperating.

After four days the NSA had unearthed nothing but a few kooks and the reality that as many as twenty labs on the campus had the ingredients necessary to make the two bombs and none of these potentially dangerous substances were kept under any serious lock and key.

Yslan was summing up all this for Harrison when she noticed that he had moved a cot into the provost's office—and that he clearly hadn't slept for days. She wondered how many.

"So you're telling me that we're nowhere. No suspects, no real leads, and frankly few stones left unturned."

"I'm afraid that's what I'm telling you, sir."

Harrison looked away from her.

"We need help, sir."

He turned back to her but before he could object she said, "I've sent our people to find Viola Tripping."

"You've got to be out of your mind. If the press ever finds—"

"They won't unless we tell them."

"They better not." He took a deep breath then said, "So did they find her?"

"Of course."

After another deep breath he asked, "When's she—"

"Tonight." Then she quickly added, "She'll only travel in the dark."

Back in her room Yslan watched her monitor as the tiny figure of Viola Tripping held tightly to the huge arm of Mr. T. She had drawn a black shawl over her head, and when she moved she looked like ET under its blanket. Ted Knight followed them, taping their every move with a tiny camera attached to his lapel. Yslan looked away from the image, and despite herself a smile creased her face. *I think of them as Mr. T and Ted Knight—like Decker does. When did that start? Shit, if someone asked me their names, I'd say Mr. T and Ted Knight!* Then, without any seeming reason, Viola Tripping pulled back the shawl and stared into the camera and screamed at the lens.

The scream seemed to pierce Yslan's heart, and she grabbed her chest in pain. For a moment she thought that she was having a heart attack.

She got the call from Mr. T a few moments later that Viola Tripping was safely in the windowless room that she'd requested. The room was down a long corridor in the basement of the old physics building. There had been rumours as to the original use of the room—World War I poisoned gas test site was the most popular, and the most likely. This university had been in bed with the military hierarchy of America for a very, very long time.

"Is she here?"

Yslan hadn't heard Harrison come into her room.

"Yes," she said.

"And she has to be in the actual place of the death?" Harrison demanded.

"Yeah," Yslan replied.

"Why?"

Yslan shot Harrison a withering look.

She didn't know why. And she knew he knew that she didn't know why. Finally she said, "We've tracked her for almost five years. We have miles of tape of her speaking for the dead. All I know is that Viola Tripping can do this, speak for the dead, as long as we obey her rules."

"Stand in the exact spot the person died?"

"Right."

"And keep her locked in a room without windows."

"Right—and one more thing."

"What?"

"Every time she stands in the place of the dead person, she can find less and less of the deceased's final thoughts."

"Are you telling me that we may have only one shot at this?"

"Yeah."

"Well, we'll record her first . . . pass, or whatever you call it."

Yslan looked away.

"What?"

"The lights may distract her. Lately she's needed to be in almost perfect darkness."

"Infrared then."

"No. She senses it."

"Well then, we'll mic her."

"Sure," but she thought, *It won't help because Decker needs to see to be able to tell if a person is lying. Recordings are unreliable for him.*

Somehow Harrison was ahead of her.

"And this Viola person can't tell if a person is lying, can she?"

"No. She just repeats the thoughts that were in the person's head just before he dies."

The reality that they'd need Decker sat there between the two of them, but Harrison shoved it aside.

"And how does she do that?"

"Senses, hears, intuits—I don't fucking know how she does it."

Harrison lit a cigarette and let out the smoke in a long straight line. Yslan could have killed for a smoke, but before she could speak, Harrison hung his head and said, "We really don't know sweet fuck all, do we?"

Yslan took a step away.

"Do we, Special Agent Hicks?" he asked more forcefully.

"We know things, sir—but not enough." She failed to add that she seemed to understand her gifted synaesthetes better as time went on—especially after the days she'd spent interrogating Decker Roberts. But she had the oddest sensation that it wasn't Roberts' answers to her many questions that clarified things—it was actually just his presence so close to her.

Mr. T stuck his head in the room. "Got the enhanced photos ready, boss."

"Good, leave them on my desk," he said.

"Will do," Mr. T said and left.

Harrison turned to Yslan. "And you're sure you want to go through with this?"

She turned to look at him full-on. "Have we got another choice? Is there something new from forensics?"

Harrison momentarily recoiled: he wasn't used to being interrogated. "Just that the bombs could well have been built in one of the school's labs."

"Right. Any idea which one?"

"No."

"Right. And how's about the two hundred twenty-seven interviews you've done? Any leads there?"

"No."

"Right, so we move to plan B."

"Viola Tripping?"

"Viola Tripping."

Yslan took a deep breath and tried to calm herself. She had been tracking Viola Tripping for the NSA even longer than she had been tracking Decker Roberts, but Yslan had never met her before. She'd just seen video—lots of video—and it scared the bejeezus out of her.

Viola Tripping was in her early forties but was many inches shorter than five feet tall and had the vacant open face of a medieval cherub. Her blond hair fell in childish cascades across the peaches and cream complexion of her face, and her milky cataract-obstructed eyes were always wide open—even when she slept.

She reminded Yslan of the two spooky Englishwomen in the film *Don't Look Now,* which cured her of any desire to see Venice— although any place that Julie Christie went . . .

Yslan punched up the last video they had of Viola Tripping. It was from a month and a half ago. The girl/woman was wearing a summer dress with no bra—with her early pubescent breasts she hardly needed one—no stockings or shoes as she entered what looked like a revival tent. It was somewhere in Florida. But she wasn't there to preach. She was not a eulogist. No. Viola Tripping's gift had nothing to do with preaching. She was a speaker for the dead. The tent had been erected over a specific patch of ground where the deceased had taken his last breath.

Viola Tripping stepped forward carefully, took several moments to adjust her feet, to find the exact spot, then she opened her arms and began to spin slowly. As she did she recounted, word for word, the last thoughts of the deceased person.

Yslan knew that sometimes Viola Tripping went back just a few moments before death. Other times she went back several minutes—in one case, almost two hours.

Yslan watched the eleven minutes of recitation then turned off the video and did her best to collect herself.

Twenty minutes later she ordered the marine to unlock the heavy metal door that kept Viola Tripping in the windowless room.

When the door opened Yslan was assaulted by the smell of human urine and feces. Viola Tripping had soiled herself, but she was not ashamed. She stared with her milky eyes straight at Yslan.

"Good evening, Special Agent Hicks."

Viola's voice was so soft and breathy that at first Yslan wasn't sure that the girl/woman had actually spoken.

Then the girl/woman spoke a little louder: "I've made a poopoo."

28

A MÉLANGE OF THOUGHTS AND ACTIONS— T MINUS 8 DAYS

WALTER NURSED HIS '84 COROLLA CAREFULLY UP THE HILL THEN under the expressway that separated Ancaster College from his basement apartment in Stoney River.

His car radio was tuned to a call-in show that only periodically broke the stream of anti-Muslim rants with news updates from the "scene of the attack." Each update seemed sillier to Walter than the last. Sunnis, Shiites, Persians—what the hell were Persians?—then experts talking about each group and their gripes against America.

As Walter parked his car on the street outside his dingy apartment he wondered if he even lived in the America that the "terrorists had targeted." He doubted it.

Then he remembered his brief interrogation by the woman with the strange eyes and said aloud, "America ain't safe if that's as good as they can do—interrogation-wise."

He opened the door and stepped into his two-room apartment and said, "Bomb this—please!"

Back in her room, Yslan found herself surrounded by the sweet smells of Viola Tripping and somehow swimming in the very fact of her. She climbed into the shower and turned on the water—hot, hard—but the smell of the girl/woman, like a baby's sweet odour, refused to leave her.

When she finally left the shower she found it, on her bed—a plane ticket and two words in Harrison's strangely prissy scrawl: GET DECKER.

29

A GLORY OF TRAVELS IN NAMIBIA— T MINUS 21 DAYS TO T MINUS 7 DAYS

AFRICA REQUIRES PATIENCE—AND DECKER WAS LEARNING TO BE patient. Learning slowly.

He and Inshakha travelled from place to place, moving whenever they sensed they were being watched. Some of the places still attracted the heavyset old Dutch who used to rule this world. They'd strut into elegant dining rooms in their short pants, huge bellies straining belts and buttons and shouting the word "nigger" whenever possible. But Inshakha took no notice. "They are the dispossessed now. Soon they will not be able to afford to even eat in a place like this, let alone order around its staff." And it was true. Already this part of the world was getting too expensive for those who used to rule it with a cruel fist.

He and Inshakha travelled as husband and wife, but at night they disrobed facing away from each other before crawling beneath the covers. But even in the cold of the desert nights they never touched. Decker knew better than to think he could sleep with his muse—for that was what he thought Inshakha was.

One night in his sleep he put an arm across her; she stiffened and moved it away.

Both knew—neither mentioned it.

And on they drove, ignoring the passing of the days.

One brilliantly sunny morning they drove around one of the few wide-sweeping curves of highway in Namibia and Decker was surprised to see several scarecrow-like human forms lined up along the side of the road.

"Stop here," Inshakha told him.

He pulled the car over and watched as Inshakha slowly, reverentially approached the four figures. Decker saw that the figures—three women and a child—were made from bits of wood and tatters of cloth. One of the women had a piece of leather cleverly folded over her stick arm to make a kind of handbag.

The figures were positioned so that they were looking away from the road up toward the corrugated iron shack in which, no doubt, their maker and her family lived.

Three faceless women and a faceless child.

Inshakha took some money from her pocket and put it in the faux purse, then turned back to Decker. It took him a moment to understand that it was his turn. He approached the figures and found that in spite of himself he was walking slowly, as if up the aisle of a great cathedral. When he reached the figures he had an overwhelming desire to kneel.

Inshakha saw it and said, "No. You must not. Just put a coin in the woman's purse."

Decker fumbled in his wallet and pulled out a few bills, which he held out to her.

Inshakha shook her head. "You must do it."

Decker reached forward and touched the arm of the nearest woman. It immediately moved and he leapt back. The thing turned— it was on a pivot of some sort. He looked to Inshakha, who said nothing but continued to stare at him. He approached a second time and put the money into the purse, which to his surprise felt cool and damp—two things you never felt in Namibia.

Many kilometres later he turned to Inshakha and said, "Tell me about those figures."

Inshakha looked straight ahead and said simply, "This is a place that believes, Mr. Roberts. It is what you would call a spiritual place. It has been that way for thousands of years. Well before your man in the mosque or your man on the cross or that other old religion. All of those beliefs are in their infancy compared to the depth of belief in this place."

When he asked her for more specifics she ignored him.

Twice more in the next week they stopped in front of what Decker now knew were called Hindi figures. Each time Inshakha approached first and Decker found himself oddly reverential. The feeling of damp and cold was again present each time he put the money into the makeshift purse or basket.

Eventually they arrived at Wolwedans, where the sun comes up so fast on the east slope of the Losberg that there is no need for a morning wake-up call. It pierces the dawn gloom and brings the high sage and mountain contours to glorious light.

The weaverbirds sing as the dance of the high desert begins.

The cloudless April sky presents its ocean of blue to the land while in the mountains the leopards cover their eyes with their paws as the oryx and zebra and springbok are grateful to have made it through another dangerous night.

You see no old or sick oryx or zebra or springbok—the leopards see to that—nor are there any bits of kill left to fester, as the bat-eared foxes and omnipresent spotted hyenas go about their work with quiet efficiency.

The high red-tinted desert feels orderly. Things are in their place—as somehow they were meant to be.

Hot water is brought to the tent and Decker makes tea—he likes tea here in Africa, although he hates it back in the Junction. He dunks the rock-hard rusks that are so treasured in this part of the world into the hot liquid and savours their earthy flavour.

The walk to the base camp is about an hour. There is an Internet connection there, but he's unsure that he really wants to contact the outside world. He knows he doesn't want them to contact him.

For a brief moment he wonders if he could live here. A hard four-hour drive to Windhoek to get the flight to Jo'burg and then from there to anywhere his truth-telling business took him. And he could use the Internet connection to supply the research for his CBC documentary, *At the Junction*. He wondered—and the moment stretched out.

Is he prepared to live as a foreigner in a country that clearly does not belong to him?

Or him to it?

But the Junction? Does that belong to him? Is that home?

Or is home just a sentimental idea? One that he should have long ago outgrown?

He thinks of Seth as a young boy. Those are his only real memories of him. Waking up each day with a smile on his face and announcing, "Pretty day, Daddy. Pretty day." It was only later that Seth learned that "pretty day, Daddy" didn't mean "good morning." Too bad. "Pretty day, Daddy" was a far better way of greeting the day—and it was Seth's alone.

Seth had been a willful but sensitive little boy who cried at films, but that sensitivity hardened into granite-like anger after his mother's death from ALS, when he saw the look of relief on Decker's face—and knew exactly what that was.

That was when the hatred had begun—and it had grown exponentially since.

Fourteen months ago, when Decker learned of his son's bladder cancer in his confrontation with the pharma CEO Henry-Clay Yolles, he immediately recognized it as the price of the gift the boy had inherited from him. Seth had the gift in its purest form. Unlike Decker, who could never tell if someone he cared about was telling the truth or not, Seth had no such restrictions. His gift was without boundaries; hence Decker assumed that's why the price was so high.

Decker remembered Seth removing his hand from his at the funeral. "You're glad Mommy's gone," he'd accused.

"No, Seth, I'm not."

Seth hadn't needed to put his head up into the pure jet stream. The boy lived in the jet stream. He didn't need to close his eyes to read his retinal screen and had simply said, "That's not true." And had begun his withdrawal.

Since then he had gone to Eddie when he needed advice or counsel. He came to Decker when he needed money.

And now he was twenty-one and living somewhere in western Canada and refusing to communicate in any fashion with his father.

It was when Decker went to log off that he saw it—news of the terrorist attack at Ancaster College—and knew his life was about to change. Again.

30

A SOLITAIRE OF MOOSE—T MINUS 7 DAYS

THE BIG MAN MOVED SLOWLY IN THE MORNING HEAT. HE WAS A fat white man in a thin black man's world.

No one remembered his coming—or a time when he wasn't there. That was just as well. Even rumours of his real age would have caused distress in the local population and no doubt parades of visiting Western scientists. But now people came to his kingdom, which consisted of a petrol station, a gift shop and of course his bakery for his apple pies. That was fame enough for the fat white man who called himself Moose.

He looked around himself but did not see what others saw. Where they saw a petrol station he saw a vestry. Where they saw a gift shop he saw a transept. Where they saw his bakery he saw an altar. And of course where they saw a stack of hubcaps he saw the boy dangling from the end of a rope.

It was the hung boy that had drawn the fat white man to this place 196 years ago.

Moose used the garage's compressed air hose to blow the dust from his hands and feet and entered his bakery. Instantly he was surrounded by the intense sweetness of apples and preserves, and he smiled. His church was ready for another day preparing for the arrival of the man from the Junction.

Moose thought for a moment of Inshakha and her admonition that the man from the Junction was being prepared.

He'd been sensing the change caused by the man from the Junction's approach for almost five months.

Awakening to the ostrich staring in the window of his tiny bedroom behind the bakery was the first of the signs.

The man from the Junction's approach confused the animals; so that packs of wild dogs could be seen at high noon and elephants drank from the foul end of the watering hole. Moose assumed that the man's approach was changing things as his world and this world tried to align.

Moose used the ancient can opener to cut around the rim of the large tin of preserved apple slices. The two-holed metal key bit into his pudgy fingers but he didn't care.

He was preparing himself to teach the one who approached.

He tilted the large tin can forward and allowed the sweet juice into a waiting jar. This was Africa, where nothing goes to waste, where human beings first stood and marvelled at the light, where one of the earth's divine portals is defended by a fat white man named Moose who made and sold deep-dish apple pies in a place called Solitaire, Namibia.

31

A HILL OF ANTS—T MINUS 7 DAYS

DECKER WAS WATCHING THE ANTS OF ETOSHA NATIONAL PARK do their level best to unmake what man had so arduously made.

They teemed from cracks in the interlocked bricks on the patio of the immaculate grass-roofed cottage Inshakha had rented for them. Only twenty yards away a watering hole drew thousands of animals every day—and allowed the roar of lions almost every night to echo and re-echo through the desert air.

On some secret signal the ants all changed direction and headed abruptly for Decker's bare foot. As they did he heard a vehicle grind to a stop, then the slamming of doors.

Two minutes later Special Agent Yslan Hicks was standing not five feet from him, her translucent blue eyes still beautiful, but now clearly tired from travel.

A few steps behind her stood her partners in crime: Mr. T and Ted Knight.

"Mr. Roberts," she began.

Decker held up his hand to stop her.

"No. Damn it, this is important."

Decker pointed toward her feet.

"We're calling in our marker, Mr. Roberts."

She stepped forward, onto a red ant hill.

Decker arched his eyebrows and once again pointed toward her feet.

"What? You don't think you owe us?"

"No," Decker finally spoke, "it's not that."

"Then what?"

"Your foot is on a red ant hill. I do believe they've already crawled up your boot and now have—"

She began to hop on one foot and swat at her pant leg.

"—gotten to your leg."

Twenty minutes later Special Agent Yslan Hicks returned. She wore a different pair of pants and was more careful where she put her feet; Africa makes you watch where you step.

Mr. T and Ted Knight had not moved from their posts.

She looked over Decker's shoulder into the cottage and said, "Who's the whore?"

Decker called, "Inshakha, come meet Special Agent Hicks."

Yslan was going to say something more but held her tongue as Inshakha stepped into the door frame. Her blue-black skin shone in the morning light and her long delicate features looked like a Modigliani painting—or rather Modigliani had done his best to paint the features that came naturally to the Herero tribe's pride and joy, Inshakha. And right now her black irised eyes bore holes into Yslan.

"I am no whore and I would suggest you watch your tongue. Words are important in Namibia—a curse once spoken cannot be rescinded."

"I meant no—"

"That is not true, Special Agent Hicks. You intended slander and harm, but you have accomplished neither."

"Right. I apologise."

"Do not apologise to me, Special Agent Hicks. It was my man you insulted. Not me."

Under her breath Yslan hissed, "You want an apology, Roberts? Then get your ass in gear before I apologise you all the way to a jail cell in America."

"This is Namibia," Decker said.

"And that should mean what to me?" Yslan demanded.

"Namibia is not America."

"More than two hundred people died in a terrorist event at a college graduation. Such niceties as borders don't mean all that much to me when all those people have been murdered."

Decker took a deep breath and said, "And you want my help." It was not a question.

"No," Yslan said. "Like I said, I'm calling in my marker. You owe me, Mr. Roberts. You are going to assist me in this investigation or you are going to jail. It's really that simple."

"Does Namibia have an extradition treaty with the United States of America?"

Yslan smiled as she said, "Who fucking cares?"

Decker rolled the last of his shirts and put it into the side of his small duffel bag beside his copy of *Love and Pain and the Dwarf in the Garden*.

Inshakha had been in the bathroom for a long time.

"You okay?" he asked.

No response.

He asked again and slid the door open. Inshakha was sitting on the side of the tub, naked except for a cloth around her waist, her beautiful skin almost completely covered in red clay.

She looked up at him.

Their eyes locked as she reached into the tub, took a handful of the red clay and pressed it slowly into the skin of her face. As she did, the sophisticated, intellectual Inshakha disappeared behind a mask. Then she said the oddest thing. "Do you like apple pie?" And before he could answer she added, "Well, you will learn to—you will learn to."

For the briefest moment she smiled at him—or he thought she did. Then she was on her feet, an untouchable African woman striding out of his cabin—out of his life.

The drive in the Land Rover from Etosha to Windhoek took four hours, and neither Yslan nor Decker spoke a word that whole time. Nor did a word come from Mr. T or Ted Knight squished together in the backseat.

Decker stared out the window and wondered if he'd ever see Africa again. Africa, where ancient aquamarine-coloured sinkholes dot the land and salt forms take advantage of the baking sun, where the simple topography is only periodically broken by mushroom explosions of rocks and humpback hills slanting west to east, brown whales on the desert ocean.

They boarded the small plane shortly after they arrived at the airport, and as the plane took off Decker leaned his forehead against the window and took in the world beneath him.

Africa from the air.

The Namibian desert, like a vast stretched cow's hide, is broken only by folds of upshot rocks and creases of riverbeds that hold only the promise of water.

The sheer size of something with so little hope of vegetation or water plagues the mind and presents a stark challenge to those who think they are brave and capable—and willing to challenge God, who had clearly signalled to one and all that this place, this land, was not for human habitation.

Across the vastness of sand and jutting rock a single two-lane road—the Trans-Kalahari Highway—dares car and driver to ante up, to bet your life on a crossing.

But there is a purity here, and not that Lawrence of Arabia crap. There's nothing much clean about clots of dust in your hair or up your nose or filling the tiny air pockets of your lungs. But there is a feeling of it all being sanitary, probably because sweat evaporates before it can dampen your clothes or accumulate in your pits or crotch, and your chest always feels dry, and there is no odour—none.

The Comair stewardesses were dressed British Air proper—and were just as haughty—but they were young and firm and black with names like Khabo, not young and firm and white with names like Patricia.

Around Decker the guttural snark of Afrikaans and the harsh crunch of German filled the air.

And outside the plane's skin, the sun beat down unhindered by cloud or hint of rain: 26, 29, 33, 39, 42 degrees Celsius. What clearer sign does the Almighty need to give that this is no place for humans?

Yet men survive here—hearty, ingenious men—and have done so since well before recorded time. They have left their marks on flat stones: giraffes for rain, lions for courage, zebra for food.

Prayers on rocks.

As the plane approached Jo'burg, lush green valleys spread out like spiders' legs from the city and belie the real wealth of the great blue funnels that rocket diamonds to the surface and Johannesburg to the map.

From there it was a direct flight to JFK, and then . . . well, that was up to Special Agent Yslan Hicks.

In the book store of Tambo, Johannesburg's international airport, Decker felt a familiar subtle pull. He turned the corner and there was a display of reissued novels of John le Carré.

"Didn't he write some movies?" Yslan asked.

For a moment he'd forgotten that she and her guys were keeping a tight rein on him.

"Yeah, they made some movies from his books."

"The Spy Who Comes in from the Cold?"

"Close. *Came in from the Cold.*"

"Yeah, I remember. Good movie."

He turned to look at her, a bit surprised that she felt that way. "Yeah. Not sure if he wrote the screenplay, but with the exception of the ending the thing was pretty faithful to the novel. And Richard Burton shows you why he was one of the great actors of his generation, if not *the* greatest actor of his generation."

"More than Elizabeth Taylor's main squeeze, huh."

Way more, Decker thought, but chose to ignore the comment. Even this clearly bright woman was not immune to the American disease of star chasing. It surprised him. He knew it shouldn't, but it did.

He turned back to the book display.

A few novels had been put back randomly. He pushed one aside and saw a copy of *A Murder of Quality,* a very early le Carré that he hadn't read in years. He often preferred the early works of great artists to the better crafted later ones. As a director he was attracted to the early works of the masters—*Baal* and *In the Jungle of Cities* by Brecht, *Peer Gynt* by Ibsen, *A Dream Play* by Strindberg. There was something about the youthful rawness that attracted him. Their desire to stretch the form—to find truth beyond the restraints of their art. Dreams too big for the piano. Paths where there were no paths before. He'd directed most of these early works, and although he appreciated the famous later works, it was the early works that continued to draw him. Like *A Murder of Quality,* he thought as he leafed through the opening pages.

"You're smiling," Yslan said. "Something funny in there?"

"No," he said, closing the book. "Something pleasing."

At the counter the girl scanned the bar code on the book cover. As she did he noticed a rack of new CDs behind her. He wondered who exactly bought CDs anymore, but he enjoyed looking at the covers. He found it easier to know what he wanted when he saw the jewel case covers rather than the tiny images at iTunes. He vaguely remembered as a kid loving the artwork on record covers—some of which he still had. And the records inside those covers, for that matter. Although it had been years since he had a working record player.

The featured CD was the new Adele release. He asked if there was a Wi-Fi hotspot in the airport.

"Not gonna buy the CD, are you. No one does. Just gonna download what you want?" she asked with a toss of her blue and gold hair.

"Yeah."

She took out a pencil and scribbled something on a scrap of paper and pushed it across to him. It was her employee access code for the airport's Wi-Fi. She smiled. He smiled back and turned to go.

"Hey."

He turned to her.

"You owe me for the novel."

He paid her, and as she went to make change his eye was drawn to the rack of CDs again—to a rerelease of an early Bob Dylan album. He nodded.

"What?" she said as she put the change into his hand.

"Dylan," he said, more to himself than to her.

"Yeah. It's an old one so you can actually figure out what song he's singing."

Decker knew what she meant. He never missed a Bob Dylan concert, but nothing did as much damage to Bob Dylan's music as Bob Dylan live.

Yslan cleared her throat loud enough to remind Decker that she was waiting.

He thanked the girl again and headed to the Wi-Fi hotspot.

He took out his iPod and punched in the Wi-Fi code the girl had given him. It promptly announced that this was the private airport code and should be used "judiciously." He just loved that in South Africa they assumed that folks knew what the word "judiciously" meant. He supplied his iPod account number and downloaded some early Rickie Lee Jones—he particularly liked the song that began "Show business kids making movies of themselves, they don't give a fuck about anybody else." After that he downloaded the new Adele and some Antony and the Johnsons. Then he punched in a search for Bob Dylan. The new rerelease of *Highway 61 Revisited* came up first, but he found himself momentarily unable to make his fingers select the album.

"What?" Yslan asked.

"What, what?"

"You've got a funny look on your face. One I've seen before."

He looked back at the surface of his iPod and wondered again why he didn't just select the album. Then—with a force of effort—he did. And immediately he felt a coldness around him, something metallic in his hand and a slickness between his fingers. He shivered.

"You cold?" Yslan asked.

"No," he managed. "When's our flight?"

As the plane lifted from the runway, Decker took a last look. Africa was a place of beginnings and endings for him—and he knew it.

And now it was time to return to a more complex world that was supposed to be his own.

This world—Namibia, Etosha, Mowani, Wolwedans—Inshakha—were really just dream interludes for him. They belonged to others—fabulous and gracious and at times deeply insightful others—but they belonged to others nonetheless.

And it would always be so—or so he believed.

But where did he belong? To Canada? To Toronto? To the Junction—to the Junction yes—but the others—that was to be seen.

Seth belonged to Canada and Canada to him—but that was different.

Theo and Leena and Trish at least belonged to Toronto.

Eddie—well, Eddie belonged to his own very special world, a world that he hoped would at some point include his daughter.

SOLITAIRE

At the intersection of Highway 6 and Highway 1 in the gift shop, petrol station and bakery that make up the entirety of Solitaire, Namibia, the fat white man named Moose finished the first of the day's eighty-six deep-dish apple pies, awaiting the coming that he had begun sensing almost five months ago. Then Inshakha walked into his bakery, smiled, and said, "He's on his way."

32

A SNIPPET OF AN AIRPLANE CONVERSATION—
T MINUS 7 DAYS

SOMEWHERE OVER THE MID–SOUTH ATLANTIC, YSLAN TURNED TO Decker and said, "The body count is up to two hundred thirty-seven."

"Could there be more?" he asked.

"Yeah."

"And when we get there you want me to do what exactly?"

Yslan considered telling him about Viola Tripping, then decided to wait until they got their feet back on terra firma, so she said, "Do whatever we ask you to do."

"That's a bit of a wide job description."

"Is it?"

"Yeah."

"Tough. There are two hundred thirty-seven people dead. You'll do whatever we tell you to do. Clear?"

"As mud," he replied, then took out his iPod and popped in his earphones. He unwrapped the complimentary sleep mask. "Do you mind?"

"No. Get some rest; you'll need to be wide awake when we get there." An image of Viola Tripping popped into her head and she repeated, "Wide awake."

Decker slipped on the sleep mask and—to the plaintive falsetto of Antony and the Johnsons singing Dylan's "Knockin' on Heaven's Door"—dozed off.

33

A PRIVACY OF THOUGHTS—T MINUS 6 DAYS

HE COULDN'T BELIEVE IT. EVEN NOW, SIX DAYS LATER, HE couldn't believe it.

It had all gone off better than he could have imagined—*ka-boom,* then *KA-BOOM, boom, boom, boom!* And such good luck; better luck than he'd ever had—ever. Not only that the bombs had worked like that snot-nosed professor had claimed they would, but he'd tricked Mr. Professor and *ka-boom boom boom* to him, too. So who's the smart one now?

And who are all those cops and FBIs and the other spooks looking for? A-rabs!

He'd seen it. They were all over the college, pulling aside brownies and ripping off face hankies and drillin' those fuckers new assholes.

They were looking for him but they'd never find him. Cause he wasn't no fuckin' A-rab. In fact he hated A-rabs—every fuckin' one of them who came to this richy bitchy college and thought they were so much better than him.

34

A CONFUSION OF RIDDLES—T MINUS 6 DAYS

HARRISON STOOD AND PUT HIS PHONE ON SPEAKER TO FIELD THE call from Mallory, the head of Homeland Security. He quickly filled him in on the arrival of Decker Roberts, although he avoided mentioning Viola Tripping.

"And you really think—"

"Yes. It's worth a try." Changing the subject he asked, "How're your guys doing with those photo enhancements?"

"Good. You'll have them by three o'clock."

"Do you have the final IT report for me?"

"Yeah, there was no unusual chatter before the attack, no one's even bothered to claim it. What have you got from your end?"

"The explosions were so massive that we're still sorting out the debris, although I doubt it will get us much of anywhere."

"Harrison, it's been almost—"

"I know. But this isn't like the downing of an airplane or the blowing up of a subway train."

"No. It was just the largest terrorist attack on U.S. soil since nine-eleven and the president is anxious—"

"For results. Yeah, I get that, Mallory."

"The stock market is down more than thirty percent."

"Did you check short sellers?" It wasn't well publicized, but al-Qaeda may well have shorted the entire market two days before 9/11 and made off with billions of dollars.

"We checked—nothing out of the ordinary. If anything, trading was long, not short."

"What about the date? Al-Qaeda's addicted to historical precedent."

"April twenty-first? Means nothing to our experts. And the claims on the jihadi websites ring hollow."

"You just said there were no claims."

"Those sites claim responsibility every time a drunk teenager drives his stupid ass off a highway in Nebraska. Besides, not a single thing we've held back from the public appeared in any of the claims. Not one. If they could stick their finger in our eye, Harrison, believe me, they would."

Harrison sat heavily in his chair. He'd actually assumed most of this before he'd picked up the phone. But now he and Mallory knew that this just might be the most dangerous of dangers—something new, an innovator, a novelist in the old sense of the word.

He ended the phone call quickly, logged its time, then waited for Yslan.

Yslan gave Decker an hour to get settled in the dorm room they'd found for him. It was what colleges call a psycho single, designed for students who just can't get along with other students—perfect for someone who "does not play well with others." And it fit Yslan's purposes. The room was on the top floor by itself at the end of a corridor. It allowed her to post a single marine guard to be sure that Mr. Roberts stayed put.

After an hour she appeared at his door and did her best to prepare Decker for what he was about to see—and experience. Finally she said, "You'll just have to see for yourself."

They left the dorm, and as they passed by the mirror-sunglassed marine, Decker shouted, "Crossing. Two crossing, boss, two."

The marine didn't flinch.

Before Yslan could say anything, Decker said, "Name that film, Special Agent Yslan Hicks, and win a prize."

"Paul Newman eats a lot of eggs—that film."

"Cool Hand Luke."

"Right."

They walked up the hill of the campus and passed two other

armed marines as they entered a low building that evidently had been built into the side of the mountain. They walked down a long, dimly lit corridor and stopped at a metal door. More guards. One on either side of the door. Decker ignored them and turned to Yslan.

"She's in there?"

Yslan nodded.

"She's just a small woman, right?" Decker asked.

"Right."

"So what's with the guards and the steel door?"

"It's the way she wants it. A room with no windows and a heavy door."

Decker did his best to maintain his calm. A room with no windows was the stuff of his nightmares.

"You all right, Mr. Roberts?"

"Sure. Just a bit jet-lagged," he lied.

"A sixteen-hour flight does that."

"Yeah. So what else can you tell me about this Viola Tripping?"

"As I told you in the dorm room, she's a speaker for the dead. Put her on the spot a person died and she'll recite what the person was thinking. In her own way her talent is as unique as yours."

Decker stared at her, then closed his eyes: straight lines—a truth.

"You think she's like me?"

"I think she's more than that."

"What does that mean?"

Yslan hesitated, made a decision, and said, "I think she's one of you."

More straight lines.

"So what do you need me for if you have her?"

"Mr. Roberts, she recites what people were thinking—just recites. If the person—"

"Lied, she'd repeat the lie. Like the twin sisters at the fork in the road to London."

"What?"

"It's just a riddle."

"What's the riddle?"

"Is now the time for—"

"Tell me the damned riddle."

"Okay. So there are identical twin sisters who live at the fork in the road to London. One sister always tells the truth. The other sister always lies, and between them they will only answer *one* question. One and only one. Because they are twins, you don't know which sister answered your knock at their door—so what's the one question you ask to be sure to know which is the proper road to take to London?"

Yslan thought, then smiled. She never used to be able to figure out silliness like this, but since she'd spent time with Decker Roberts her way of thinking, her perception of the world had changed.

"So?" Decker demanded.

Yslan spoke slowly, completing the idea even as the words came to her lips. "If I was to ask your sister which is the correct road to take to London, what would she say?"

Decker nodded then said, "And?"

"And whichever road the sister said, take the other road. The honest sister will honestly repeat the lying sister's lie and the lying sister will lie about the truth that the truthful sister would say—so both sisters would point you to the wrong road."

"Very good," Decker said, but it troubled him that she could figure it out.

"What?" she demanded.

"Nothing," he lied, then he turned to her. "I thought deathbed confessions were accepted in most courts. So why do you need me at all?"

"These folks didn't know they were going to die—that's an important element in a deathbed confession. They thought they were going to see another sunrise. They had no idea the end was around the corner."

"I assume under their feet."

"Yeah—that."

"Okay, but Viola repeats people's final thoughts—their thoughts. People don't lie to themselves."

Yslan's stare brought her brilliant translucent blue eyes into clear focus. And, as at the first time he met her, Decker was not able to hold her gaze.

"You think people lie in their thoughts?" he asked.

"Don't you?"

"No."

"Really?"

"No."

"Come on, people prepare lies in their thoughts. In their hearts sometimes. Speaking a lie is the end product, that's all."

Decker heard far more than the words. A profound Z behind the Y that led to her statement. A rich subtext of pain was bolstering Special Agent Yslan Hicks' statement. He changed tack. "How many of us are you tracking?"

"You're not that special, Mr. Roberts."

"How many?"

"More than thirty."

Swirling lines—a lie. "That's not true!" He turned to leave. Immediately guards stepped forward to block his way. These were the marines he'd seen at the front of the building. When had they come in?

Decker turned back to her. "Where are Ted Knight and Mr. T?"

"Around," she said.

"At least that's the truth. So spit it out, Special Agent Yslan Hicks; what do you want from me here?"

"Start by telling us which, if any, of Viola Tripping's recitations are true."

"If I can."

"You'd better."

"Or what?"

She hesitated, then said simply, "Or I won't tell you where your son, Seth, is."

Decker couldn't find words to reply.

Yslan said nothing. She just pointed toward the heavy metal door that led to Viola Tripping's windowless room.

"And after I finish will you—"

She took a key from her pocket and reached for the door.

Decker stared at her. "You locked her—"

"She wants it that way."

35

A READING OF MINDS—T MINUS 6 DAYS

VIOLA

*The light from the open door is behind
him, and—his silhouette—his death
shroud—surprises me. It has such depth
and pulses in the light. Never seen a
death shroud like that. The door shuts
behind him and someone turns the key.
He lurches at the handle and tries to
pull the door open. It won't open—it's
locked. Good.
Then he doubles over and almost falls.*

DECKER

*The door's locked.
The room has no windows!
No fucking windows!
The small figure across the way takes
a step toward me. I'm falling—down
a well, backward, at night—fuck, I'm
going to vomit, but I don't. I look up at
her. So small—so very small and fragile.
And I stand. I don't feel any nausea
at all.*

"Why don't I feel—"

"Sick?" the small creature asked.

"Yeah."

"Cause I'm not a pukerator to you or you to me. We're through the great woods. We're in the clearing—the others are lost in the woods unable to find the path to the clearing. But we are together in the clearing. Don't you know that? We're not at the glass house yet, but we're looking for it."

Decker shook his head, trying to rid it of random thoughts that were whizzing back and forth—clearing? great woods? glass house?—but he asked, "Pukerator?"

"Pukerators make people like you and me puke—pukerators. But you and I are in the clearing in the middle of the great woods so we don't make each other sick."

> DECKER
> *In the clearing? I remember the*
> *profound nausea I felt when I was near*
> *Mike Shedloski and that guy Emerson*
> *Remi—and the admonition years ago*
> *from the pianist, Paul Scheel: "Your*
> *forest will infect mine."*

"Those lost deep in the forest who can sense the clearing but can't find the path to it—"

"Make those of us in the clearing sick?"

"Right."

> DECKER
> *Two worlds out of alignment.*

He closed his eyes—cold surrounded him—two perfect cubes.

> VIOLA
> *How funny he doesn't know that—I*

thought all of us in the clearing knew
that. He's holding up a hand.

DECKER

Don't come closer, I tell her.

VIOLA

Why? I ask him.

DECKER

I shriek, Don't!

VIOLA

I retreat to a far corner of the room
and make myself even smaller than I
usually am. He draws his sleeve across
his mouth.

"Why have they locked you—"

"They haven't locked me anywhere. I need to be in enclosed spaces."

"You're an agoraphobic?"

"Big word."

"Frightened of open spaces?" She didn't answer, so Decker asked again. "Are you frightened of open spaces?"

VIOLA

I shake my head. My hair falls across
my face. I like my hair across my face.

"Then what?" Decker demanded.

"I like the dark. I like closed spaces."

"Like Tourette's?"

"No, I'm not sick and neither are you."

VIOLA

Then I stop speaking.

DECKER

She's holding back.

She turned her face to the wall. "And?" Decker demanded.
"And?"
"Come on, and what?"
"And . . ."

VIOLA

I hesitate. I've never told anyone before,
but his death shroud is so unique, so
deep, so pulsing . . .

"And . . . in a closed room I know there's no portal."

DECKER

It stuns me. I never thought of it that
way before. Portals—I know of the one
in Houston at the Rothko Chapel and I
sensed I was near one in Namibia.

"How many portals have you seen?"
"None."
"What? None? You've never seen a portal?"
"Once I see the hanging boy, I run."
"What?"
"The hanging boys. They mark the portals. Haven't you seen
them?"
"No. But I've sensed the portals."

DECKER

Why can this creature see the hanging

boys but not the portals? And where was
the hanging boy in Houston? But before
I can think about my own question
I know the answer. Mark Rothko was
the hanging boy—his suicide was his
hanging boy.

VIOLA
Then I'm screaming, "No more, no
more, no more."

DECKER
I put up my hand. I understand, even
talking about the portals is panicking
this strange creature. Then Special
Agent Hicks' words, "one of your kind,"
slide through my consciousness and
other words float up in my head. My
daughter—this girl is my daughter.

"Have you worked for the NSA before?"
"Who?"
"For Special Agent Yslan Hicks?"
"Funny name. Pretty lady."
"Have you worked for her before?"
"Worked?"
"Been with. Helped?"
"No. Pretty lady."

VIOLA
Then I stand and turn slowly with
my arms out like when I speak for
the dead—when I am awake and
dreaming at the same time. When I do I
always float in my dreams—arms wide,

*upside down and spinning, the tips of
my long hair just brushing the ground
while my waking self has arms wide
and spinning but my feet are on the
ground—like I'm spinning now.*

DECKER
*She is turning slowly, almost elegantly,
and somehow she's older and taller
and incredibly beautiful, her hair now
long to her waist, her smile so intense
it seems to light the room and draw me
to her. And then I am spinning, with
her, and old—we are both so old, like
ancient trees on Vancouver Island,
then he is there, Seth getting into his
wet suit—and crying, oh, Jesus he's
crying—his hands to his face, tears
squeezing through his fingers. Then her
hands are on my face.*

"Don't cry. He's just on another path. Just another path."

DECKER
*The same words Crazy Eddie had used
to describe his wife's ALS all those years
ago.*

36

A FOLDER OF FILES—T MINUS 6 DAYS

DECKER DIDN'T EXACTLY REMEMBER LEAVING VIOLA TRIPPING. Somehow the door opened and a marine or two were there—he was confused—and he found himself, before he knew it, in Yslan's small makeshift office.

Yslan looked up as he entered. "Are you okay? You look terrible."

"Thanks."

"Want to tell me how it went with Viola Tripping?"

"No. Want to tell me where my son is?"

"When this is done. Okay?"

"Do I have a choice?"

"No."

"Yeah, I get that."

"Good."

"Why bother asking me how it went with Viola Tripping; you had the place wired, surely."

"Naturally." Yslan stepped to one side and pointed at the photographs on the table. "I need you to see this."

"This is the best—"

"Yes." She didn't bother mentioning the work Homeland Security was doing on the photographs. "Some parent at the very back of the graduation tent took this shot two and a half minutes before the first blast."

"Surely every parent had—"

"No. The college forbids photographs during the graduation."

"So the parents have to buy the video the school shot?"

"Yeah."

"So where's the video?"

"It was destroyed in the blasts."

"Completely?"

"Yeah."

"Wasn't there a wireless feed to a hard drive?"

"You'd think, but they were economizing."

"This country's excuse for everything."

"Be that as it may."

"So, all you have is this photograph of the faculty members on the stage waiting for the ceremony to start? How could you ID them from that?"

"We have our ways."

Decker didn't like the smile on Yslan's face.

Yslan handed him a large folder containing an outline of the achievements of each of the dead faculty members. Each had his or her own file within the folder. Several had red dots in the right-hand corner of the folder. Two had blue dots.

"What's with the dots?"

"Red means they had highest security clearance."

"And the blue?"

"Those considered potential security risks."

Decker looked at her. "You mean they were commies or something?"

"Let's leave it at 'or something.' "

"I thought the McCarthy trials ended long ago."

"You have a problem with the McCarthy trials, Mr. Roberts?"

"Every thinking person has a problem with that little part of American history."

"Why's that?"

"A lot of innocent people got hurt for no goddamned good reason."

"Really? You don't think that Stalin, a man who was willing to kill thirty million of his own people, was a potential threat? And he had the bomb, at least in part thanks to the work of the Rosenbergs, which is a fact that the released KGB files confirm. Those same files, by the by, also confirm that Alger Hiss was, as Senator McCarthy claimed, a Russian spy."

"Paranoia," Decker snapped back.

Yslan threw a wide-angle shot of the carnage at the graduation on the table. "Is that paranoia too?"

It was the first time Decker had seen the devastation caused by the bombs. It took his breath from him. He pushed the photo aside, picked up the files with the précis of the professors, and said, "Mark the professors' names beside the chairs they were sitting on and Viola and I can—"

"Yeah, when we have that information each chair will be numbered. The number will correspond to those on the top of each of the files."

"Is the site secured?" Decker asked.

"Not yet. It'll take some time. In the meanwhile"—she pointed toward a laptop—"start with these." She pressed two keys and the paused image of a very frightened swarthy-skinned man came up. She tossed Decker a thick yellow pad and a pen, turned, and left.

37

A PILE OF JUNK—T MINUS 6 DAYS

TWO HOURS LATER DECKER TOOK THE HANDKERCHIEF FROM HIS
pocket and dabbed at his eyes. As he did he noticed that his hand
was shaking. It was doing that more and more since he'd returned
from Namibia.

The door opened and Yslan entered. He handed her his notes.

Another taped interview came on the screen. He tapped his pen
against the pad and waited. Finally he said, "I don't need to see these
opening questions. I don't need a baseline like some kinesics person. Just cut to the chase. Ask them if they had any knowledge of or
participated in any way in the bombing at Ancaster College."

"Yeah, well." Yslan paused. "We didn't know that, so you're going
to have to sit through the entire thing."

"How many have I done?"

"Twenty-one so far."

"How many are there?"

"So far they've completed two hundred and seventy."

"And how many are they going to do?"

"As many as they need to, Mr. Roberts."

"Give me a ballpark figure."

"Say six hundred, give or take three hundred."

Decker let out a low whistle then said, "Next."

Yslan said, "Enough for now. Get your coat."

"Why?"

"We're going on a field trip."

* * *

The low-hanging sun's light glinted off the windshield as Yslan sped the government-issued Buick through the upper New York State countryside.

"I thought I was here to help with Viola Tripping."

Yslan tipped down her sunglasses so her translucent blue eyes were staring right into Decker's. "You're here to do whatever the fuck we want you to do." She flipped back up her sunglasses and turned left without bothering to signal.

"Well, that's fair."

"Try to get it through your head that you work for us."

"I don't work for anyone."

Mr. T, who was sitting behind him in the backseat of the car, grunted some sort of response, then moved a heavy duffel bag on the seat beside him. Then he grunted again.

Decker turned to look at him. "I knew I shouldn't have given you that dictionary."

"What?" Mr. T said.

"Lenny Bruce."

"Who?"

"Never mind."

"Enough, Mr. Roberts. Think of it as you're on our team."

"I'm not on your team—or any team."

"Not even Seth's team?"

"That's subtle."

"More than two hundred people are dead; I've had it with subtle. Get it?"

"Yeah. I got it."

"I hope they'll have made the site safe for you and Ms. Tripping soon."

"Okay. So where are we going now?"

"To a junkyard."

"Sounds like fun."

"Shut up."

"More subtlety."

"You're just here to tell us whether this guy's lying."

"I only know when someone's telling the truth. Got it?"

"Yeah, I get that. But as I said, from here on in you shut up."

The rest of the drive was done in silence. The rolling countryside was recovering from yet another harsh winter. Beneath some of the trees and in the depths of some of the ditches there were still patches of snow and ice locked in the brown leaves.

As they drove away from the college, things changed—rural, impoverished America reasserted itself on the landscape. Those who had been left out of the economic miracle, who watched on their TVs the lives of others. Decker felt for them and was appalled by them: their overarching religiosity, their clannishness, and their deep distrust of "city folks"—read liberals.

The junkyard was right on the side of the road. Nothing but a cheap chain-link fence separated it from the blacktop—and, oh yes, there were two snarling German shepherd guard dogs. B film here we come. Then right out of central casting, a grizzled overalled man in his late twenties or early fifties—it was hard for Decker to tell—shooed away the dogs and opened the gate for them. He turned his back and walked through the piles of junk to the north side of his lot. He stopped in front of what used to be the front seat of a Subaru.

"So, on the phone you said you wanted to show me something."

Mr. T unzipped the heavy duffel bag he'd been carrying and dumped the contents on the ground. Maybe two hundred pounds of metal scrap.

"Could this have come from your yard, Mr. Johnston?" Yslan asked.

"Johnson, not Johnston."

"Sorry," Yslan said. "Could this have come from your yard, Mr. Johnson?"

"Is this from that—"

"Just answer my question, Mr. Johnson."

"Sure. It could have. It also could have come from somewhere or anywhere else, too."

"Do you sell—" Yslan didn't complete her question because Johnson pointed behind her to a pile of metal scrap perhaps nine feet tall and twenty feet in diameter.

Yslan blinked back her surprise then asked, "Have you sold any of it—"

"Lately? Nah. Business is bad."

Yslan looked at Decker. He opened his eyes and asked, "May I speak?"

"Sure."

"He's telling the truth but—"

"Thank you, Mr. Johnson."

"Sure," he said and spat out something viscous and brown that had been in his cheek.

As Mr. T packed up the metal scraps Yslan turned to go. Decker caught up to her. "Can I speak again?"

"That guy was telling the truth. Right?"

"Yeah, but only to that question."

"What?"

"Ask him if he's *ever* sold some of that scrap." Yslan stopped and looked at him. "Then ask him if he remembers the last person who bought scrap metal from him. Then ask if he knows that person's name. Your questions have to be precise for me to help you. This works best if there's a simple progression." Before Yslan could question that, he added, "Don't ask me why."

She turned and headed back toward the trailer where they'd first seen Johnson. As they approached the dogs began to growl.

Johnson stepped out of the trailer. "Now what?"

"People come here sometimes to buy scrap metal?"

"Yeah—that's why I keep it. I don't use it to decorate."

"Do you remember the last person who bought some?"

"Yeah, I guess."

Yslan looked at Decker.

"Do you remember, Mr. Johnson?" Decker demanded.

"Yeah."

"Do you know the person's name?"

"No. This is a junkyard, not an antique shop."

Yslan looked at Decker. Squiggly lines on his retinal screen. He shook his head.

"Mr. Johnson, I'm a federal agent. We are investigating the killing of hundreds of people."

"At the fancy college, right?"

"Right."

"Maybe they got what they deserved."

"That's not the point, Mr. Johnson."

"Really?"

"What did the guy look like who bought the scrap from you?"

He spat on the ground again, this time much closer to Yslan's foot than was necessary. "He looked like a girl is what he looked like. Tits and everything."

38

A STATUE OF SCRAP—T MINUS 6 DAYS

VALERY PALMER ADJUSTED HER BRA FOR THE HUNDREDTH TIME that day. Since she'd found that lump—even though they claimed it was benign—she'd been unable for some reason to wear a bra that didn't pull or itch or just damned well hurt.

After another effort she gave up, turned on the acetylene and lit her welding torch. The flame was instantly reflected in the hundreds of metal surfaces of the huge sculpture she was working on.

Yslan approached with Mr. T behind her and Decker at her side. "Ms. Palmer?" she asked.

Valery Palmer turned her whole body in the direction of the voice, which momentarily pointed the lit torch right at Yslan's chest.

Then she snapped it off and flipped up her welding mask, allowing her blond hair to fall to her strong shoulders. "Yes, I'm Valery Palmer—to my student, Professor Palmer."

Decker noted the use of the singular "student."

Yslan introduced herself then said, "You're not all that easy to find."

"Well, I'm the only fine-arts faculty member of the only fine-arts department on this science campus, so they kinda hide me away."

"That must be—"

"Nah. But I'm only here because they can't legally get rid of me. Twenty years ago two graduates from the school set up a trust fund that had to be spent on a fine-arts faculty member. They wanted there to be at least some contact with the arts for these science nerds. Seems that they missed contact with what they called the 'other world.' So here I am—in the far-off corner."

Yslan nodded.

"So, what can I do for you folks?"

"Mr. Johnson from the junkyard said that you bought scrap metal from him."

Valery pointed at the sculpture and said, "Yep. By the carload."

"Did you use all the scrap you bought?"

"Well, not all."

"Why not all?"

Valery leaned down and picked up a few pieces of scrap from around the statue. "Cause I make mistakes sometimes. Or I change my mind. Or I make mistakes and I change my mind."

"You mentioned a student."

"My one and only student. Poor kid takes a razzing from his buds. The college doesn't even credit it as an elective."

"Can we have his name?"

"Sure."

39

A STUDENT AFFAIR—T MINUS 6 DAYS

AS YSLAN INTERROGATED THE YOUNG MAN, DECKER LOOKED AT the two large Dylan posters on either side of the kid's closet. One before his Evangelical transformation, one after. Both had "Highway 61" marked in thick red felt pen across them. Decker opened the kid's closet and was surprised to see a fine reproduction of an early Mark Rothko painting. In the back of the closet he found a large portfolio of the young man's etchings, each one an effort to reach toward Rothko—just as Richard Dreyfuss's sculptures in *Close Encounters of the Third Kind* reached toward what he had seen in his dream.

Over his shoulder he heard Yslan demanding an answer to a question.

"Am I a suspect or something? Do I need a lawyer?"

Decker turned back to look at the art student. He wasn't cowering, but he was clearly frightened.

"Just answer this," Decker said. "Did you ever take scrap metal from Valery Palmer's studio?"

"You mean Professor Palmer?"

Decker looked at him oddly—there was something here.

"Yes, Professor Palmer."

"I never took anything from her."

Decker closed his eyes. He felt a solid shot of cold then something metal in his hand and blood between his fingers. Random lines crossed his retinal screen. "That's not a truth," he said as he looked at his empty right hand.

"What is this? Just because I took a class with her, I'm guilty of something?"

Of something, Decker thought, then he signalled to Yslan that he wanted to ask another question and she nodded. "Are you having an affair with Professor Palmer?"

"No. I mean, why's that important? But no. No, I'm not."

Decker didn't need to close his eyes to know that the young man was lying.

Throwing her arms up in the air with a "what-the-fuck" gesture clear for all to see, Yslan turned and left the room.

When Yslan was gone, Decker reopened the closet and pointed at the Rothko print. "Have you been to his chapel in Houston?"

"No. Am I in trouble? I just—"

"Yeah. No. I don't think you're in trouble. I think you're looking for something." He pointed to the Rothko a second time and said, "Houston—you might find it in Houston."

Outside the dorm, Decker met up with Yslan, who was clearly upset.

"What?" Decker prompted.

"This whole thing! Rich, entitled students. Destitute townies serving them. Older women having affairs with students! Jeez! You taught in a university for a while, didn't you?"

"Yeah. At the University of North Carolina at Chapel Hill for a bit and then up in Toronto at York."

"And did shit like this go on there?"

Decker took a breath. "I didn't fit in well at universities, so my opinion of them is jaundiced. Look, did you go to college, Special Agent Hicks?" Decker asked.

"State school."

"Well, this isn't a state school. This is an elite institution for the elite in this country. This country is wealthy because of the brain power that schools like this produce."

"You went to an elite institution like this, didn't you, Mr. Roberts?"

"For grad school, yes. You know I did."

"So you know more about how they work than we do."

"By the end of his or her first semester any freshman knows more about how these places work than you and the NSA do. There's bound to be an old codger in the town who can fill in some details for you. These places usually have an amateur historian—often he was the local newspaper's editor, and since he doesn't teach he wouldn't have been at the graduation."

Yslan nodded and checked her BlackBerry. After a bit of scrolling she said, "Yvgeny Smukler."

40

A SMUGNESS OF SMALL MINDS—
T MINUS 6 DAYS TO T MINUS 5 DAYS

YVGENY SMUKLER SAT BEHIND HIS PAPER-LITTERED DESK IN AN old office in a converted industrial building. There was no computer in evidence and not a single empty space on his floor-to-ceiling bookshelves.

"I am the living history of this place, Special Agent. A fossil that refuses to sink into the mud."

As Yslan made nice-nice, Decker took in the man. He was not an old academic, although he emulated one. He didn't have a pipe, corduroy slacks and leather patches on a well-worn tweed jacket, but he might as well have. Decker had always found such people either the very best that Calvinist America could produce or the very worst. In this case he withheld judgement, although he was surprised that the man was not as distraught as one would expect him to be over the killing of so many of his fellow residents of this small town.

Yslan had just expressed her disgust with the sculptor and her affair, and Yvgeny Smukler nodded sagely—everything about him was sagely. Then he said, "How very unfortunate."

For a moment Decker thought he was going to launch into a discussion of the mistake that Ancaster College made when it went co-ed in the early 1970s. But he didn't.

"You must understand that institutions, like Ancaster College, are stuck in aspic."

Yslan looked to Decker for clarification.

Decker enjoyed not offering any.

Finally Yslan asked, "Aspic? Can you explain that?"

"Certainly."

Unfortunately for Yslan, Yvgeny Smukler was enjoying his momentary notoriety.

Like the old woman who lied in Twelve Angry Men, Decker thought.

Yvgeny Smukler shifted his long body and grimaced. With a smile he explained, "A disk in my back."

"Aspic, Mr. Smukler?" Yslan prompted.

"Yes. These institutions are hermetically sealed. A tenured professor has to be caught in flagrante with a pregnant Chihuahua selling term papers in a stolen car before he or she can even be considered for dismissal." The man smiled, crinkling the already crinkly skin of his face—he was clearly pleased with his turn of phrase. "But, and here's the big but, they're not paid well. They often have in excess of nine or ten years of postsecondary education but they make less than an autoworker makes, in some cases less than a kindergarten teacher. The only happy ones are the professors who make more money outside the college than in."

"As so many did."

"They were the fortunate ones who the military found to be of value."

Substantial understatement there. Professors at Ancaster College had been called on as experts in things ranging from the nuclear threat in Iran to the actual functioning of drone aircraft, which they in private called sneakers. Well, they could call them whatever they wanted because they'd invented much of the technology that allowed the things to do their deadly work.

"And was there much jealously over their successes?"

Yvgeny Smukler smiled. "Does the pope wear a dress? Yes—some of their less successful colleagues were not pleased."

"More anticapitalist nonsense?"

The older man shrugged his sloping shoulders. "I'd prefer to keep politics out of our conversation, but I think it true to say that many of those at places like Ancaster College who can't get outside work turn inward. To them perks become everything."

"And sleeping with students is a perk?"

"To some of them. To others it's the vacation time—better than fighting over closet space."

Decker saw that Yslan was losing patience and asked, "Could you elaborate?"

"Certainly. When there's nowhere up to grow, stupid things like having a closet in your office—or a window overlooking a court-yard—become the be-all and end-all."

"Things become that trite?" Yslan asked.

"And of course, academia can also become self-protective and incestuous."

"Swell," she said.

"Despite all that, Special Agent Yslan Hicks, they also sometimes manage to produce the most important of all resources."

"And what are those?"

"You know what they are. Special people. Gifted people. Folks with the brainpower to keep this country strong—and in a science and math place like this, to keep the country's military might such that the home-land is safe."

Back on the campus, Yslan turned to Decker and said, "So tell me what else I don't know about places like this."

"Let me count the ways."

"What?"

"Nothing. Have you read le Carré's book *A Murder of Quality*?"

"The one you bought at the Johannesburg airport?"

"The very one."

"No. Why?"

"Well, he talks about discontent in small-town universities. In that case it led to a murder."

"In this case to a terrorist act? Are you out of your mind or are you just making a really bad joke?"

"Fine. I thought you wanted me to—"

"Okay—so tell me."

"There's lot of discontent in places like this."

"Enough to—"

"There are science labs here, aren't there? So there are the chemicals in those labs—and certainly the know-how necessary to make a bomb. Right?"

"Yes, so?"

"Well, who has access to those chemicals?"

Yslan nodded.

"Check on lower-level faculty members. Places like this shamelessly use nontenured teachers. They hire them on what they call CLAs—contractually limited agreements. And they pay them peanuts. Year after year they dangle the possibility of turning their one- or two-year contracts into fully tenured positions. They seldom if ever come through. It keeps these folks on a string—it also allows this place to offer the education they do without breaking the bank." Decker waited for a response but got none so he added, "That would piss me off; wouldn't it piss you off?"

"Not enough to do that," she said, pointing in the vague direction of the blast site.

"Yeah. Well, you have a future ahead of you. You don't feel the world is using you. You don't look around every day and see your peers quadrupling your year's salary in a month or that almost all of the students you teach have trust funds greater than your potential lifetime earnings."

Yslan looked to Mr. T, who nodded and headed out of the room—to collect a list of the Ancaster College's CLA workers, Decker presumed.

"What else?" Yslan demanded.

"The academic journals in which everyone has to publish are nests of vipers. The government in Kabul could learn things about corruption and kickbacks from these folks."

"How do you—"

"Everyone has to publish, right?"

"Yeah, publish or perish—yeah, I know that."

"And the only place to publish is in these journals—all of which are supposedly juried."

"What does 'juried' mean?"

"A panel of your peers is supposed to read your submission and okay it for publication."

"So the folks on these juries have a lot of power."

"Literally over hiring and firing. No publish—no job."

"So who gets on these juries?"

"They're appointed."

"By whom?"

"It's where the corruption comes in. Academics get on the juries by doing favours for powerful academics—sometimes agreeing to nix an article of an enemy, sometimes agreeing to allow a friend's article to go to publication when the work is dubious at best."

Yslan thought about that for a moment then asked, "Who juries the juries?"

"Now there's a good question. Who juries the juries? No one."

"Swell."

"See who on the senior faculty at Ancaster College sat on the juries. Who they've said no to. Who now hates them."

"Hates them enough to—"

"Having someone stand in your way—blocking your progress—can be a powerful motive."

"But to kill all those people?"

"Maybe to cover the fact that it's only one of those people he was after."

Yslan looked at him, then turned to Ted Knight. The man nodded and headed out.

Yslan's cell phone buzzed and she flipped it open. "When?" She evidently heard the answer and then hung up.

"When what?" Decker asked.

"When can you and Ms. Tripping go to the blast site."

"And the answer is?"

"Not tonight. Forensics isn't anywhere near finished."

"Okay. I want to see Viola."

"You'll see her when I say you see her. Understood?"

"You speak a precise if oddly accented English—so, yeah, I understand."

* * *

The marine shook him into waking. Decker rolled over and groaned, "Hey boss—what shakes?"

The marine left the room.

"Get up, Mr. Roberts."

Yslan.

"What time is—"

"Time to go to work."

She turned away from him to allow him some privacy as he dressed but didn't leave the room.

"Another field trip, Special Agent Hicks?"

"Yeah, you could say that."

Outside the marine stepped aside to allow them out into the cold night air. She led Decker quickly across the campus to what looked like a classy cafeteria. It had the odd name of "Fred" emblazoned across the front portico.

Decker assumed it was a donor's last name, although he'd never heard of "Fred" as a last name. Nonetheless the students here were left with having to say "Let's eat at Fred" or "I'll meet you at Fred." Sounded very odd to Decker's ear, but then again, this whole place was odd.

In the dimly lit cafeteria sat thirty or forty bleary-eyed people. Some were clearly in their late twenties or early thirties; many others were substantially older.

"What the—"

"Every CLA contract teacher who worked at Ancaster College in the last sixteen months."

Decker turned to her. "How the hell did you find them so fast?"

"It took us three days."

"But I just told you about them yester—" He stopped himself. "You already knew before I told you, didn't you?"

"You really ought to stop underestimating us, Mr. Roberts. It's really quite stupid on your part to think that we are dumb."

One of the oldest of the CLAs, dressed in a sixties-style peasant dress, began to complain loudly that they had rights.

Decker watched as the others joined the chorus of complaint.

Then without warning, the lights in the place were snapped off and the sound of high-powered hoses filled the air—along with a few "What the fucks," "this is Americas" and a whole stack of "stop its."

The lights clicked back on and the two NSA officers holding the fire hoses turned them off.

A soggier group of loser academics Decker had never seen—but more, he was shocked at how little it took to cow these people. These folks surely knew their rights, yet no one reached for a cell phone to call a lawyer, no one put up anything that could even be called a fight.

Yslan stepped up on a cafeteria table and said, "I apologise—"

"Who are you?"

Yslan introduced herself then said, "This can take the three remaining hours before dawn or up to five days—it's totally up to you folks."

One by one the CLA contract workers were led to a far end of Fred and sat across a table from Yslan and Decker.

After six hours of interrogation Decker had identified sixteen people who had not truthfully answered Yslan's carefully crafted series of questions: (1) What's your name?; (2) How long have you been on a CLA contract with Ancaster College?; (3) Was there ever an insinuation or outright promise that one day you'd be put on a fully tenure tracked contract?; (4) Were you resentful of not being given a tenure-track contract?; (5) Resentful enough to plot and/or execute the bombing at the graduation ceremony?

The sixteen people whom Decker identified as having prevaricated or at least failed to tell the truth did so on question 2 (seven, all older CLA workers; Decker assumed they were simply embarrassed that they had foolishly accepted CLA contracts for so long) and question 4 (where all sixteen claimed they were not resentful).

But all were telling the truth when saying no to question 5.

When the last of the CLA workers left their table, Yslan asked Decker, "You're sure?"

"Your question makes no sense."

"Why?"

"Are you sure that the day follows the night?"

"Yeah but—"

"Well I'm that sure when someone tells the truth."

She stared at him. "You're cold." A statement, not a question.

Decker nodded.

"And what's that wiping your hands against your jeans thing about?"

Decker wasn't going to tell her about the approaching cold or the feeling of blood between his fingers when he lifted his head into the jet stream to do the truth-telling. So, he just shrugged and said, "A tick."

Yslan didn't believe him but let it go and arranged for the release of all but the sixteen whom they'd interrogate further.

Decker waited by the exit of Fred; the marine whom he'd begun to think of as "his marine" had barred his exit.

When Yslan finally came up to him he said, "Breakfast. I need some fuel and this place is a cafeteria. They're bound to have a bun or a steak somewhere."

"We'll get it on the road."

"The road to where?"

"Lovely downtown Rochester, New York."

41

A JOUST OF JOURNALS—T MINUS 5 DAYS

ROCHESTER STRUCK DECKER AS A LOST CITY—ITS HEYDAY DUE TO the Erie Canal and then Kodak now well in the past.

Border cities, especially in the northeast, always surprised Canadians, since Canadian wealth lived, huddled, along the U.S. border—directly opposite much of destitute America.

Yslan guided their car along a wide boulevard that no doubt used to house Kodak execs and pulled into a long driveway near the south end of the street.

"Care to tell me who lives here?" Decker asked.

"A professor—"

"From Ancaster College?"

Yslan nodded.

"Then why wasn't he—"

"At the graduation? Come meet him and you'll see why."

They got out of the car, but Yslan stopped him. "Something else about him."

"What?"

"He's the editor and publisher of three of the science journals you talked about."

"Ah." Decker said.

"Yeah—ah."

An African-American maid in full uniform answered the door and led them through the grand old house to a room that was, no doubt, called the library. Full Professor Giuseppe Got awaited them there.

Despite the mild day outside, the radiators were on full blast, hissing merrily away. And in the middle of the room sat Professor Got in an old-fashioned wheelchair with a shawl over his thin shoulders and a heavy rug over his knees.

For a moment Decker couldn't figure out why this struck him as familiar, then the penny dropped. One of the Raymond Chandler novels adapted to the movies—or was it a Dashiell Hammett? Yeah, with Bogart but also that newer movie *The Big Lewinski*—no, *The Big Lebowski*.

He smiled at his mistake.

"Is there something humourous?" Professor Got's voice was deep but not produced properly, so it rasped in his throat. Then he coughed.

Yslan started with "Thank you for seeing us," then quickly segued into questions about the journals he edited and the juries for those journals. Then a surprise.

"I often overrule the juries. The journals only exist because of my foundation's support of them, so I rule as I see fit." He puffed up his chest, which caused him to cough again.

"So you overturn some jury decisions?" Yslan asked.

"Dozens of them."

"May I?" Decker asked Yslan.

Yslan shrugged.

"Was it ever made public that you did this?"

"Of course."

Yslan stated, "You didn't attend graduation this year." Professor Got vaguely indicated his wheelchair. "Yes, but did people expect you to be there?"

"I assume. This is the first one I've missed in many decades."

Decker asked, "Can you give us the names of academics whose papers you rejected in say the last sixteen months?"

The old guy's memory was sharp. Without referring to notes he named seven academics. Four died in the blast. The other three were from universities other than Ancaster College.

* * *

Associate Professor Ruth Judring sat in her office at Hislop College just down the road from Ancaster. A garish plastic painted bust of Elvis Presley sat on the windowsill behind the henna-haired professor. She was way too old for kitsch to be cool, but evidently didn't know it.

"Giuseppe Got—you mean Hitler in a wheelchair?"

Yslan looked to Decker, who did that shrugging thing. He'd have to stop that. He'd shrugged more in three days with Yslan than he'd done in the previous three years.

"Don't like the old guy?"

"Loathe him. Death couldn't come soon enough to that dinosaur."

"Dinosaur?"

"Yesterday's news. A genuine throwback to the time when the rich controlled everything including the universities of this country. He probably worked for a dollar."

"Can you explain that?"

"Sure. The old-time rich guys didn't need the college's money, so they often taught for a buck. Course they had trust accounts up the wazoo—shit, have you seen the house he lives in?"

"Yes."

"The Got estate. You know where the money came from?"

"No."

"His grandfather invented that liner in the top of the Coke bottle cap. He received some percentage of a cent for every one they sold—gazillions, fucking gazillions. So it was no hardship for him to work for a buck."

"Did he refuse a paper of yours for his journal?"

Without hesitation she said, "Several times."

"Do you know why?"

"Cause he's an old sexist? Cause his knickers were in a twist? Cause he can't read or think anymore? Who knows."

Yslan looked to Decker.

"Professor Judring, did you know that he wasn't going to be at the graduation ceremony?"

"No, I didn't even know that he still attended them."

Cold; slime on his fingers; two perfectly parallel lines—a truth.

* * *

Assistant Professor John Augustery's office had a large sign on the door: "This office is safe and open to gay, lesbian and transgendered students."

Yslan knocked and there was a scuffling sound from inside. When the door finally opened, Professor Augustery was in somewhat of a sweat.

"Professor Augustery? I'm Special Agent Yslan Hicks, I called earlier today."

As if something finally fell into place in his head he smiled and pointed to a seat. "I was just practicing for the maypole dance." Seeing the confused look on Yslan's face he added, "Maypole dancing takes place every May first."

"Does it?"

"Yes. Now how can I help you?" he asked as he pulled his long black hair back into a ponytail.

"You teach advanced chemical engineering here, don't you?"

"Yes. Have done at Prestwick College for many years."

Decker asked, "Were you denied promotion when your last three papers were rejected by Professor Got's journals?"

A moment of anger crossed the man's pleasant features, then it was gone—like a cloud moving to reveal the sun. "Yes. Unfortunately Professor Got controls the three journals that I need to publish in for advancement."

"That must hurt."

"It does—but I'm tenured."

"Yes, but still an assistant professor."

Again that anger moment. "In these hard times having a tenured position of any sort is an honour."

Cold; slime; two perfect trapezoids crossed his retinal screen. He nodded to Yslan.

"Are you sorry that Professor Got was unable to attend the graduation?"

After only a slight pause he replied, "Many fine people lost their lives. Unfortunately the higher power, in his wisdom, decided to spare the life of an ancient rat. Unfortunate, wouldn't you say?"

Professor Ron Masinger was on the phone when they approached his office down the hall from Professor Augustery. He was evidently in full flight—yelling into his speaker phone. From what they heard it sounded like he was shouting at a Hollywood producer.

He waved them into the office and pointed to seats.

They sat.

He continued his rant, then with a theatrical flourish punched a button and the line went dead.

"Serves them right," he said, then strode forward and introduced himself. His handshake was firm, his red hair receding. He wore clothes more appropriate for a man many years his junior.

"On the phone to the coast?" Decker ventured.

"Right you are," he said and slapped Decker's knee.

"A film script?"

"*My* film script. They've had it for years."

Decker knew from past experience that yes or no came quickly from Hollywood. Keeping a script for years was their way of not offending. So they must think they need this guy for something. "Do you do consulting on films, sir?" Decker asked.

"Yes. Boring, so boring! But it pays and it's a foot in the door."

To the restroom, Decker thought, but he asked, "Explosives?"

"Yeah. They always want to know about shit that blows up other shit."

"But that's not hard to find on the Internet, is it?"

"No. It's all up there, but they like a full professor's name to put on their film—gives them a sense of legitimacy."

Decker looked to Yslan. She was clearly annoyed with this guy. "Professor Masinger, do you hate Professor Giuseppe Got?"

"Yep."

"Are you sorry that he wasn't at the graduation ceremony?"

"You bet, sister."

"I'm not your sister, sir."

"Just an—"

"Did you have anything whatsoever to do with the explosions at Ancaster College?"

"Yep."

That gave Yslan pause.

"Exactly what?"

"Well, not with the blast, but with the forensic work after. They've contacted me several times, and my lab has analysed several of their samples."

"And that's it?"

"Until they ask me for more."

"No. Is that the extent of your involvement with the bombings?"

Finally getting their drift he put hand to heart dramatically and said, "Yes, that's it."

Yslan looked to Decker.

He didn't need to close his eyes for this one—he just slowly shook his head.

By the time they got back to campus it was cold and well past sunset. Decker was beat, but too tired to sleep.

42

THE SANCTITY OF CHAPEL HOUSE—T MINUS 5 DAYS

DECKER STOOD ON THE MAIN CAMPUS'S CENTRAL QUAD. SUCH places were the stuff of many a nightmare for him. And one that he'd never been able to figure out. Always in a place like this. Alone and either late for a class that he had to take or that he was supposed to teach. And the appointed time was approaching and he was completely lost—unable to figure out even which direction he ought to go.

As a wave of fear took him he reminded himself that this was not about him teaching or studying; it was about finding out who murdered more than two hundred people—and earning the right to know where Seth was.

Decker forced himself to his feet, then ordered those feet to walk.

He followed his nose and wandered up the steep sides of the college hill. On the very top, as far from the science labs and engineering classrooms as could be, sat a modest, low-slung two-building complex.

Decker immediately knew that this was not like the rest of the campus. As he walked, motion sensors turned on powerful overhead arc lights that illuminated the first of many plaques: "Chapel House welcomes anyone of any religious tradition—or none."

Decker pulled on the heavy door and entered. The arc light went out behind him.

A pamphlet near the entrance informed him that Chapel House was a gift from an anonymous donor who requested that her name never be mentioned, since "she was an old woman who would soon be going over to the other side."

Decker crossed a flagstoned courtyard, passed the small rock fountain on one side, and entered Chapel House proper.

The silence there pleased him. He felt his heartbeat slowing. There was a reading room whose shelves were filled with volumes covering the world's great religions, a music room holding hundreds of recordings of religious music evidently from the earliest times to the latest experimental compositions, and a chapel that was set up more for contemplation than services. He was pleased to see that the only dedication read: "This chapel is consecrated by the worship of those who use it."

In the chapel another pamphlet informed him that "no specific discipline is imposed, no instruction given, no lectures offered."

Decker knew that the openly liberal tradition of this chapel was in stark contrast to the fire-breathing Baptist missionary types who had set up the college. But as a psychiatrist who was a student once assured him, "We get better. We forget and get better."

Decker walked past the gossamer-curtained windows and sat in one of the straight-backed chairs and felt comfortable. Here, amidst this horror, this place was a possible refuge from the world—a way out.

Decker closed his eyes and gratefully saw nothing on his retinal screen.

He awoke moments, minutes, hours—he didn't know—later to a gentle touch on his shoulder.

The man standing beside him was about his age and had a pear's shape to him. *A sort of modern Friar Tuck,* he thought.

"You were snoring," the man said.

"I'm sorry," Decker responded.

"That's not why I woke you. You were beginning to rock—I was afraid you'd fall off the chair and hurt yourself."

Decker wanted to ask "Was I talking in my sleep" but settled for saying, "Thank you."

"No need to whisper. Only you and I are in the chapel."

The man straightened out a few chairs and ran a cloth along an altar railing.

"Do you work here, in Chapel House?" Decker asked.

"No. I come here as a retreat. There are five modest rooms one can rent. As soon as I heard what happened here . . . I went to school here a long time ago. And I thought they'd need my help now."

"You're a priest or a pastor?"

"No. Not a priest or a pastor." Decker saw a kind of twinkle in the man's eyes. "Definitely not," he repeated. Then the man leaned in close to Decker, completely unconcerned that he was staring. "You have a faraway look my friend. The look of a man in need of a path."

Fortunately three people entered the chapel at that moment, grief and shock written clearly on their faces, and the man moved to them.

Decker headed toward the exit. Before he got there an exterior arc light snapped on, revealing the sharp silhouette of a figure behind one of the gossamer curtains.

Decker froze—someone behind the curtain?

He willed himself to leave but couldn't. He approached the curtain. When he pulled it aside he almost fainted.

"It's a Hindi doll figure from Namibia," the pear-shaped man said. "Isn't it beautiful?"

How had this man managed to creep up on me? Decker asked himself. He mumbled a vague affirmative reply to the man then stepped past him to the door. In the door he turned back to the chapel. The pear-shaped man was sitting with the newcomers, clearly offering them some solace. Yes, this was a path, but he sensed that it was a dangerous path for him, a cul-de-sac. One that offered him a chance to lay down his burdens—in return for living out his life in a windowless room with a locked door.

That night his dreams were laced with horror. Twice he woke with a scream in his throat.

His marine woke him late in the morning and brought him the laptop, some breakfast and a message from Yslan: *Work on these interrogations. The CLAs you singled out are being interrogated although I doubt that will go anywhere. We're also checking the alibis of the people who were "juried out" by Professor Got. But, again, I doubt that will be anything. So on to plan B—be ready this evening."*

As he watched the sun set through his dorm window he heard a sharp knock on the door. Without a word except Decker's "How they hanging, boss," his marine led him back to Yslan's makeshift office.

"Are they ready for us?" he asked.

"Close."

"My understanding is that she needs to stand in the exact spot where the person died."

"Yeah. That's my understanding, too."

He looked at her—two straight lines, a truth . . . and lingering cold.

"They've put up scaffolding to get the floor up to the right level and put plywood over everything," Yslan said.

"We'll start at eleven o'clock."

"That's my call, Mr. Roberts."

"Eleven o'clock. She doesn't like people looking at her."

"Yes, but time is—"

"Special Agent Hicks! She doesn't like people looking at her."

"I get it."

"Good."

"You going to record—"

"What she says? You bet."

"With your trusty digital tape recorder?"

"It worked just fine in the past; I see no reason to change methodology now. Do you?" He smiled at her.

She did not smile back.

He leafed through the file with the information on the dead faculty members then he asked, "And what about the students?"

"One hundred and forty-seven."

"That's not my question."

"Mr. Roberts, we don't have a photograph of them in their seats.

The most we have is the order they were supposed to enter in—and hence sit in."

"Why just supposed to?"

"Most of them had been drinking at least since Friday, their final exam. This place kicks out kids in their final semester of their fourth year. They crack the whip here and keep cracking it."

"So at graduation the kids blow off steam and refuse to follow any more rules?"

"Exactly. Shit, I would."

"Yeah. But you have the names of the dead, surely."

"Yeah," Yslan said, pushing another folder across the desk to him.

Decker took the file, then asked, "But without identifiable body parts how are you sure who died in the—"

"Their parents. Their parents reported them missing."

Decker thought about that for a moment. "But it is possible that one or more of them set the bombs then disappeared to places unknown?"

Yslan nodded. "Anything's possible."

Decker knew if there was one undeniable truth it was that—that anything's possible.

"Give me your digital recorder."

"Why?" Decker demanded.

"Just give me the damned thing." Yslan's voice was hard as granite. He handed it over. She took out a small disk and attached it to the back.

"A transponder?"

"Hardly," Yslan said. "It's a high-powered transmitter. We'll be receiving everything you and she say. If you need to contact us, just tap the button on the side. It acts like the best cell phone there ever was."

When, just before eleven o'clock, he was let into Viola's room, the tiny girl/woman was sitting beside a small lamp—the cone of light didn't illuminate her face but did the book in her tiny hands.

"You like Shakespeare?"

"No."

"Then why read—"

"This is *Pericles,* a play Mr. William probably didn't write all of."

Decker had directed the piece a long time ago. A great deal of it was clearly not Shakespeare's writing, no matter what the academics argued. Just put the text in the hands of good actors and it becomes obvious. Shakespeare had been an actor as well as a playwright. If you are in a scene for no conceivable reason—or your character should have exited many lines ago—then you are not in Mr. Shakespeare's writing. If your character has already made his point but there are still dozens of lines to say—not Shakespeare. If your character arrives, says what needs to be said, then splits—Shakespeare. It's actually quite easy to determine—with good actors. The reunification of Pericles with his daughter in the fourth act carried all the hallmarks of the master—concise, incredibly insightful on the nature of human emotion and heartbreakingly simple.

Decker took a step closer to Viola and asked, "Have you read the Shakespeare play with the character who has your name?"

"There is no such play. Don't tease, I don't like it. I don't."

The force of her words surprised him. And although *Twelfth Night* certainly featured a character named Viola, he wasn't going to press the point.

Then she said, "There are no Shakespeare characters named Viola Tripping."

He smiled. Of course. For the umpteenth time he reminded himself that inaccurate questions solicited inaccurate answers.

"Are you ready?"

"In a minute," she said. She turned her face back to the play and for just over a minute continued to read. A single tear came from her left eye and rolled down her cheek. With the tear hanging from her pointy chin she closed the play and said, "I'm ready."

Harrison watched Yslan framed in the provost's office door, light behind her, her face in shadow. Then she stepped into the office and the overhead light brought her out of the darkness and literally into the light. *From out to in, from darkness to light, from there to here—from one world to the next,* he thought.

He looked at her closely. She'd sprouted worry lines on the sides of her eyes since she kidnapped Decker Roberts sixteen months ago. "So they're ready?"

"Yes, sir."

"And?"

"They seem to be able to communicate."

"That's nice."

"I mean, not everyone can communicate with Viola Tripping."

"I knew what you meant."

He turned from her. She saw the sweat stain on his shirt. She'd never seen him anything but coiffed and immaculately dressed. She looked at his reflection in the windowpane. As she did, the first drops of a spring shower hit the glass. The water on the windowpane made it look like her boss, Leonard Harrison, was crying.

It momentarily terrified her—then he turned back to her. His face was without tears, although rage was slowly filling his features. "What else do you need, Special Agent Hicks?"

She hesitated. Viola Tripping could tell them who was thinking what before the explosion and Decker Roberts could tell her which of them was truthful, but if there was a pattern to be found she wasn't sure that these two could find it. Only one of her other gifted synaesthetes could do that—and he was presently housed in Leavenworth Penitentiary. Just thinking of him sent a shiver up her spine.

"Let me see if they can get started." She turned to go, then turned back to Harrison, "Forensics . . . ?"

"Nothing new," he said and turned to the now rain-filled windowpane.

Yslan took a quick final look. She was pretty sure that the strongest man she'd ever known was indeed crying.

In the steady downpour Ted Knight was organizing the final planking over of the seating area while Mr. T, using a photo of the previous year's graduation to guide his work, helped move platforms to re-form the stage. Some of his men, referring to a chart, were painting numbers in luminous paint on the chair backs.

Yslan approached Ted Knight. "When'll it be ready?" Before he could answer her she said, "I need it by eleven o'clock."

"Why then?"

"It's dark enough then."

"And there's no moon tonight."

"Yeah," Yslan said, "and there's that."

43

A VOYAGE OF DREAMS—T MINUS 5 DAYS

SETH GLANCED AT THE SLEEP GOGGLES HE WAS REQUIRED TO wear. They looked like something out of an old sci-fi film—a cheap sci-fi film.

But the computer monitors that the goggles were hooked up to were clearly state of the art.

It was late. Seth didn't know how late since the clinic didn't permit clocks of any sort—"They attach you to the world that made you sick."

His day had been filled with clinical examinations—and yet another painful cystoscopy. The nurses seemed efficient enough, but the two doctors who did the exams were sometimes clumsy with the instruments.

Then of course there was the afternoon counselling session; it seemed more like a quiz to Seth than counselling.

He picked up the sleep goggles.

They were supposed to help him lucid dream. Evidently the first step in his cure. He'd told them he didn't need help lucid dreaming, that he'd been lucid dreaming since he was a kid. That he was a dream navigator he was so good at it. He kept reminding them that he had bladder cancer and that's why he was here. They assured him that they knew that and still insisted he wear the goggles when he slept—"As a first step toward balance and health."

He wondered yet again whether he'd wasted his father's $20,000 in this California clinic.

He'd done his due diligence before contacting the place, although he couldn't remember where he'd first heard of it. Maybe someone had suggested it to him at the public library in Victoria. Or had it just popped up on his Gmail sidebar? It just seemed somehow ordained. So he'd contacted them and they'd sent him further materials and dozens of testimonials, all of which he'd looked up online and all of which seemed legitimate. All the people had returned his phone calls and spoke in glowing terms of the groundbreaking work of the clinic. Finally he'd had enough looking. All that he really knew was that he had to do something or he'd never see his twenty-fifth birthday.

The particularly virulent form of bladder cancer he had would eventually have to be operated on, but the doctors in Victoria had been clear with him that even if the operation was a complete success his life would be significantly altered. A young man without a prostate is a young man outside the realm of young men. The operation also chanced spreading the cancer to the rest of his body.

He lay back and thought of the ocean—of the surf and wildness of Vancouver Island. Then he threw the goggles across the room—and instantly was deep in a dream he'd had a lot lately, about a world (no, worlds) where there was no dreaming. Where humanity had years before "for fear of nightmares abandoned dreaming." And the few dreamers who were left hid their "gift" and if exposed were hunted down and imprisoned. Until suddenly something happened and the world—no, worlds; there were many worlds in his dream—woke up to the need for dreamers, for people like him.

44

A CELEBRATION OF GROUND ONE THOUSAND— T MINUS 5 DAYS

THEY WERE THE ODDEST COUPLE WALTER'D EVER SEEN. THE hunch-shouldered tall guy walking hand in hand with the little girl—no, she was a little woman. A dwarf or a midget maybe. He didn't know what the difference was. Just short, real short, and the umbrella the guy held to keep the rain off her was one of those huge red and white golf ones—it could have kept twenty of her dry.

Walter had learned over the years working at Ancaster College how to look but not let people know that he was looking. After all he was only the help. He was supposed to be invisible. Invisible when they groped in the corridors. Invisible when they vomited in the urinals—just there to clean up for them. A fixture, no more important than a white-painted wall. Useful but not something you ever thought about—or saw looking at you. So these two didn't realise that he was watching them. *Who the fuck are these two, anyway? And what are they doing? Especially at this hour of the night—and walking right toward the blast site—my blast site.*

Then the girl or woman or dwarf or whatever she was pulled on the man's hand and both turned in his direction. He stepped back into the storefront and pretended to look at the chocolates there, a box of which cost more than he made in a day. What was wrong with a Baby Ruth or a Mars bar—why did these people have to have chocolates like this shit in the window? He counted to one hundred like he used to do when the kids laughed at him in school and then turned back to the street. The two of them had disappeared behind the barrier that now hid his masterpiece.

The fucking Arabs had ground zero. Well, Walter Jones had ground one thousand.

45

A WORLD OF WONDERS—T MINUS 4 DAYS

YSLAN HAD ARRANGED TO HAVE THE POWERFUL ARC LIGHTS THAT overhung the blast pit dimmed to their lowest level. The few remaining streetlights in the town had been unscrewed, and heavy curtains covered every street-side window that remained.

With no moon the darkness was as Viola Tripping had requested.

A quick glance at his illuminated watch face told Decker it was just past 11:05 p.m. He understood they had about six hours until the dawn's light would interfere with Viola Tripping's work.

The rain came down harder.

The woman/girl's slender fingers intertwined with his as she led him—as if it were brightest day—onto the creaking boards that were bolted to scaffolding and now covered the blast pit.

Rows and rows of stacking chairs had been set up—a few of which, those whose student occupants the NSA had been able to identify, had numbers in luminescent paint on their backs.

She led him down the centre aisle toward the raised stage.

It seemed an unbelievably long walk to Decker—and filled with images from a specific day in his past: a happy day in a May long ago when he and Sarah had walked down an aisle hand in hand, before her ALS, before Seth, when he thought his life was going to travel a simple, straight path. Long ago.

He found it hard to orient himself in the pitchy black, and he wasn't pleased with the springiness, let alone the groaning, that came from the rain-slick plywood boards that covered the pit. Then they were mounting steps to the reconstruction of the stage where the professors had sat.

He had no idea why she wanted to start on the stage, but this was definitely her show, and only she knew the rules by which she worked.

She tugged at his hand and he stopped.

He reached into his pocket and turned on his small digital tape recorder.

"Here?" he asked, not knowing if he ought to whisper. It certainly felt like he ought to; the air seemed somehow thick. *With the presence of souls?* he asked himself. *No,* he answered his own question. He knew that death didn't leave a thickness—it left an emptiness. Like when Sarah died in Crazy Eddie's arms, like when his house was torched, like when he found that Seth had left. With a shock he realised that much of his life was constructed around a profound emptiness. *To keep it at bay?* he wondered. *To stop me from falling into it? Like you could fall through a portal?*

Viola Tripping squeezed his hand. He came back to the present and looked down at her. She didn't speak, but she stopped and waggled his hand up and down, so he assumed they were in the right place.

"I need to know who . . ." He didn't know how to complete his sentence. "Can I turn on a light for a second?"

Again she waggled his hand.

He flicked on the small flashlight Yslan had given him and shone it at Viola Tripping's feet. The number 27 had been painted on the planking there. He consulted his chart and found number 27—Dr. Paul Dack, PhD in chemical engineering and computer sciences, red dot. He had full clearance.

In the penumbra of the flashlight he saw Viola Tripping take a step away, then stop, then turn, then take a half step back, then repeat the process. *As if she were a dog finding a place to defecate,* he thought.

Then she stopped, raised her arms over her head and slowly

began to turn—like a figure skater's spin but in slow motion and far more elegant, smoother, otherworldly.

The words from Dylan's song "Knockin' on Heaven's Door" bloomed in his head as he watched, never wondering how she managed to turn at such a consistent slow speed, seemingly without moving her feet, or how somehow she was bathed in a subtle greenish light, which seemed to come from her.

Then her jaw sagged open and her head lolled far back, sending her hair almost to the floor—and she spoke—but what came from her mouth were not her words or her voice. And as her eyes widened, suddenly able to see, the final thoughts and the voice of Dr. Paul Dack, PhD in chemical engineering and computer science, aged forty-four years and two months, now deceased—no, fuck that, assassinated—poured from Viola Tripping's small mouth as her eyes roamed the heavens.

Although eerie, the thoughts of the good professor were nothing particularly surprising. A concern about the length of the upcoming ceremony, the need to catch a plane, the hope that someone named Amanda would answer his phone calls, the need to upgrade his BlackBerry—then no thought, just the half word "Jee——"

Viola Tripping stopped spinning and looked in Decker's direction. Clearly for a moment she couldn't place who he was, then she smiled. "Did that help?"

Decker took a moment to find his bearings. Had he just seen what he thought he'd seen? Finally he shrugged. Her recitation clearly didn't help in the NSA's investigation, so Decker didn't bother testing for truth. She suddenly seemed deflated like a little girl who had disappointed her dad. He smiled at her and said, "One down; who knows exactly how many more to go. Come on, we have a lot to do and not all that much time."

Viola Tripping repeated the process at chair 28, which had at one time been occupied by Dr. Ines Buchli, PhD in aerospace technologies and linguistics. Dr. Buchli's thoughts were more business oriented but hardly revealing of any complicity in a mass murder.

And so the night proceeded until they got to chair 67 in the back row—Dr. Neil Frost. It took Viola longer than usual to find the exact spot, and this time her spin seemed more erratic, but the voice of Dr. Frost was clear, British accented, concise and disturbing:

Deny me full professorship, will they? Won't give them the chance or the satisfaction to do it again. We'll see just who's smart and who's not. They thought that anyone with a shred of self-respect would have gotten the hint and moved on. Well, I got the fucking hint, but Neil Frost isn't moving on—you're all moving on. Every damned pompous one of you. Moving on to hell.

I'm fuckin' fifty-three and I've been summoned here like some stupid pimply undergraduate—and I hate this damned robe.

That's right, everyone, ignore me—ignore Neil Frost. Look the other way—then look down and that'll be your last look.

Neil's laugh erupted from Viola's throat. It hurt to hear. Viola Tripping stopped spinning. Her arms came down to her sides and tears coursed down her cheeks so that Decker couldn't tell if it was rain or tears.

"Are you all right?" Decker asked.

"So much hate. So much hate." She held out her arms to him.

Decker enfolded her to his chest then sat on one of the folding chairs and pulled her onto his lap. He felt her entire body heave as she wept. Finally she stopped, slid off his lap and moved back to the final resting spot of Dr. Neil Frost, hater.

She opened her arms and it was as if someone yanked her head back—she screamed, then held out her arms and began to rotate, and her mouth opened and Dr. Frost's vitriol spewed out.

Fuckin' graduation and graduants and the rest of this idiot faculty. Full professors. Everywhere full professors. Morons!

I only came to get my final paycheck. What kind of sophomoric idea was it of the provost's to withhold final paychecks if you didn't attend the fuckin' graduation?

But this graduation is going to be like no other. No—this is going to be a momentous graduation. One that no one will ever forget. No one.

Look at them all. All so excited. So expectant. So young. Way too many are brownies and slant-eyed bastards! It'll serve the lot of them—the whole lot of indulged, pampered, preening pancakes. The Chinese, Japanese and Koreans—pancakes. The Southeast Asians— brownies. The Americans—puffed pastries. And the women—all of them—cunts, just cunts.

Pancakes, brownies, puff pastries and cunts—I'm saving you from being eaten alive by the American military-industrial complex the way I was. Saving you, you ungrateful peons.

Twenty minutes to show time. Time for me to make my ever so polite excuses—my bowels, you know, must have been something I ate, sorry, so sorry—and then like Snagglepuss make with my exit stage left—"

Decker felt the cold and the slime between his fingers then saw the perfect squares enter his retinal screen and knew beyond knowing that this man's words were the truth—at least the truth as he saw it. He opened his eyes and stared at Viola Tripping. Waited, but she put her arms to her sides and stared into space. "No more?" he asked.

"That was the last thing he thought."

Decker nodded, then read the file of one Professor Neil Frost.

As he did, back in the provost's office Yslan and Harrison turned from their receiver and flipped open their copy of the professor's folder.

Neil Frost was a perennial assistant professor—the definition of an academic failure. He had been denied full professorship three times. He was fifty-three years of age and rented an apartment west of the village. He had no other address. Divorced twelve years ago, a sixteen-year-old daughter—whereabouts unknown—wife remarried, three kids, new husband works for the Pentagon, had been Frost's contact there. What other business contacts he'd had since then hadn't panned out. There was a note from the Pentagon warning that he was an unstable individual, and a reference to Gerald Bull that drew a scowl from Harrison.

There were several student complaints about his insulting language and one about a sexual harassment allegation that had been settled on the quiet.

His departmental evaluations were below average, but it was noted that although he was tenured he saved the department big bucks by accepting a pittance of a salary to teach the introductory courses.

There was also a note about a petition he tried to start to stop the provost's new rule that required all faculty members to attend graduation to receive their last paychecks.

His security clearance was minimal, but there was no sticker on the front of his folder to indicate that he was a security risk.

"And we're sure that he died in the—"

Yslan held out another folder and nodded. "Dental match, came in yesterday."

"Get a team over to his apartment. I want it taken apart piece by piece."

"Let's wait for Decker."

"Why?"

"I hope he can tell us whether this is truth or fantasy."

They didn't have to wait long for Decker to contact them.

"I assume you got the Frost stuff?"

"Yeah, Mr. Roberts, we got it. So?"

"Who's we?"

"Not your concern. So, is it true?"

"As far as I can tell, yeah." He didn't bother to mention the three perfect rectangles that crossed his retinal screen as Viola Tripping spouted the final thoughts of Dr. Neil Frost.

"And you're sure he was surprised by the blast?"

Decker didn't answer.

"Mr. Roberts, was he surprised by the timing of the blast?"

After a pause Decker said, "I think so."

"You think so!"

"Hey, this isn't my usual way of working, so all I can say is that I think so."

"Okay. Anything else strike you as possible?"

"No, just a whole lot of grocery lists, textbook requests, thoughts on how to avoid coming to graduation—stuff like that—but nothing else all that interesting."

"How's Viola holding up?"

"I don't know. I've never seen anything like this before. I have nothing to compare it to. She seems okay."

"How far have you gone?"

"We've done the professors on the stage—at least the ones we could identify. And part of the first two rows of students."

"Anything there?"

"Yeah, a couple who were giving each other hand jobs while they waited, and they apparently had invented a porn site that they've sold for a bundle. Wanna hear the name of said porn site?"

"No."

"Well, too bad. It was Reachoutandfuckapornstar dot com. They received just short of three million dollars for their little invention—I guess their hand jobs were celebratory."

"And who says America is falling behind in research and development."

"Not me."

"What else have you got?"

"The need for a coffee. I'm beginning to lose focus."

"Will do—strong, black, in a mug. It's on its way."

Two hours later Decker and Viola Tripping came across the first hint of how the bombs might have been linked. A student named David Pern had been sitting in the fourth row awaiting his turn. He'd evidently been either talking or thinking to himself, because Viola Tripping's words came out in torrents and her spinning was unusually fast.

I turned down three major job offers. Three. Everyone else here is going to work, but I'm going home. Home to Momma. Four years away from her has about killed me. All the phone calls weren't enough and going home to La Porte was so expensive. Just getting to the airport cost a hundred dollars. But I did it and every time I brought home inventions I'd made to make Momma's final years more endurable.

I wish you could have been here for this. I think you'd be proud of me. It was so hard, but I did it. I did it for us.

What the . . . Flash of light from the stage. Jeepers. I know what this is—I'd warned them about it. My terrorist projection model had the graduation of the science class at MIT number four on the hit list.

Blood and flesh and bone on the proscenium arch of the stage—the dead on that stage were yesterday's news. Oh, shit—me and my class-mates are the future.

A scream—then a single thought,

Who's going to help Momma now?

Decker contacted Yslan again.

"Is he telling the truth, Mr. Roberts?"

"You mean *was* he telling—"

"Okay, *was* he?"

"Yeah. Not sure if this kid's observations are of any value. But they at least confirm the sequence."

"They do more than that," Harrison said to Yslan. "Get this David Pern's terrorist threat assessment paper. I want to know exactly who read it and when. It could have given someone an idea."

Agents were sent scurrying.

Just an hour before dawn Viola Tripping uttered the word "jihadi" for the first time. She was speaking the final thoughts of a chemical engineering student named Ahmed Veladi, who was in the seventh row.

Viola Tripping's spin this time was like a slow minuet. Her words though, were accented—clearly a South Asian, either an Indian or a Pakistani.

I don't love America—but I don't hate it, either. And I don't take

*orders from illiterate beardos with cheap plastic glasses who believe
that every word in some dumb book was supposedly dictated by God
himself, like the Evangelicals in this country who believe the same
thing about their silly book. These two groups deserve each other.
Best two out of three mud wrestling would be good. Maybe an HBO
pay-per-view special. The Christian Right against the Muslim Brother-
hood—cheerleaders against women in burkas!*

*Sure, I've been approached—fuck, every brown chemical engineer-
ing student has been approached. Everyone has an uncle's friend's
father's mechanic's third cousin who has jihadi contacts.*

An ugly snicker.

*If the West knew the extent of the jihadi movement they wouldn't
allow a single Muslim from outside the country into America's places
of higher learning.*

What's that? Shit! This shouldn't be happening to me. It's not fair.

A scream of pain, then an even uglier snicker.

*How stupid. Stupid of me. Who the hell said that there is fairness in
the world except these foolish Americans?*

Decker reported this only because of the jihadi reference, but
Harrison latched on to it and got the information directly to the head
of Homeland Security. Shortly this kid's dorm room was swarming
with FBI agents.

Twenty minutes later Viola Tripping stopped her spinning and began
to giggle. The sound of her innocent laughter was so odd in this
place of death that Decker wondered if this was all too much for her.
Finally he asked, "Do you need a rest?"

She shook her head slowly, but she was smiling.

"What was this—" he checked his chart to get the name—"Charles
Roy thinking?"

She looked away from him but giggled again.

"What? What was he thinking about?"

"About touching Jelena's booby."

"That was his last thought?"

"No his last thought came after the blast."

"And that was?"

She giggled again.

"Come on."

"It was "Shit, now I won't be able to touch Jelena's tit again.""

"Fine All-American thought for the end."

"He wasn't all American."

"No?"

"No, he was Indian. He was thinking about India—how much he felt the responsibility to return home and help his country, how he should marry the girl his mother had found for him. Then he thought of a job offer from Siemens and the chance to live in London—in London with money! There he could find an Indian girl on his own—well, actually he wanted to find a Croatian girl. He liked Croatians—and they seemed to like him."

"And I suppose Jelena was . . ."

"Croatian? Yes."

With her small hands she made the most innocent indication of a large-breasted woman Decker had ever seen—and amidst the horror—the two laughed.

Then she stopped and said, "He named the probable explosive components when he heard the bomb from the stage and said, 'Whoever made this explosive device had a heavy hand with the RDX.' "

"And when he heard the bomb behind him?"

"He wondered if Siemens would honour the insurance policy in the contract he had signed. Then he got upset that he wouldn't be able to touch Jelena's breast again."

The only other student they encountered whose final thoughts were of interest was a boy who evidently was sitting by himself. And all Viola Tripping could get was:

So that's why; now it makes sense. I should have known. The turd, the damned turdlet.

Harrison and Yslan assumed the kid was cursing his fate—granted, in an odd way, but a boy's curse nonetheless.

Decker wasn't sure. The phrase "now it makes sense" wouldn't leave his head.

Along with his marine guard he walked Viola Tripping back to her room, then went to the town square and sat in the gazebo. The rain had stopped and a milky sun was rising.

Yslan approached him. She had her files in one hand. "You okay?"

He looked at her. He had no way of answering the question, so he just shrugged.

"Something specific troubling you?" she asked.

He thought for a long moment then asked, "What was the kid's name who talked about the turd?"

Yslan glanced quickly at her files. "Grover Cleveland Rabinowitz."

"And what dorm room was he in?"

Yslan checked her file again and answered his question. Then asked one of her own: "Why?"

But before she could get an answer her phone buzzed. It was Harrison and he was in a hurry.

46

A TALE OF TWO PADS—T MINUS 4 DAYS

YSLAN SAT BESIDE HARRISON AS THE CASCADE OF THE POLICE cherry-tops scolded across his now hard-set facial features. They drove fast out of Dundas and raced under the thruway that divided the rich college town from Stoney River, the dilapidated village that housed the workers.

Passing the liquor store, the only store with a neon sign on Main Street, and the two dollar stores—each a one-dollar store—and the inevitable Greek pizza joint, they sped down by the river.

There they found 137 Demerit Street and unit 21—Professor Neil Frost's apartment.

They didn't bother with the niceties of warrants or finding the landlord—these were poor people and they knew better than to challenge authorities.

In apartment 21, a one-bedroom with a stained bedsheet covering the street-side window, they had a view into the life of an unsuccessful academic—i.e., one who tried to live only on the salary the college paid. Successful academics made less than 40 percent of their salary from their universities, the rest from private industry. First-class professors of math, physics and chemistry—not to mention computer science—were in great demand in the private sector. The universities often had policies against taking on outside work, but they couldn't do anything about it. They needed A-list computer, math and science profs to attract the kind of students they wanted, who in turn would contribute generously to the endowment funds without which the universities couldn't function.

Neil Frost was not, as was evident from his digs, a first-class or A-list anything.

Discoloured popcorn ceilings, 1970s appliances in the kitchen, bookshelves made of stacked bricks and warped boards. A faux leather couch that had a rip in the seat of the centre sectional piece and a clearly sagging foundation—one leg was missing and it was propped up by what looked like dozens of test booklets. The only up-to-date thing in the whole place was a huge HD flat-screen TV filling most of the living room wall.

First they searched for a computer—none.

In a stack of papers—mostly takeout menus from various fast-food restaurants—they found his Dell laptop warranty. They decided that he must have taken it with him to the graduation, so it—along with his cell phone—was history. The place had no land line.

"Get his cell phone number from the college. I want his phone records. And see if he has a computer in his office," Harrison barked.

"The professors were expected to provide their own computers," Yslan said.

"How do—"

"I checked."

"Let the forensic guys know that anything at the blast site that could even possibly be part of a hard drive is to be bagged and brought to us right away."

Yslan nodded, although she had already ordered that on the day they arrived.

The fingerprint guys were already hard at it, but it was quickly becoming obvious that there were many sets of prints in the place. The dear professor had clearly not applied himself to cleaning, so some could be weeks if not months old.

It was Yslan who found the only real clue in the whole place. Beneath the filthy George Foreman grill was a large sheet of paper evidently used to catch drippings. On the back side of it was a shopping list. "Sir, I think you'd better—"

She didn't get out the rest before Harrison had the sheet of paper in his hands and was shouting, "Damn it to fucking hell!"

* * *

Outside the apartment, on Demerit Street, Harrison huddled with Yslan and Mallory, the head of Homeland Security.

"And you're sure?" Mallory asked.

"It's a bomb maker's shopping list."

"Not really, Harrison," Mallory insisted.

"Okay. It's a list for components to build a detonator for a bomb."

"I buy that."

"Mallory, he could get the stuff to make the actual bombs from any one of more than a dozen labs on this campus."

"And you're convinced this Professor Frost person died in the blast?"

"We got lucky with dental records," Harrison said.

Yslan looked at Harrison. No one had told Mallory, or anyone for that matter, about Viola Tripping. Surely Mallory was wondering how they'd gotten to Professor Frost's apartment.

"So it was a suicide bombing," Mallory said.

Yslan breathed a quick sigh of relief and snuck a look at Harrison. Both knew from Viola Tripping's recitation that Neil Frost had every intention of sneaking away before the bombs went off. This guy was no martyr. Of that they were sure.

"Did he have an accomplice?" Mallory asked.

"There had to be," Yslan piped in.

"Or two or three," added Harrison. "Assembling the bombs wouldn't be hard. And if the shopping list Special Agent Hicks found proves true, then the bombs were detonated from a cell phone signal. But the bombs were surrounded with metal shards. This was a tent, not an enclosed space. The shards did more killing than the bombs themselves. And it must have been several hundred pounds of scrap to have done this much damage."

"So accomplice or accomplices," Mallory said, putting his hands behind his back and pacing.

To Yslan he looked like Alec Guinness in *Smiley's People*—sans the big specs, and Guinness's obvious intelligence. She stopped herself. Alec Guinness? *Smiley's People?* Had she even seen those things or was she somehow seeing from Decker's eyes? She didn't know.

"Check his students. Perhaps he had a cadre."

With that Mallory strode to his waiting black Mercedes, where the uniformed driver held a back door open for him.

Yslan had an odd look on her face.

"What?" Harrison demanded.

"Cadre? What's a cadre?"

Decker looked around Grover Cleveland Rabinowitz's Spartan dorm room. It occurred to him that the boy's parents must have cleaned up after they came to retrieve what remained of their son. There were tape marks on the walls where posters must have hung. The bookshelf over the bed was empty, as were the desk drawers, the closet and the armoire

Decker sat on the bare mattress and tried to understand what this boy could have meant when he said, "So that's why; Now it makes sense. I should have known. The turd, the damned turdlet."

He reminded himself that he taught actors not to work on the meaning of the words but rather on what could have caused the character to say those words. The Roberts Method: work backward— Z to Y to X. So what could have made Grover Cleveland Rabinowitz say, "So that's why; now it makes sense. I should have known. The turd, the damned turdlet." Well, clearly he didn't know something before. But then—at the blast—something came clear. Something about a turd.

Then he noticed the blue paper-recycle bin tucked under the bed—and a transparent folder. He picked it out and was surprised by the title—"The Science Behind Microwaving Human Fecal Matter with Appendix of Turd Occurrences."

47

A TALE OF TWO MEN—BEFORE

HE'D BEGUN TO EXPERIMENT WITH HIS TURDS SHORTLY AFTER what he thought of as "the incident" with Marcia.

What a stuck-up cunt she was!

Just like all the rest of them. They all claim they're so liberal, so open, so progressive —Democrats. Not him, he'd be a Republican if he ever got around to voting. Not some fucking communist.

Well, he was sweeping the men's basketball court. What a joke. What did these nerds need a basketball court for? They were braini-acs, not athletes. If there was a Division XX they'd be at the bottom of it. Not like Louisville—his team.

Well, the basketball court was his to clean on alternate Thursdays, and on a Thursday in late January was when he'd heard the music from the small gym next door and went to check it out.

Well there they were—maybe six of them, in shorts or tights and halter tops, sweating as they worked out to some hip-hop. He care-fully tried the door—locked from the inside—so he rested his broom against the wall and watched through the window portal. They were all facing away from the door—what a sight that was!

But he'd forgotten there was a mirror on the far side of the gym, and one of them must have seen him watching. And they all turned toward him.

He quickly retreated down the corridor and ran into a broom closet before any of them could find him. And he hid there, like some fucking criminal, for almost a half an hour before he let himself out. But he made a note of the time, and the next day he snuck up into the rafters to watch, but they weren't there. He thought it might just have been a one-off, but he tried again in a few days and they were back at it. And he'd watched them from the rafters, and . . .

Slowly he learned their schedule. Mondays and Thursdays and early on Saturdays. And each time he'd watch, some of the girls were different except for the one they called Marcia, who seemed to lead—she certainly led him.

And she was damned perfect. Like an old *Playboy* centerfold. Blond and beautiful. And big. He liked big women—or at least he thought he liked big women. His mother had caught him once with an old skin mag in his bedroom. He'd found it in the garbage can and carefully cleaned it and brought it home, and she'd caught him with his . . . and she'd walloped him good with a belt and screamed that he was just like his father. It was the only time she'd ever talked about his father. But hey, like father like son. And when she'd walloped him she'd been in her bathrobe and it had opened enough for him to see, so it didn't hurt, and when he'd made a mess on the bed she'd screamed at him even more.

Sometimes at night he heard her screams in his dreams. They would echo and echo and sometimes it woke him up—and it always caused the headaches. Real bad headaches. They'd gotten even worse the day of her funeral. It was snowing. He was freezing and the clothes they made him wear itched and he didn't know what he was supposed to do. So he'd just stood by the grave until some guy who he didn't even know told him to say good-bye to his mother. So like an idiot he'd stepped forward and at the side of the grave said really loud, "Bye, you old bag." Someone yanked him back from the edge of the grave. He couldn't remember who. Maybe the first of the foster parents he'd have. Fifteen sets in the next seven years—some sort of record he guessed—until he was sixteen and got a job at the college, a real job, and a real place of his own, and he'd changed his name, and he'd held his head as the headaches came more and more often. Until he met Marcia.

It was a full month after he first saw her that he got dressed up real nice and made sure he was outside the field house when the girls finished exercising—and Marcia came out. It was a cold day but she still had on her shorts and only a thin university sweatshirt over her halter top—and a towel around her neck.

The sweat on her face and neck made her shimmer in the bright winter light, and after she said good-bye to the other girls she looked right at him.

That's when he did it—he spoke to her.

And she smiled and spoke back.

To him!

And ended by saying, "Gotta shower. Hey, see you around."

He sailed home that night, and passed up his usual session of porn on the computer. It just didn't seem right after he'd spoken to Marcia. No—more than that. She'd spoken to him, and she was look- ing forward to seeing him around.

So he'd made sure that he was outside the field house the next time she came out, glistening.

"Hey," he'd begun.

"Hey back at you," she said, putting her hood up on her sweat- shirt.

"So now's around," he'd said, and she'd looked at him funny—very funny. So he quickly said, "I've got class to get to. See ya soon."

And she'd said, "Sure," or maybe she'd said "Maybe," or maybe she hadn't said anything.

He'd had an angry porn session that night, and the headache was very bad.

But three days later he was mopping down the central hallway in one of the older chemistry buildings when he looked up and there she was—staring at him.

He mumbled, "I'm sorry."

"For what?" she asked.

He looked at the mop and the pail.

"Hey, there's nothing wrong with working your way through school. I admire you for that."

Then somehow he'd asked her out—and miraculously she'd agreed.

* * *

He'd borrowed a car and went to pick her up in front of the campus bookstore, which everyone called the "Coop" for some reason he couldn't figure out. Some sort of secret he guessed. As he stood waiting there for her he hoped that no one recognized him, that one of the other campus workers—especially a janitor—didn't come by and see him just standing there, all dressed up, his hair slicked back and wearing shoes he'd just bought at the Price Right. They hurt his feet, but they were shiny. Everything about him was clean and no body hair—none. But it was fucking cold, and because his winter coat had a rip in it he only had on a spring jacket—and she was already twenty minutes late. Maybe she wasn't coming. Maybe she and her friends were watching him from one of the dorm room windows and laughing. Yes, that's what was probably happening. They were laughing. I mean, one of these girls going out with a janitor—I mean, how stupid could he— Then she was there, like a vision. In the car they talked about how his day went, what was his major, which dorm did he lived in, and he answered every question as if he was a student at the college—one of them.

She'd never been to the restaurant he took her to—three towns over. He'd scoped out the place to be sure he knew how to get there and that he could afford it. But the moment he walked in with her he had a bad feeling—she didn't like it. But he thought they all liked fish places. Actually he hated fish, but he'd taken some Pepto-Bismol before so he wouldn't gag on the food—or fart. The headwaiter eyed him funny as he led them to a table in the middle of the large, almost empty room, but Marcia called the waiter over and said they would prefer to sit by the window overlooking the lake.

"Is that okay with you?" she asked after the waiter had made a face and then gone to clear the other table.

"Yeah. By the lake would be good." Then he added for no particular reason, "But it's frozen."

"Yeah—duh—it's winter."

Was she making fun of him? He didn't like the "duh"—the way she said it. But once they were settled at the table he ordered a whole bottle of pink champagne, the most expensive thing he'd ever ordered in a restaurant.

"It's pretty great stuff, pink champagne."

She looked at him funny again. As if he were pulling her leg. "Pink champagne?"

Suddenly he wished he hadn't ordered the champagne. That he'd allowed her to order what she wanted. But the champagne arrived quickly and it was already open so he couldn't send it back, even if he was brave enough to send it back—which he wasn't.

She took a small sip of it and giggled. "It fizzes."

"Yeah, the bubbles are the whole point." He didn't know why he'd said that, and for a moment he just wanted to get up and leave. But when he looked at her, reading the menu, he felt heat all over his body.

"You're staring," she said. "Not polite."

But she wasn't angry. It occurred to him that she liked to be stared at—and was often stared at.

She ordered a whole lobster that almost made him gag when it arrived at the table. He ordered halibut fish and chips—and lots of ketchup.

Several times during dinner she tried to draw him out on where he came from, what he was studying at school and what his goals were.

When he hesitated she supplied answers to her own questions. She liked talking about herself, her family, her studies (chemistry) and her desire to work in the third world—"To make a difference." He thought, there's a third world just around the corner from your damned college—why not make a difference there? Then she was talking about how excited she was by her future—her fucking future.

And the waiter kept eyeing him. He didn't fool that guy for a moment—he could smell who Walter really was and looked at him like dirt. Living in a basement apartment, cold as hell in the winter, cooking soup in the can on a hot plate—this guy saw right through his combed hair and his cheap shoes.

And she saw the waiter see.

When the bill came the waiter had already added on a hefty tip—which came to more than he made in a week. He'd have to borrow some money to pay his rent. But he paid without complaint—he didn't dare complain in front of her.

As he drove her back to campus she looked out her window and didn't talk to him. He tried a few times. She didn't answer him. But when he said, "It's a good restaurant." She looked back at him, saw through him. She said, "It's a dump—and you're not a student at Ancaster, are you?"

He stared straight ahead and thought about driving the car off the road and slamming into a telephone pole. *It would serve her right,* he thought. But he didn't drive off the road. Nor did he say another word—all the way back to campus.

She got out of the car without even looking at him and disappeared back into the protection and privilege of her dorm.

He sat in the car in the dark for hours just smelling her perfume.

And the rage came upon him, and ideas—awful ideas began to find their way deep into his head and lodged there—and grew. They bloomed as the headache struck him with such force that he put his head against the cold of the window. He woke up hours later when a cop tapped his nightstick on the outside of the window, and the fucker made him take a breath analysis test right there and then. He'd never have done that to one of the students at the college. No, they get to drink all night although they're underage—and no one does anything.

This whole country's set up for them to have a good time while the Walters of the world serve them and cops like this one who are closer to Walter than to them go out of their way to protect them.

Like that waiter at the restaurant. He'd never have eyed one of them the way he'd eyed Walter. Never put such a big tip on the bill. Never have opened the champagne in the kitchen then brought it to the table. Never treated one of them with the disrespect he treated Walter.

* * *

Two days later he found out which was her dorm room, and the night after that he spied on her as she necked with one of the boys from her dorm. He even arranged to switch with Fat Juanita so he could clean that stretch of dorms.

That's when he microwaved his first turd and put it in that boy's bathroom in Lyndon Dorm.

A week later he discovered how to unlock Marcia's door and stood there—in her private place—and did his private thing, and felt strong and alive and the better for it.

He found her schedule online and when she was in class he was in her room, on her bed, in her dresser drawers—in her life.

Then he'd made the mistake. He'd been dreaming—really dreaming—of her and had fallen asleep on her bed, where she found him and screamed like his mother had and he'd made a mess in his pants.

Neil Frost hated committees. Like most professors he did his level best not to live up to either his contractual research requirement or his assigned administrative duties. Even in the sciences, if you knew the right people it was easy enough to get published. You have a contact on a journal's board, he published your crap, then you sat on the board and you published his crap. You both kept your cushy jobs—taught maybe four hours a week, took four- or five-month vacations—then bitched and moaned about the difficulty of the job. Yeah, sure, there were real research papers in those journals from real researchers. But Neil had given up on that after he had juried a set of articles by Gerald Vincent Bull, a Canadian engineer who had developed a supergun that could launch a satellite into space or throw a missile hundreds of miles—like from Saddam Hussein's Iraq to, oh say, Israel. Dr. Bull had called it Project Babylon. And from Neil's calculations, the thing actually could work. He thought of Bull as a genius and was going to say as much in his report. He also submitted an article to the journal in enthusiastic support of Bull's work. In fact he'd set up a meeting with Gerald and was going to use his article as a way of getting in on the ground level with this genius. Finally a horse to ride, an idea that had real legs, and cash and all the things that cash could buy. Then the Canadian was assassinated outside his apartment in Brussels. It was speculated that the Mossad was behind the assassination. Then the fucking Jews who controlled everything in America rejected his article, and his contact at the Pentagon had refused to return his phone calls and the university denied his application for promotion to full professor.

And now he didn't even have the seniority to choose which committee he had to sit on and he actually had to do the committee work like some fucking slave.

He was assigned several committees like a damned lecturer, not the assistant professor he was. One of them was Student Complaints. It dealt with housing complaints and anything having to do with the staff of the university. Not the faculty—just the staff.

That's where he met big-boned, big-busted Marcia and first heard the complaint about a janitor named Walter Jones.

And he'd liked the scrawny janitor from the moment he'd set eyes on the kid's pimply face. Something chemical seemed to reach out from him. Neil found the young man's rage refreshing, clean—useful.

So he'd stick-handled around bouncy Marcia's complaint—sent it to committee, the academic form of deep-sixing something—then called Mr. Walter Jones to his office.

"So, you owe me, Mr. Jones."

"For what?"

"For what, *sir.*"

"For what . . . sir?"

"I solved your little misunderstanding with the lovely Marcia."

Walter thought about that and put what he thought of as his "Spidey senses" on full alert. Finally he asked, "How did you—"

"I told her to fuck herself."

"You didn't."

"Not in so many words. I did it metaphorically."

Walter didn't know what that meant, but he decided it was best not to say anything.

Neil saw the open confusion on the young janitor's face, and he liked it. He liked it a lot.

"How's about I buy you a beer, Mr. Jones?"

And so the dance began. Two men angry at a world that had rejected them—one with access to the basic compounds that could make explosives, one with the rage to plant and detonate them.

One who thought he was smarter than the world, and one who knew he was cleverer than a failed professor named Neil.

It surprised Neil to learn that young Mr. Jones had access to so many parts of the campus. But as Walter so simply put it, "Everywhere gets dirty and needs to be cleaned, don't it?"

Neil thought of correcting his use of the English language then decided against it, thinking, *Fuck, what's the English language ever done for me?*

"Do you have a computer, Walter?"

"Of course. Who do you think—"

On his laptop Neil showed Walter how to download the PROMP-TOR anonymity program.

After that initial drink they communicated through their PROMP-TOR protocol and met at infrequent intervals, both knowing that the meetings were not casual, both knowing that they were building toward something—something big.

They agreed on the idiocy of Ancaster College.

They agreed on the obnoxiousness of the students.

They agreed they were aggrieved (Neil's word), pissed off with the way things were (Walter's words).

Then Neil took the first real step and showed Walter how to take three basic household products and blow up an abandoned outbuilding on a farm . . . and Walter loved it.

Then of course there was the deer—or buck or stag or whatever the fuck it was. Neil Frost wasn't big on zoology. But that was on their fifth meeting.

In their second Neil had shown Walter how Mentos and Diet Coke produced an interesting reaction. When he went to explain how it worked, he saw Walter's eyes glaze over—a look Neil was only too accustomed to receiving in his lectures, so he backed off and handed the younger man a pack of Mentos and a litre bottle of Diet Coke, and the kid had a ball.

On their third meeting Neil escalated his attack.

"Do you know what C-4 is?" he'd asked.

Walter had heard the term many times because he loved action movies, so he said, "A bomb thing."

"Yeah, it's a 'bomb thing.'" He saw the young man retreat; he'd have to stop doing things like that. The kid was sensitive to mockery. "Sorry. You wanna make some?"

"Maybe."

"Come on—I'll show you how."

They went to the local discount department store and began to purchase things—twenty packs of Silly Putty, a tub of Vaseline, a wax candle, 12 ounces of rubbing alcohol, a box of cornstarch, 24-ounce bottle of canola oil, two packages of clear gelatin, and a package of pipe cleaners.

Then Neil brought him to a part of the town that used to belong to the college but was now abandoned buildings.

"Where are we going?"

"One of the old labs. Not used anymore. But some of us still have keys." Neil dangled his key ring like a kid who had just found a way to get at his parents' liquor cabinet.

In the lab, Neil measured 4 cups of tap water and put it into a Pyrex bowl on a burner. He increased the temperature until it boiled, then added the gelatin and mixed it thoroughly. Then he took it off the heat.

"Now what?" Walter asked.

"Now we wait till it cools, and once it does we add the cooking oil and stir."

Walter noticed that Neil was smiling. It struck him as odd, but it—well, this interested him.

Once the mixture was completely cooled there was a thin layer of solids on the top. Neil used a small spatula to scrape it off and then put it in a dish and into the freezer.

Walter went to ask what he was doing, but before he could Neil said, "Light the candle. Allow the wax to accumulate in that other bowl."

Walter did as he was instructed, although he shivered when he saw the wax, the memory of the pain on his skin almost making him want to run.

"Good. Now mix in the petroleum jelly—"

"The what?"

"The Vaseline. And the cooking oil, the Silly Putty and the corn-starch—put them in that bowl and mix them together."

Before Neil could stop him, Walter reached into the bowl with his hands and mushed the mixture together.

Neil watched him; the kid was having fun.

Neil went to the freezer and removed the mixture there and walked it carefully over to the bowl.

"Why are you—"

"Moving slowly? Because these crystals are highly unstable." He carefully put them into the mixture that Walter had prepared.

"Now mix," Neil said.

Walter hesitated.

"Once it's in the mixture it's stable again. So just mix it in care-fully—no need for speed. A mistake and neither you nor I will have any problems left in the world."

"What are—"

"If you are rough with it, it will explode and take you and me and most of this building to hell. Is that clear enough."

"Yeah," Walter said, then, using a spatula this time, he slowly mixed in the crystals.

Neil watched from across the room and said, "Once it has the con-sistency of ice cream, stop."

About ten minutes later, Walter announced, "Ice cream."

"Good," Neil said and moved over to take a look. Then he turned to the younger man and said, "So what shall we blow up?"

"What can we with this?"

"Take a little and it'll blow up something small; take a lot and it will blow up something big."

That night they blew up an empty barn way out on the highway. Then Neil Frost showed Walter Jones how to make RDX—the king of explosives.

That fifth night Neil met him in his rusted-out Volvo outside Dundas just as it began to snow.

"Fuck, it's cold; why can't you just pick me up at my place?" Walter complained as he hopped into the car, rubbing his hands and holding them up to the heating vent. "Does this car have heat?"

"Some. It has some heat." Neil pulled away from the curb and his car swerved on the newly slick pavement. "So ask me again."

"What?"

"Ask me again, Walter."

"Okay. This is dumb. But okay. Does this car have heat?"

Neil smiled. "No, not that question, the other one."

"Why can't you just pick me up at my place—that one?"

"Yeah. So ask."

"I hate this. You ain't my teacher or anything."

Neil hit the accelerator and the car complained but picked up speed.

"I get that. So here's the answer to your delightful question: because we have to keep this secret. That's the reason I showed you how to use PROMPTOR, that's the reason we never meet on campus or at your place."

They drove on in silence, taking a wide sweeping curve at over seventy miles per hour. As they did, the back wheels slid slightly.

Walter thought to mention that they were going too fast for the increasing snow but didn't want to seem like a sissy, so he kept his mouth shut. Finally he asked, "How's about meeting at your place?"

"You don't know where my place is."

Walter nodded and said, "Yeah," although he'd figured out where

Neil Frost lived several days ago. But he saw no reason to tell the smartass that he wasn't all that clever.

They were picking up speed on a downslope so they could climb a steep hill. Seventy-five, eighty, eighty-five miles per hour. They zipped up that fuckin' hill like a dragster.

Then they crested the hill and the car actually came up off the pavement—and there it was, standing in the very center of the highway, its antlers proudly challenging the sky, its eyes huge and round and black.

Smack—crunch of metal—a scream—an air bag slammed Walter in the chest. The Volvo did a three-sixty and ended up in the ditch.

Blood came from Neil's forehead and nose, but Walter staggered out of the car without a cut. After checking that Neil was okay, he approached the buck.

Neil pulled himself from the car and watched the young janitor walk through the pelting snow to the animal, which lay on its side, its feet kicking, antlers raking against the pavement. Neil was about to say something but stopped himself as he saw the young janitor kneel down near the head of the buck.

Walter saw the terror in the creature's eyes and reached forward to grab one of its antlers.

The velvety smoothness surprised him. He ran his hand down the antler to the bucks head and felt the life there.

Neil was transfixed by the young man. The animal seemed to calm under the young man's touch.

Then the knife was out and a spray of bright arterial blood fountained from the buck's throat and Walter Jones stood in the now deep snow—lit by the headlights of Neil's Volvo—blood showering down on him.

And any doubts that Neil had that Walter Jones was his man—vanished.

48

A REALITY OF TV SHOWS— T MINUS 4 DAYS

THE TALL, SLENDER MAN WITH THE LONG GREY HAIR HAD USED craigslist to recruit people to populate the Wellness Dream Clinic. What they'd been told was that it was a reality television show called *The Institution. No experience was required: Apply to the code above.*

Then the listing had added: *About the show: Each actor will be assigned a role in the mental institution: some as orderlies, some as cooks, some as cleaners, some as patients. Each will be given a scenario which they must faithfully follow. Every moment will be filmed by more than 300 hidden cameras. Anyone acknowledging that they are playing a role, at any time, will immediately be taken off the show and forfeit the $1,000 payment. Please read the release below and sign it before you apply.*

The tall, slender man with the long grey hair had been inundated with folks anxious for their fifteen minutes of fame. So he'd cast his show then brought in its star—Seth Roberts.

Once Seth had abandoned the goggles, the man took to watching him sleep, although the fact that the boy slept with his eyes open was disconcerting. And then there was all that rapid eye movement. The kid seemed to dream from the moment he fell asleep, then on and on through the entire night.

Such dream behaviour was completely outside the norm.

The man tied back his long grey hair, pulled up the video of Seth in the Duomo from the synaesthetes website again and watched carefully: for the thousandth time he examined the joy on the boy's face.

Then he looked through the one-way mirror again—the boy was awake. It was time.

49

A LEVERAGE OF PROMPTOR—T MINUS 3 DAYS

IN WHAT SEEMED TO DECKER LIKE ONLY A MINUTE AFTER HE'D left Mr. Rabinowitz's dorm room and crawled, exhausted, into his bed, he was yanked to his feet by strong hands—Mr. T's hands.

In the morning light streaming through his open window he saw Yslan and a tall man standing beside her—a sort of beat up leading man, sans the charm and currently scowling.

Mr. T held out a towel to him.

It was only then that Decker realised that he was naked. He took the towel and wrapped it around his waist.

"We need more on Professor Frost so we need her to go back in," Yslan said.

Decker pointed at the window. "It's daylight."

"Yeah, that happens at ten thirty in the morning," the scowling man said.

"Who's the ghoul?" Decker asked Yslan.

"Never mind that. Get her to go back."

"I assume you've tried to convince her."

Yslan nodded.

"Give me a minute to get dressed."

It was then that Decker looked out the dorm window and saw the moon just above the horizon, despite the intensity of the sun. He turned back to Yslan and the others and thought, *The marines marine, the cops cop and everything goes on as before—except that like in Namibia the moon is out in broad daylight.*

And there it hung like a ghostly presence in the brightness of the day.

* * *

As Decker entered the locked, windowless room he was once more struck by the profound connection he felt with the strange diminutive creature who sat on the floor against the far wall.

VIOLA

His death shroud's grown.

DECKER

She's been crying.

"They want you to go back," Decker said.

"Tonight."

"Now."

"I said tonight."

"They say now."

She stood but she didn't look at him. Somehow she seemed larger—fuller. Then she turned her eyes to him. "Are you of the clearing or not?" Her voice was deep and centred. The lightness and lisp were gone. This was a warrior speaking, one who could wield a flaming sword. "Are you one of them or one of us?"

Decker resisted saying what he always said to such questions: *I'm not one of anything.* He grimly remembered the endless comments on his grade-school report cards: "Does not play well with others."

Then she demanded, "Or are you of the enemy?"

He was surprised to find himself on his knees and even more shocked as he heard his voice say, "I am no enemy of Viola Tripping."

"And of the clearing?"

He held out his arms. "I don't know. I don't."

They heard knocking at the door and shortly thereafter Yslan's voice—but they ignored both.

Just after sunset he emerged with Viola Tripping and they reentered the blast sight. All night they moved slowly from numbered chair to numbered chair. Over and over Viola Tripping settled her feet and raised her arms, but her spin, when it came, was slow and awkward. And quickly her arms came down and she looked at him. Her features were drawn—old. She added a few snippets to their knowledge but nothing significant.

When she stood where Neil Frost breathed his last she momentarily opened her mouth, but no voice came. She tried a second and a third time then looked sadly at Decker and said, "It's gone." For a moment Decker wanted to ask "What's gone? How does it work?" but he realised that Yslan had asked him the same things when she kidnapped him from the restaurant in Manhattan sixteen months ago. He'd found her questions ludicrous. As no doubt Viola Tripping would have found his.

Long before the sun rose Viola Tripping was back in her locked room and a bleary-eyed Decker sat in the provost's office with Yslan and the scowling man, whom Decker finally was introduced to as Leonard Harrison, head of the NSA.

Harrison addressed Yslan as if Decker weren't in the room. "So the shards led us to a junkyard, which led us to a professor who slept with her student."

"Right," Yslan said, clearly not pleased with the tone of his voice.

"And the student was cleared?"

"He was with her."

"Swell. So they alibi each other."

"And Professor Palmer's roommate and her building super both saw them together at the time of the blast."

"So she wasn't even hiding her affair with the kid?"

"Evidently not."

"Why wasn't she at the graduation?"

"No one she taught was graduating and she's not a tenured faculty member. She's paid from a trust fund so she didn't have to attend to get her final paycheck."

"Okay. So she couldn't be Frost's contact?"

"His cell phone records show no calls whatsoever to her."

"Well, what do they show?"

"Calls to take-out restaurants. To a publisher who refused to publish his biography of Gerald Bull. To his bank. That's about it."

"What do you mean 'about it'? What's the rest?"

"He called the chemistry department secretary at least once a week."

"Why?"

"He called in sick more than any other faculty member in the university."

"Was he? Sick, I mean."

"There's no record of it. We checked every doctor in town and none of them saw him in the past three years."

"So no calls to a potential accomplice?"

"Not that we could find."

"There're pay phones on campus," Decker said.

Harrison slowly turned to Decker. "So?"

"So he may have used them to make his phone calls."

"Fine, but how exactly are we to know which calls from those pay phones were his?"

"I don't know," Decker said.

"Neither do I," Harrison snapped. Decker heard it loud and clear—the expert to the dilettante: "Keep your fucking mouth shut!"

"So how else did he communicate?"

Decker saw Yslan shuffle her feet, then she said in a remarkably small voice, "We traced a PROMPTOR protocol from the campus server to his URL."

Harrison whirled on her and let her have it.

Decker knew some fine profanity that even the *Maledicta* didn't know, but his was kid's stuff compared to the swill that poured from Harrison's mouth. And the length of the obscene tirade put Christian Bales on-set blow-up to shame.

Anonymity and security have always been at odds.

But Decker found himself smiling—he knew that PROMPTOR fascinated Crazy Eddie. And for the first time since he was whisked away from Namibia he thought he might have access to a little leverage—and Decker knew he badly needed some leverage.

50

A BIBBLE OF EDDIE—T MINUS 3 DAYS

EDDIE'S CELL PHONE RANG. HE TURNED ON HIS GPS MAP AND saw the dot he'd been following since Decker left the Junction, then flipped open his phone. "To what do I owe the honour of your phone call?" Eddie asked.

Decker walked quickly across the campus green toward his room as he recited the prologue to act 3 of *Henry V,* knowing it timed out to just under two minutes. Enough time for Eddie to light up a bomber, plug his phone into his computer and find out exactly who else was listening in on their conversation.

Decker passed by his marine stationed in the hallway, shouted, "One boss, one," and entered his dorm room. As he did Eddie said, "We have visitors, young man."

Decker was six months older than Eddie, but when it came to things digital Decker was definitely Eddie's junior. With the exception of a few genius hackers in Russia, India, the United States and Israel, almost everyone in the world was.

"Visitors! *Quelle surprise,*" Decker said. "Out of curiosity, how many?"

"Impossible to say."

"Okay. It is what it is."

"Exactamundo, Kemo Sabe. So what's shakin'?"

"How's your business with our New York lawyer friend going?"

There was a moment of silence, then Eddie said, "In the planning stages still." His voice was hard.

"Any word from Seth?"

"Yeah."

"What, Eddie?"

"He's been in touch."

"That's all you're going to tell me?"

"Yeah."

Another silence followed.

"You in Dundas, New York?"

"Yeah."

"They come and get you from Namibia?"

"Yeah."

"Then this attack is for real?" Eddie was no conspiracy nut, but he had a profound distrust of power and those who wielded it. He was always sceptical about what they chose to tell the populace and what they chose not to tell the populace.

"Yeah."

"Yeah what? Try to be specific."

"There are still body parts . . ." He didn't add "stuck in the mud," although he wanted to.

"Oh."

"Yeah. Oh."

"So outside of seeking an update on my efforts with our lawyer friend to what do I owe this missive?"

"How much have you found out about the PROMPTOR program?"

"You have computer access?" Eddie stood. His brace clacked.

"Yeah."

"Go online. You know where." Eddie hung up.

Decker opened his browser and called up the synaesthetes' website. The front page had a new video of the Human Camera. Decker admired people like Stephen Wiltshire and Daniel Tammet but he knew they only provided cover for him. So when people inevitably had to label him they called him a synaesthete, although he was in actuality only a distant—very distant—cousin of synaesthetes.

A pop-up of the young monk in the Duomo came up, but before Decker could watch it the second prompt appeared. He hit shift F7. It immediately gave him what Eddie called a side door to the Pro

Actors Lab website. He carefully moved his cursor back and forth over the Pro Actors Lab title page—an etching of two French commedia performers having a late-night drink. Back and forth—back and forth. Finally the cursor hopped and the carafe of wine on the table between the two actors changed colour for just an instant. If Decker hadn't been concentrating he would have missed it. But he *was* concentrating and moved the cursor to the carafe and typed in his access code: Sethcomehome.

The carafe tipped forward and the wine spilled across the table until it covered it like a large tarp. Then the table tilted forward filling his screen with darkness. Instantly Eddie's unique script bibbled across the top.

Why do you want to know about PROMPTOR?

Because I want to trade it for information about where Seth is, he wanted to write but instead he typed, *They think one of the terrorists used it to contact his coconspirator.*

And they can't break PROMPTOR?

If they could I wouldn't be—

Yeah. I get that.

So, Eddie, can you help them break PROMPTOR?

Maybe. Eddie relit his bomber and inhaled deeply. He'd been making slow progress on breaking into the guts of PROMPTOR. But of late things were changing out there in cyberland. The Israeli STUXNET virus opened up all sorts of new possibilities for someone with Eddie's computer prowess. As well, as the Arab Spring took hold, tens of thousands of young Middle Easterners had downloaded PROMPTOR to keep their communications safe from the local secret police. So many that the system crashed several times. Eddie monitored every crash because each time the system started back up it gave him more and more access to its inner workings.

What does your maybe mean? Decker wrote.

What if I could get them to the guy who wrote the program?

They already know who wrote the thing, but they can't touch him.

What if we tell them they have the wrong guy.

What?

Eddie took another long drag and let the sweet smoke bounce off his computer monitor. *Don't you think something like PROMPTOR has a lawyer's fingerprints on it? A New York lawyer's fingerprints? Perhaps someone who lives on Patchin Place—and likes to fuck with other people's lives?*

Decker smiled, then wrote, *Get them the PROMPTOR e-mail contacts for one Professor Neil Frost and I'll try and trade it for them caging Charendoff.*

Sounds like a plan to me.

Good. Now tell me about Seth.

Decker, you know I can't.

Yeah, yeah. My son swore you to secrecy.

He did.

Well, tell me this at least. Did he cash the $20,000 check I gave you to get to him?

For a moment the screen was blank, then Eddie replied, *Last Friday.*

Not going to tell me where?

Come on, Decker, you know that I promised Seth not to pass on information about his whereabouts to you. You know that. And you know why he insisted on that.

For an instant he was back at his wife's graveside. Seth's tiny hand in his. Then the boy's eyes turned to him—shock on his face. "You're happy Mommy's dead."

"No, Seth. No."

"You're lying to me. Lying to me." The boy had taken his hand back—and he never held Decker's hand again, or let him into his life.

Decker didn't know what to say so he asked, *Any news from the ol' neighbourhood?*

El Junctioni?

Yeah, the Junction.

Trish Spence and Theo keep leaving messages for you.

Forward them to me.

Something about CBC not liking the hung man in that documentary you're working on. CBC have an objection to male size, do they?

Who knows what CBC objects to. Just forward their messages to me. Others?

Leena left a message.

What did it say?

Are you okay.

That's it?

That's it.

Okay.

Then there's that guy.

What guy?

Preppy looking—hanging out on our street. Finally knocked on the door.

And?

Said his name was Emerson Remi and that you knew him. Do you?

Decker remembered his feeling of nausea every time he'd met Emerson Remi. Was Mr. Remi in the woods looking for the path to the clearing like Viola Tripping had suggested? If so, was that why he was knocking at their door?

You still there?

Yeah. No, I don't know any Emerson Remi. Any other news?

Nothing except yet another church on Annette is being converted to condos.

Decker lifted his fingers from his keyboard, careful not to write what was in his mind: *That's not good. The churches keep the evil in check.*

You still there? Eddie bibbled.

Yeah. What's featured in Theo's shop?

The used-book shop?

Yeah.

Why?

Just tell me what's on display in his window.

Calling it a display is generous, Decker.

Okay—what's there?

It's Camus this week—dozens of different editions of L'Étranger.

Decker nodded, thinking, L'Étranger, *the stranger . . . no, the outsider. Like the girl who just wanted to watch,* but what he wrote was, *How long on the PROMPTOR thing?*

Two days at least—but I'll have to get lucky to manage it in two days. Anything else, my friend?

No.

Then adios, comrade.

Then Eddie's distinctive icon—a cross-legged yogi with a large erect phallus smoking a huge bomber—popped up, waved and disappeared into the nothingness of land digital, Eddie's kingdom.

51

A COLLISION OF LIBRARY BOOKS AND RED MUD—
T MINUS 3 DAYS

DECKER OPENED HIS DORM ROOM DOOR AND SHOUTED TO HIS marine in the corridor, "Hey, boss. One going out, boss!" He was rather pleased with the way the line sounded coming from his mouth, not Paul Newman, but not bad.

Decker left the dorm and noticed that the large library building across the way had its lights on despite the late hour. He watched students coming and going. It amazed him. It was the middle of the night and the place was clearly in full use. Decker couldn't remember if he'd even bothered to get his library card validated when he was an undergraduate at University of Toronto.

He crossed the quad and entered the building. As he did he recalled sitting in on a student-actor evaluation at a university theatre program where he was appalled to hear a senior teacher turn to a young actor and say, "Just go to a library and wander the aisles— something will catch your eye. Read that."

Stupid advice to a student who, like so many of them, had so little knowledge of literature. But for someone like Decker who knew books, it was a good idea.

He called Yslan. "Can you get me a library card?"

"If you've got too much time on your hands—"

"Can you get me a library card?"

The phone went silent for a moment then Yslan came back on the line. "It's waiting for you at the front desk. Present your ID and they'll give you a two-week card. And Mr. Roberts . . ."

"What?"

"Your real ID, not the fake one you used at Gatwick."

He hung up and got his two-week library card from the indifferent student who was manning the night desk.

He quickly found a copy of Camus' *L'Étranger,* then, allowing himself to meander, he found himself slowly walking the aisles of the fiction section. He'd done this many times in the past.

When he told Crazy Eddie about this kind of thing his friend had asked, "You're looking for truths. Right?"

"I wouldn't use those exact words, but yeah, truths."

"So why look at fiction?"

"Because fiction is just fact filtered through a specific mind. If the mind is good, the truths are distilled, refined."

Decker stopped halfway down one of the many rows of books and turned to his right. At eye level was a copy of a John Fowles' collection, *The Ebony Tower.*

He checked out the two books and left the library. As he did he stepped into a puddle and swore. Then, in the bright light from the library windows, he saw the dull red mud on his shoe. He reached down and scraped some off with his finger. He looked at it—red mud. He put it to his nose and was instantly surrounded by the earthy smell of Inshakha. Here in upper New York State the red mud of Mowani brought back his final image of her—on the edge of the bathtub, stripped to the waist, applying the very same red mud he had on his fingers to the beauty of her face.

He looked around him, but all was as it should be. A campus on a hill in upper New York State. The cold of the night solidifying its grip before the sunrise drove it back to the other world.

Three hours later, back in his dorm room, he finished making notes in the margin of both the John Fowles book and the John le Carré novel he'd picked up in the Johannesburg airport and was pretty sure he had something valuable at his fingertips. Then he started on *L'Étranger.*

The door opened and Harrison and Yslan entered his room.

"You could knock . . ."

"We don't need to knock, Mr. Roberts," Harrison said as he tossed a stack of papers onto Decker's desk. Decker glanced at them—they were his reports on the first interrogations.

"What am I supposed to do with these?" Harrison demanded.

"If the U.S. government is short of toilet paper, I assume—"

"Enough," Yslan said.

"I thought you were the truth expert, Roberts."

"It's not as simple as that."

"Really? Why's that?"

"Look," Decker said pointing at the stack of paper, "these folks knew they were being interrogated. Knew that they were suspected of doing something that they probably had nothing to do with."

"Why do you say that?"

"Simple math. I've gone through almost two hundred and fifty interrogations. It's not possible that all of them had something to do with the attack. Not possible."

"Yet more than two hundred of them you've marked as suspicious."

"No. As potentially untruthful."

"Same thing."

"No, it's not. These people may be hiding something. Sure, but fuck, it could be anything. Maybe they're illegal in the country, maybe they cheated on their taxes, maybe that they hate America, maybe they oppose democracy, maybe they despise Chicken McNuggets—could be anything."

"And why would that make them lie?"

"Oh, come on. You're the bad guys as far as they're concerned. They don't think you're questioning them to help them—or keep them safe. They think you're there to accuse them of complicity. So they hedge their bets."

"They lie," Harrison said.

"No. I didn't say that. They could be prevaricating or equivocating or paltering."

"Or fucking lying."

"Yeah, or that. All I can tell you is that I think they weren't telling the truth on the sections I underlined. But I have to tell you I'm not confident in even that. First, I wasn't there to see them talk."

"And that's important?"

"It's sometimes crucial to me."

"And this time?"

"I don't know."

Harrison turned to Yslan. "I want them all questioned again. This time about their contacts with Professor Frost." Then he turned to Decker. "You have just short of two hundred interviews left to review."

"Maybe you folks are barking up the wrong tree by interviewing Muslims."

"Really, Mr. Roberts." He paused, evidently in some sort of argument with himself. He just as evidently came to some sort of resolution and said, "Do you know who Gerald Bull was?"

"No."

"Well, Dr. Bull was a crazy-assed weapons inventor who was dealing directly with Saddam Hussein, and our dear Professor Frost had business dealings with that creep. So it's logical that his accomplice or accomplices were from the Muslim community, wouldn't you say?"

Decker ignored the rhetorical question but asked one of his own. "That's why the minimal security clearance on his file?"

"Yeah," Harrison said. He pointed at the computer on Decker's desk and said, "The interviews are there for you to download and analyse. I want your opinion by nightfall."

Decker had never heard the word "opinion" used as an obscenity before. But before he could say anything else, Harrison turned and left his room.

Yslan went to follow, then stopped herself and closed the door.

"You don't buy it, do you."

"Buy what?"

"The jihadi connection to Professor Frost."

"It's not for me to say. It's not why you brought me here."

"But you don't buy it," she pressed.

Decker reached into his backpack and took out two paperback books. The first was le Carré's *A Murder of Quality*. The second was Ancaster College's library copy of John Fowles' *Ebony Tower*. He handed them to her. "Read the underlined passages."

Yslan accepted the books, put them on the desk and pulled up a chair.

"Explain," she demanded.

"Just read the damned books."

"Why?"

"I find books helpful," he said.

"Okay. But that's just because you know literature, right?" Yslan said. "At least modern literature."

Decker didn't answer. He hoped she was right but had a sneaking suspicion it had something to do with his other gift.

"Well, isn't it? You've done adaptations of a bunch of novels for the stage, haven't you? *Lady in the Lake, The Great Gatsby, A Canticle for Leibowitz, Brazzaville Beach* and *Rapture of Canaan*."

"I only started work on those last three, I—"

"—never produced them. Right. But you did get to adapt and direct *The Dwarf,* didn't you? In Cincinnati as I recall. "

"You know very well I did."

"Yes. I do recall that."

"That's how you found me, wasn't it? Through the Cincinnati Playhouse. That led you to Steven Bradshaw, who led you to me?"

Yslan didn't answer.

She didn't have to.

A look Decker hadn't seen before crossed her face. "Wanna know what's up with your supposed friend and accomplice in that little Cincinnati episode, one Mr. Steven Bradshaw?"

"Is this some kind of bribe or trick?"

"Neither. But I'm tired of you thinking of yourself like some kind of saint." Before Decker could protest she continued, "After you used him—yes, that's the right term Mr. Roberts—used him, he had a seizure, then about two hundred more over the next month."

"And is he—"

"All right now? No, I wouldn't say that unless you think that living in a vegetative state is 'all right.' Perhaps you should be more careful, Mr. Roberts."

More than you could possibly imagine, he thought as he remembered finding Seth's diary in the hostel on Vancouver Island—with its eight by ten photograph of the dead boy from Stanstead, Quebec, whom Ira Charendoff had had killed. But more than the photo he remembered Seth's cutline on the bottom: "This is what happens when you get close to people, Dad. Stay away from me."

Decker had used Steven Bradshaw's good services to contain Henry-Clay Yolles of Yolles Pharmaceuticals, but the last time he saw Steven the young man's eyes were glazed and he was seemingly unable to control the movement of his limbs.

Decker turned away. He couldn't allow Yslan to see his eyes.

"So, tell me about you and these books. This isn't about you and truth-telling. What's this—another parlour game of yours?"

Decker assumed his ability to walk down aisles and aisles of books and somehow find something of relevance to him was another subset of his gift. Like his ability to tell people's ages and backgrounds and his ability to find order in events—what he called "semblant order." But he wasn't sure he wanted to share any of this with Special Agent Yslan Hicks.

"It's not a parlour trick."

"Fine, what is it?"

"Before you met me, could you have worked out the riddle of the two sisters in the house at the fork in the road?"

Yslan opened her mouth, then shut it.

"Don't do that. Just answer my question and remember I know if you're telling the truth."

After a moment she said, "No. I don't think I could have figured out the riddle."

"Right. But I always could figure out things like that. Always. A library is just another kind of riddle."

"Books speak to you?"

"I won't answer snide questions like that."

"Fine," she said and pointed to the computer. "Back to work with you." She turned to go.

"Read the books," he said.

She turned back to him. "And *L'Étranger,* should I read that, too? You still don't get it, do you?"

"Get what?"

"The moment you picked up that le Carré book in Johannesburg I had someone read and annotate it for me. You got the John Fowles book and *L'Étranger* from the library, they immediately reported it to us and they're being annotated, too."

"Like Coles Notes."

"What?"

"Canadian reference."

"I can Google it or you can tell me what the fuck you're talking about."

"They publish précis of books so school kids don't have to read the whole thing."

"Ah, CliffsNotes. America invented that."

"Another fine American export." Decker remembered Eddie's admonition that there was no shortcut to living your life. "So, did you read the précis?"

"Yes, and the full books."

"Good. Okay, so what did you think?"

"Well I get that the le Carré book implies that college towns are incestuous pits of liars and cheats, which we've found to be absurdly true. But I don't get what attracted you to the John Fowles book or *L'Étranger.* Or *Fanny and Alexander* while we are on the subject."

"How did you—"

"Never mind. Tell me about the books."

"Okay, remember the 'Ebony Tower' short story in the book?"

"Yeah, the old writer goes to a cabin on the moors to complete his novel. A young thug comes in, ties him up and robs him."

"Not as simple as that. The kid robs him but then promises to call the police to tell them to come and free the guy. Then he makes sure that the restraints aren't too tight, that the guy is comfortable."

"Right," Yslan said. Her eyes brightened as she said, "Then he sees the almost-completed novel."

"Yeah, and when he learns that the old guy had written it what does he do?"

"He tightens the bonds, burns the novel and never calls the police. The old guy almost starves to death."

"And what does the professor make of the thug's change in behaviour?"

"Something about those who—"

"Those who feel part of the secret of the written word and those who know that there is something special out there but they can't comprehend it. That they know they are being left behind. Left out of what some Irish poets call 'life's roar.' Outsiders . . . *l'étrangers*." *Lost in the woods,* he thought, *unable to find the clearing.*

"Not outsiders like an anchorite, though," Yslan said.

Decker looked at her. "A what?"

"Nothing. Just a random thought. But you think—"

"That it's more likely you're searching for an outsider. Someone who feels he's been looking in the window of an expensive restaurant knowing he'll never have the money—or perhaps even the taste—to enjoy the secret in that place."

"Stoney River."

"Yeah, a whole town that works here but is on the other side of the glass—outside the secret."

Yslan was suddenly on her feet. "And this person could have access to the entire university."

"Yes. Access to the labs. Access to the graduation ceremony."

"So a worker, a lab technician, a teaching assistant."

"Or a janitor."

She looked at him sharply.

"Read this," Decker handed over Grover Cleveland Rabinowitz's paper on the microwaving of human fecal material.

Yslan quickly scanned it and was about to speak when Harrison barged back in, his face contorted with anger.

"What?" Yslan demanded.

"The president's changed his mind."

"Well, that's a relief."

"Not really."

"Why's that?"

"He's decided not to come in four days, he's decided that the nation can't wait so he's coming the day after tomorrow."

52

A MIXING OF THE GREY-HAIRED MAN AND FUNERALS—T MINUS 2 DAYS

THE WALL-SIZED FLAT-SCREEN WAS ON AS THE GREY-HAIRED MAN entered his three-storey loft. CNN was flashing a bulletin that the president had moved the funeral at Ancaster College forward.

He put aside his coat and watched the rest of the coverage, then poured himself a drink of pure rainwater as he thought about funerals.

He liked funerals. No, that's not the correct way to put it. He found that in the midst of the grief and grieving he was able to catch a whiff of their feeling. For a while he'd attended many funerals but never got exactly what he wanted from them. But this funeral in the small upper New York State town was something different, in both size and scope. So many people grieving at one time in one place—so much feeling in the air to wrap around himself.

He hit number 2 on his speed dialer and when the other end was picked up he said, "You know who this is."

An affirmative response.

"I want a seat for the memorial at Ancaster College. Can that be arranged?"

Another affirmative.

He disconnected, then hit number 4 on his speed dialer and said, "Get the crew and plane ready."

53

A KILLING OF A SUPERVISOR—T MINUS 2 DAYS

SO THE PRESIDENT IS COMING TO BLESS WHAT I HAVE DONE, Walter thought. *Good. Very good. Very right. Yes, it's right that he comes and sees what I have done.*

He almost used the word "wrought." As in "See what I have wrought." He knew that word from Sunday school. His teacher told him that the word meant "done." He recalled asking her why they didn't just say what they meant. Then he remembered the girl beside him laughing at him.

He wanted to grab her long, narrow nose and pull it and pull it and pull it. But of course he didn't. He never did anything he really wanted to do back then—when he was a boy.

But now that he was a grown-up . . .

The president would speak at the church on Main Street, of course, he thought. *No, not the church where my mother made me go to Sunday school—no, that wouldn't be good enough. And—and oh, yeah, of course—I won't be invited. Not invited. Left out, again. Laughed at.* He wanted to do more than pull someone's nose this time—much more.

He felt the headache begin and he tried to keep his eyes away from the setting sun. The sun sometimes made it worse. Then he felt himself smile, before he knew he wanted to smile.

But no, he thought. *I have to be there. It wouldn't be right if I wasn't there.*

Then he asked himself: *But how?*

He knew that the Secret Service agents were already securing the church. *Who had cleanup duties on the church?* he wondered. Then he knew that it wouldn't matter who was scheduled. It would be left to the head supervisor and his assistant, both of whom had clearance to go anywhere on campus.

"But if only one of them showed up to clean before the ceremony? What would they do then? Cleaning the church was usually a four-man job. But if only one showed up . . ."

He considered that for a moment. He went to the cupboard and pulled out a pack of animal crackers. He liked animal crackers, although when he bought them in the grocery store he always had to pretend they were for his nephew—even though the girl who checked out his groceries had known him since high school and probably knew he didn't have a nephew.

He stacked together two tigers and bit their heads off and felt better. He took his box of animal crackers over to his computer and turned it on. He had a momentary tug to go to his favourite porn sites but he resisted.

He opened his PROMPTOR account and waited to get the all-clear signal. Once PROMPTOR announced that he was anonymous he searched for an address for the head supervisor and to his surprise he found it under the Rotary Club listing for the town.

Twenty minutes later he was standing outside a grey clapboard house with a rusted boat trailer—but no boat—on the front lawn.

He looked up and down the patchwork street of tiny houses, then, not seeing anyone, walked up the cracked paving stones to the front door and pressed the button.

The supervisor answered the door in his bathrobe and boxers. Hair sprouted from his ears, his pits and over the top of his wife-beater T-shirt.

"Who are you and whaddaya want?"

Walter didn't know for sure until the man spoke that he was going to kill him, but his tone of voice and not even knowing who Walter was after all these years, and then there was all that hair—well, it was just so disgusting.

54

A CACOPHONY OF OUTSIDERS—T MINUS 2 DAYS

"HOW CAN IT HURT?" DECKER SHOUTED.

"Some kid mutters something about a piece of shit and all of a sudden he's the access to—"

"Look at the essay he wrote. The kid was a fucking scientist. The thing interested him as a scientist. So he kept notes. Times and places. Just get the records of which janitor cleaned that restroom and cross-reference them with the appearances of the piece of shit."

"Why? Is this more of that outsider stuff?"

Decker stared at her. "You called it something else."

"What are you—"

"An anchor—something."

Yslan sighed then said, "It's a Catholic thing—an anchorite."

"What's an—"

There was a knock at the door.

"Yes," Yslan said without looking to the door.

Mr. T came in and handed Yslan an elaborate security pass.

"I already have a pass."

"Not for the church service you don't. Everyone who's going gets a new pass." He turned and left.

Yslan held the pass up to the light. Even from a distance Decker could see the intricate metal threads in the plastic and the large hologram imprint on the front. Decker didn't know much about such things, but he assumed it cost a minor fortune to produce these gizmos.

"Well, Special Agent Yslan Hicks, you do get invited to the finest of parties," Decker said.

"Yeah, I'm a real . . ." Her voice trailed off, and she shot Decker a look.

He nodded.

"I'm an insider, right?"

"Right."

"And he's an outsider—*l'étranger.*"

Decker nodded again and waited for her to piece it together.

Finally she said, "And he'll try to get in, won't he?"

"If I was an outsider I would."

"Get into the church to see the funeral!" She swore softly under her breath, then said, "Give me the kid's notes and I'll meet you in the provost's office in half an hour."

While Decker waited for the half hour to pass he googled "anchorite"—and what he read shocked him.

55

A CALLING TO ORDER—T MINUS 2 DAYS

DECKER ARRIVED ON THE DOT IN THE PROVOST'S OFFICE AND immediately didn't like what he saw.

Harrison was clearly in charge of the room. Yslan had been relegated to one side.

And they both were scowling.

"What's—"

"Wrong?" Harrison demanded.

"Yeah, I guess that's my question."

"Well a few things, Mr. Roberts. The first is that apparently the janitorial staff at the university regularly sign in for one another on those time sheets. Second, there are nineteen listed janitors, but there are also thirty subs who come and go."

"So how many of them were potentially on call on the day of the explosion?"

"Almost fifty."

"So, interview them all."

"We can't."

"Why?"

"Only six are kept on for the summer. The rest have eight-month contracts."

"What? Does this university treat these people like itinerant workers? Can they do that?"

"Money-saving crap again," Yslan said.

"The rest have left to find work for the summer, probably field work, picking. We'll be lucky to find half of the total. But there's another problem."

"Most of the signatures on the time sheets are illegible," Yslan said.

"Find the supervisor and ask him," Decker replied.

"That's the last and biggest problem."

"What is?"

"He's missing."

56

SCORPIONS AND THE SOUTHERN SKY— T MINUS 2 DAYS

THAT NIGHT DECKER ACCOMPANIED YSLAN AND HARRISON AS they interrogated the few janitors they could find. Over and over he closed his eyes, felt the cold and blood between his fingers and saw perfect geometric shapes—all of these people were telling the truth. Exhausted, he climbed into his bed. It was just past 4:00 a.m. when he heard it again.

Clattering. He'd heard it every night he'd slept in the dorm room, but now it was louder. He flicked on the light and there standing on his desk, its tail raised and ready to strike, was a large scorpion. He stared at it. This wasn't the Southwest. This was upper New York State. Then the thing turned and Decker saw its heart pulse in its thorax.

He pulled on his coat and yanked at the door handle. It was locked. He banged on it and his marine opened the door. "Tell her I'm not staying in this room. Tell her now."

"You can't—"

"Yeah, well what are you going to do? Shoot me?" He pushed his way past his marine and strode out into the cold night.

The sky was cloudless and the stars pierced through the darkness and made Decker shiver. The moon was above Venus, the four stars of the Southern Cross were to one side, and Scorpio dominated the western sky, its red heart-star pulsing.

Decker turned quickly—this couldn't be. Fucking upper New York State was way up in the Northern Hemisphere and yet above

him was the southern sky of Namibia. Then he thought about that—
above him, above him, not above everyone, just above him.

His phone buzzed, and Eddie's excited voice whispered, "Mission
accomplished."

"Eddie are you—"

"Sure? Hell yes, otherwise I'd never quote George W."

57

AN AGREEMENT OF TRADE—T MINUS 1 DAY

"YOU THINK YOU CAN TRADE WITH ME!"

"Yeah—you and the NSA, and that grumpy guy."

"I can have you arrested."

"I know that."

"Mr. Roberts, the president arrives in four hours and there are more than two hundred people dead and you at least claim to have the information as to who did this, so—"

"So trade, Special Agent Yslan Hicks—trade. I give you the URL at the other end of Professor Frost's PROMPTOR account, and you pursue a certain New York City lawyer as if he were the inventor and head of PROMPTOR itself."

"That Charendoff shit again?"

"Bingo. Haunt him, make his life a misery with the PROMPTOR stuff, and I'll give you the URL at—"

"Yeah, I get that." She thought for a moment then said, "Crazy Eddie figured it out, didn't he?"

"Yep."

"How?"

"Apparently something to do with the Arab Spring and thousands of people wanting PROMPTOR accounts so your counterparts in repressive regimes can't track them down."

"Don't compare me to—"

"Fine. I don't compare you. You work for the good guys—as you no doubt believe—hence using the same tactics as those who work for the bad guys is okay."

"You're on a tangent, Mr. Roberts." Decker recognized the line as something from an early Sean Penn film—something based on a Springsteen song.

"The Arab Spring?" she prompted.

"Eddie says there were so many requests that PROMPTOR couldn't handle them. So they began to pass them off to subsidiaries who didn't have the refined protections that PROMPTOR has."

"So he got into the system itself."

"Is that a question?"

"No."

"Well, you're right. He got inside and now he can navigate within PROMPTOR and hence has the information that you are so desperate to find."

"And you'll trade—"

"For you and yours making Mr. Ira Charendoff—lawyer of Patchin Place, New York City, probable killer of that boy in Stanstead, Quebec, and definitely the one who forced Crazy Eddie to betray me—make his life a living hell. So that he can't even think about coming after me again. Accuse him of being the mastermind behind PROMPTOR. Eddie will supply the information."

"But it's a lie."

"Yeah, well that may be, but it'll take him almost all of his considerable resources and probably the better part of five years to prove that it's a lie."

"And that's what you want in return for the identity of the terrorist?"

"It is. And I'm not prepared to negotiate my terms."

That was when Harrison barged in with Mr. T and Ted Knight—and a set of handcuffs and shackles.

58

A VISION FROM ON HIGH—T MINUS 1 DAY

WALTER WAITED OUTSIDE THE CHURCH. TWICE HE NODDED TO the Secret Service guy on the steps and the guy nodded back. Eventually the supervisor's assistant came out on the front steps looking for the supervisor, as Walter knew he would.

"You not doing anything, William?" the guy asked.

Walter didn't bother correcting him but climbed the steps and acknowledged that he was free. "Do you need a hand?"

"Sure as hell do. Come on. The fucking supervisor thinks that cleaning's beneath him."

"Does he?" Walter asked innocently.

"Yeah. And my back's killing me."

"Okay, I'll give you a hand."

The assistant supervisor turned to the Secret Service guy and said, "I can't do this alone. This is William, I need him to help me."

The Secret Service guy recognized Walter from days earlier when he had cleaned the church and this very guy was overseeing security.

More good luck, Walter thought. But he corrected himself: *This is more than good luck.* He didn't know the word "omen" except as the title of one of his favourite horror flicks, but he intrinsically understood and believed in the concept. And the security guy being the same one who saw him before was a sign. A sign that this was meant to be. *Yes,* he thought, *this whole thing was meant to be.*

"Okay," the Secret Service guy said.

Walter entered and went directly to the basement, opened the far door as if to air out the place, then emptied the dirty mop water into one of the industrial sinks. He put aside the mop and slowly made his way back past another Secret Service guy and up the stairs to the main sanctuary.

The supervisor's assistant was making a final inspection of the place. *Mustn't be dirty for these rich kids' folks. Mustn't have these privileged folks put their butts into filth.* Walter thought, *They ought to see where I have to live.*

"Good, William," the supervisor's assistant said, taking off his rubber gloves. As he headed out the front door he said, "I'm trusting you to do a good job, William. Everything in its place, everything in perfect alignment."

"Walter."

"What?

"Nothing, sir."

"And be sure you put things away properly."

Then he was gone.

Walter looked around, then began to clean. The properness of the place drove him nuts. Everything had a perfect match across the way. Everything was perfectly twinned—actually squared. It was nuts, just nuts as far as Walter was concerned. He waited for the Secret Service guy he saw downstairs to come upstairs then he retreated to the basement and put away his cleaning equipment—carefully looked around to be sure that he was alone—then he undid the screws the Secret Service guys had used to fasten the panels leading to the ductwork of the church. They'd used screws that were supposed to be impossible to remove, but Walter was a janitor and had faced off with the smartest, often most secretive kids in the country. So he'd seen screws like this and had long ago figured out how to undo them. He did just that, then slid open the panel and crawled up into the ductwork. He went in feetfirst to allow him to slide the grating back into place and the screws back into their holes so that from the outside it would appear like nothing had changed.

It was tight work and his hands began to sweat. The top two screws went into their sockets with little trouble, but the bottom left one almost made him cry it was so hard to get it into the hole.

Finally he got it in and was about to work on the final one when he heard a Secret Service guy come back into the basement.

Walter stopped moving and cupped the final screw in his hand so that it wouldn't fall and clatter against the metal ductwork. Then he heard the Secret Service guy call out, "Did you see the janitor leave?"

Walter slipped the screw into his breast pocket and pulled the zipper closed.

Another voice called out, "I'll check."

Walter cursed himself. He didn't have to be here. To chance this. But he did. He needed to see what he had done. To be part of this—this "thing." He wanted to claim it, but he knew better than to do that. But now no one could say that he was nothing. He wasn't nothing. He was the one who blew up all those fucking privileged people—all of them.

Through the grating he saw the Secret Service guy check the bucket and take the mop from the closet. Then he looked around him. The basement was pretty barren. Nowhere really to hide. Walter lost sight of him as he went to check the fire door at the back of the basement. Then he heard him call, "He must have gone out this way, the thing's open."

Walter smiled to himself. *I'd done that—smart—yeah, Walter's smart.*

From up the stairs he heard the other Secret Service guy call, "Okay. Lock and seal it then come on up here. We're doing a final sweep."

Walter heard the guy using an electric drill to seal the fire door shut, then saw him walk right under the ductwork and head up the stairs.

Walter realised that he'd been holding his breath. He let it out in a single long exhalation. Then he turned in the tight space and began his climb upward. The screw in his pocket scraped against his chest as he moved. Forty-five minutes later he peered through an ornate grating and looked down on the church's altar. He had a bird's-eye view of the proceedings—of that which he had wrought.

59

AN ARRIVAL OF A LONELY MAN—T MINUS 1 DAY

AS THE SMALL PLANE HE'D RENTED BANKED AND APPROACHED the single landing strip airport to the north of Dundas, New York, the grey-haired man sat back and turned on his laptop. He watched the video of Seth singing single notes up into the dome and then allowing the chords of music to cascade down on him.

Clearly touching glory.

60

ANOTHER AGREEMENT OF TRADE—T MINUS 1 DAY

THE OVERHEAD LIGHT IN DECKER'S ROOM SNAPPED ON AND HE went to turn toward the door, but the shackles stopped him.

"You stay facing the wall, like any common criminal." It was Harrison's voice.

Decker said nothing.

"We're prepared to trade, Mr. Roberts." It was Yslan.

"A wise—"

"Shut up, you damned freak." Harrison. Definitely Harrison, although they were precisely the same words his father had used when he was kid.

"Hard for me to negotiate when I'm not allowed to—"

"Your friend Eddie is in custody in a Junction police station." Harrison again.

Decker closed his eyes—squiggles of lines then forming up a perfect square. An untruth and then a truth. Decker assumed that the true part was that Eddie was in a police station—the lie that he was in custody. Canada was not so quick to act on requests from the likes of Leonard Harrison. Something like, "Arrest this guy as a material witness." Yeah, they'd take him to a police station to question him, but it's unlikely they'd hold him in custody. Besides, Eddie was surprisingly canny when it came to the law. His efforts to get his daughter back had led him to read many a legal textbook.

"Not a truth," Decker said to the wall. He wished his shackles would have allowed him to see the look on Harrison's face, but they didn't have any give in them at all.

"We let your friend go if you tell us who received Professor Frost's PROMPTOR e-mails." Harrison.

"We tell you where Seth is, then." Yslan again. Decker was sorely tried, but he'd promised Eddie, and somehow he knew that there was a semblant order to events and Charendoff came before Seth.

"No deal," Decker said. "You know my terms. Either meet them or fuck off—I have some fine wall viewing that you're interrupting."

A door slammed—he hoped Harrison. Then he felt the mattress sag a bit behind him. Yslan must have sat on the bed. A stab of pain in his wrists, then the sound of a key in a lock. Then his shackles loosened. He turned quickly on the bed and found himself face to face, eye to eye, lips to lips with Special Agent Yslan Hicks. And once again he was taken by the unusual colour of her translucent blue eyes, and the remarkable pallor of her skin.

For a moment neither knew what to do, both acknowledging the peculiar connection between them. Then the moment was gone and Yslan stood. She handed him the keys and he quickly undid his shackles.

Then she passed him a cell phone.

"It's a deal. Call Eddie."

Decker closed his eyes—two perfect interlocking squares floated from left to right across his retinal screen. Suddenly the cold was so intense that he winced. Then the metal thing in his hand and the slime between his fingers.

"What?" Yslan demanded.

"Nothing." He held out the phone to her and said, "Cleanmyass at hotmail dot com."

"That's the guy's e-mail address?"

"Yeah. His name's Walter Jones."

Less than a half hour later Mr. T kicked in the door of Walter Jones's basement apartment. Harrison rushed in, followed by Yslan and Decker.

It was a clean if extremely modest place. On a Formica kitchen table they found an old desktop PC with an early edition of

Windows that took more than a minute to boot up. Once it did, they found more than forty e-mails from Professor Frost's PROMPTOR account that Walter had saved.

Harrison quickly organised a search for Walter Jones. Photos of the suspect were e-mailed to every cop, FBI agent, Homeland Security officer and Secret Service officer who protected the president.

In less than two hours the president was scheduled to speak in the church on Main Street, and the tension was palpable in the room. Harrison was issuing orders and Mr. T and Ted Knight were urging the forensic guys to hurry.

It was as Decker heard Harrison say into his cell phone, "Security Code One lockdown—repeat, Security Code One lockdown," that Yslan came out of the bathroom and said, "Better take a look."

The men followed her into the small bathroom. She pulled aside the streaked shower curtain to reveal what could only be called a shrine.

A shrine to a girl named Marcia.

Decker looked closely at the collection and knew it was not random. It had been carefully organised and displayed. But something was missing.

Then Yslan shoved her way past him—a tendril of her perfume caught his attention and he turned back to the shrine.

And there it was—a small space, now empty, that at one time had (Decker was pretty sure) been filled by a bottle containing Marcia Lavin's perfume.

At the church the six Secret Service officers who oversaw security for the president scowled when they heard the order to execute a Security Code One lockdown. The eldest of the six looked around the church then up at the open grating for the ductwork high, high above the altar. "Ladders, guys. Big fucking ladders. And get me the portable welding kit. I'll seal the ones in the church proper—you guys look after the basement and the vestry."

61

A SCREAM OF VIOLAS—T MINUS 1 DAY

IT WAS JUST FIVE MINUTES LATER WHEN VIOLA TRIPPING BEGAN to scream, and the marine guard immediately contacted Yslan.

Ten minutes after that, the locked door to the windowless room was opened and Yslan Hicks stepped in.

The tiny creature turned her cataract-blurred eyes toward the NSA special agent.

"Viola?"

The girl/woman screamed louder.

"Viola, what's wrong?"

More screaming. Yslan didn't have a clue what to do, then she found herself kneeling and holding out her arms to the tiny woman.

Silence.

Viola Tripping's mouth opened wide but now no sound came from it. Her head moved slowly from left to right then canted, as if trying to bring the image of the NSA special agent into proper focus. Then she slowly walked forward and climbed onto Yslan Hicks' lap, rested her head against Yslan's chest, and heaved a sigh.

Yslan never dealt with children, leaving that to those she thought had the motherhood gene. But she found herself slowly rocking Viola Tripping and then much to her surprise, singing a lullaby— the words to which she was surprised that she knew. "There was a young cowboy who lived on the range . . ."

Twenty-five minutes later Yslan eased the sleeping girl/woman from her lap and Viola Tripping's eyes snapped open.

"When?" It was more a demand for information than a question.

"When what?" Yslan responded.

"When's the memorial?"

For an instant Yslan wondered how she knew about the memorial service, then she quickly told her when the ceremony was going to be. Before she could ask if Viola wanted to attend, Viola said, "I must be there. I must—with him."

62

AN OCEAN OF GRIEF—T MINUS 1 DAY

GRIEF HUNG IN THE AIR OVER THE SMALL TOWN THAT MAY FIRST day, like a tarp thrown over all this.

What remained of the church on Main Street was draped in black cloth.

Security personnel were everywhere and made no attempt to hide their presence or their weapons.

The austere, perfectly symmetrical interior of the Calvinist church was as closely guarded as any property on the planet. Every entrance had been sealed shut and every grate of every duct had been welded into place. Sniffer dogs had barked, but nothing had been found.

Each seat on the hard wood pews was carefully marked with a name card. The seats for the grieving parents of the deceased students were up close to the altar, followed by seats set aside for the relatives of the dead faculty farther back.

The day had dawned with a brisk north wind and despite the fact that it was the first day of May the chill intensified when the rain came.

Harrison and Yslan were busy organizing the search for Walter Jones while trying to help the Secret Service agents with security responsibility for the president. So much so that no one kept the press back—and they had a field day.

A massive memorial for young people, students, was by its nature a ghastly and heart-rending event—and one to which the American public insisted upon having full access. So the cameras were everywhere as the sorrowful parents and siblings of the deceased made their way into the church.

Flashbulbs broke the gloom, and video cameras panned to get the best shots.

But the one that captured the public imagination showed a tallish man holding hands with what looked like a dwarfed girl wearing wraparound sunglasses despite the rain as they waited in line to enter the church. In hours it appeared on the front pages of newspapers around the nation and led thousands of newscasts.

As soon as everyone had taken their seats, the head of the Secret Service signalled the president, who looked up from his BlackBerry and gave the head of the CIA a thumbs-up.

The doors of the church opened. A hush fell over the mourners.

The president's entrance to the church was done in silence with a solemnity that befitted the profound sorrow that filled the church like a thick fog.

His athletic figure looked a little stooped, his features a bit haggard. His handsome wife walked at his side. They did not hold hands. Their two little girls did not attend.

Everyone rose as they entered, and every Secret Service officer tensed. Movement of any kind was not a friend of security, and mass movement in a confined space was an outright danger.

High above, Walter pressed his face hard against the grille and strained to get a look at the president.

Far beneath him in the seventh row, the grey-haired man found himself unimpressed by either the president or his wife, although he liked the feeling that the grieving all around him produced in his chest.

The president's wife sat in the front pew as the president ascended the four steps to the raised dais alone. For a moment he glanced at the pulpit that projected out into the church like the massive prow of a sailing ship. An image of Orson Welles delivering the whaler's sermon bloomed momentarily in his head.

He signalled for the crowd to sit and they did.

The president touched the tie he was wearing and allowed his eyes to roam upward.

Walter grinned, although he wanted to whoop and cheer. The president of the United States was looking at him, and he was looking back—an equal. Equal to him. No better. Equal. He wished Marcia could see that.

The president pulled his eyes away from the ceiling and looked at the assembled mourners.

Viola Tripping squeezed Decker's hand. "There's an active death aura around him."

"Active?" Decker asked. But before Viola could respond, the president began. "This is a day unlike any other I can recall. It is a day completely devoid of joy."

Decker leaned back in the pew, exhaustion finally taking hold of him. His eyes shut before he realised—and much to his surprise—no, shock—random lines entered his retinal screen. The president of the United States when he said, "It is a day completely devoid of joy" was not telling the truth.

The service progressed. There were tears and the odd cry of anger, but on the whole the mourners were grateful for the president's words of solace. Yslan and Harrison were even more grateful when the president finished and was whisked away to the safety of Air Force One.

Once the door to the plane was shut he demanded, "So?"

Leon Panetta, head of the CIA, said, "It's confirmed. He's there."

"So tomorrow?"

"Yes, Mr. President, tomorrow."

A final hymn was sung and the congregation rose. The mourners began to leave the church down the centre aisle. Parents clung to each other; children bewildered by the sudden change in their lives cried openly, as much from fear as anything else.

For a moment the line stopped, and right in front of Decker stood a late-middle-aged couple who wore their grief in the deep lines of their faces—faces that Decker was pretty sure belonged to the parents of Grover Cleveland Rabinowitz. The resemblance to the mother was startling.

"I'm sorry for your loss, Mr. and Mrs. Rabinowitz."

The older man looked at Decker. "He was a good boy. A very good boy."

"I'm sure he was," Decker responded.

"He was our reason . . . ya know?"

Decker didn't know but was grateful that the line of mourners began to move again before Mr. Rabinowitz could clarify that Grover Cleveland was their very reason for living. From the man's large strong hands Decker assumed he was a blue-collar worker—perhaps a warehouse worker—not a scientist like the son of whom he had clearly been so very proud.

The last of the mourners finally passed and Decker and Viola Tripping stepped out into the aisle. Once he did, Decker saw Yslan standing to one side. He threw her a questioning glance and she mouthed the word "nothing."

High above Walter saw the man with the dwarf girl and again wondered who they were. Then he settled in to wait. He was good at that—he'd waited all his life for rich people to finish this or that.

Outside the church, government-supplied limousines picked up the mourners and drove them away.

Suddenly Decker felt someone looking at him. He turned. A tall man with long grey hair wearing a very expensive suit was openly staring at him.

Then Yslan was at his side and between him and Viola Tripping. "Hey!" Decker protested.

"Viola needs to come with me," Yslan said.

"Just a second," Decker said, stepping in front of Viola. He was standing three steps down from her on the church's front steps, so they were eye to eye. "What did you mean about the president's death aura?"

"Someone's going to be killed—soon."

"Who?"

"Someone with a huge aura. The president's carrying that aura."

Yslan stepped in and said, "She's exhausted, Mr. Roberts. This chitchat can wait." She turned the girl/woman and marched her quickly back toward her locked and windowless room.

As Decker watched them go he wondered if the huge aura Viola saw the president carrying had anything to do with the president's lying when he said it was "a day completely devoid of joy." Was there something good in this day? If so—what?

It was May 1, 2011. Navy SEALs were taking their final practice run in their mock-up of a certain Pakistani compound, completing the end of a nine-year search. The final sighting of bin Laden in his lair had been relayed by the watchers to the SEALs, who had passed it on to the president. For both the Seals and the president of the United States, May 1, 2011 was not a day "completely devoid of joy."

Mr. Bin Laden had one day left to live; the countdown was nearly over.

63

Cussed when she saw the photo of Decker and Viola Tripping on the front page of the *National Post.* Then she yelled at the photo, "Decker, phone home!"

She tossed the paper aside and noticed the mess of her apartment. How the hell had it gotten so out of control? It never used to. But even as she wondered where she had put the vacuum cleaner she forgot about the apartment's disarray and turned her powerful mind to the professional problem at hand.

Why the hell had the CBC insisted that she cut any reference to the Hung Boy in the sixth episode of the documentary series that she and Decker were working on?

She reran the meeting at CBC in her mind.

She'd stared in disbelief at the pin-striped CBC executive across the desk from her. No doubt he lived in Riverdale. Trish often thought that if you fired twenty shots at random in Riverdale you'd rid the world of at least ten of these stuffed-shirt bureaucrats who spent their time at the public tit while claiming they were protecting Canadian art. Then she'd looked to Erika, the CBC-appointed show runner.

Erika shrugged then looked away, as if something in the atrium was of more interest than the show that they'd been working on for almost eighteen months.

"So it's settled," pin-stripe said and picked up a file from his desk as he made the traditional motions to indicate (a) that the meeting was over and (b) that Trish should get out of his office—that he was a busy man, a "doer" and this bit of biz was done, done, done.

When he glanced up he was surprised that Trish had not moved; and more, it looked like he'd need a forklift to move her from her seat. He'd opened his mouth, but Trish beat him to the punch.

"Why? Just tell me why you want the material on the boy who was lynched in the Junction cut from a documentary series about the Junction. Just, in twenty words or less, tell me why."

After a sigh clearly meant to indicate that such explanations were beneath him, he said, "It's gratuitous."

"The racist crap we found, the anti-Semitism we uncovered, the presence of over fifty percent of the prison halfway houses in the city and the out of control violence of the thirties—those weren't a problem, but this one gay boy's death—his murder—is a problem?"

"The dead boy's cut. Got it?"

She always hated the way CBC bureaucrats pretended they were Hollywood moguls. These guys were grant writers, not producers.

Trish turned again to Erika. "Anything to say about this, or did you already know? Fuck, you already knew."

"Language," pin-stripe interjected.

"The buyer's always right," Erika said.

"What CBC hymnal's that from?"

"What?"

"Erika, what if the buyer's an idiot?"

Pin-stripe almost rose to the bait, then turned away.

Something in all this struck Trish as particularly odd. She wished that Decker were here—he was good at reading stuff like this.

"Well?" pin-stripe asked.

Trish rose, turned on her heel and left the office without agreeing to cut anything.

She'd placed more than a dozen phone calls to Decker, none of which had been returned. She needed his help to find out why CBC wanted the dead gay boy cut from the show. What issue could they possibly have with the fact that a gay boy had been lynched in 1902 across from the library in the Junction—and that his murder had never been transferred to the police blotter of the Toronto police force when the Junction, suddenly and for no discernible reason, joined the big bad city?

She looked at Decker's photo in the newspaper again and muttered, "Come on, Decker. Decker phone home."

EDDIE

Stared at the photo of Decker and the tiny woman on the front page of the *Toronto Star* and wondered who the small creature was. Then he wondered if Decker was okay. Helping at Ancaster College was a far cry from going on truth-telling sessions. And breaking into PROMPTOR was exposing both of them to scrutiny in a way that they'd never been exposed before.

He studied the photo carefully. Was it a girl or a very small woman at Decker's side?

He pulled his desk light closer and bent it down toward the photo.

The girl/woman drew his eyes. There was something about the way she held her body. But what? Then he understood: it was the same way his own daughter in far off Portland, Oregon, stood—after she'd been crying.

THEO

Was looking at the photo on the ninth page of the *Globe and Mail*. Theo was naturally surprised to see Decker in the midst of a U.S. calamity. As he folded the paper he thought of his friend.

"How much do I know about you, Decker?" he said aloud to the thousands and thousands of books in his used-book shop.

Then he smiled. "Not much, I guess. Not much."

The phone rang and he picked it up. "Pizza Tarantino—viscera on the side, viscera on top, your choice, heart attack discount available upon request."

"Hey, freak face, has Decker called you?"

"Nice to hear from you, too, Trish."

"Yeah. Have you heard from him?"

"No. Did you try Eddie?"

"The other freak face. Yeah I tried."

"And?"

"Yeah, he's spoken to him but that's all he'd tell me."

"Then leave a message."

"I did. Twelve to be precise."

"Well then . . ."

Trish Spence had hung up.

EMERSON REMI

Looked at the image on his iPhone in the wood-panelled bar of the spooky old CPR hotel, the King Edward, on King Street in downtown Toronto—and smiled.

He hadn't filed a story for the *Times* in almost eight months. Nor had he returned phone calls from his Princeton friends. Or from anyone. He just sat in the bar every day—and waited.

And today that which he was waiting for—really from the time he'd last seen Decker in Cincinnati in the old synagogue some sixteen months ago—had come back to him.

He allowed his index finger to trace the lines of Decker's face and said aloud, "Hello brother, welcome home. So very nice to see you again." And finally he didn't feel so profoundly alone—such a freak—a man with a brother is never really alone.

LEENA

Saw a reproduction of the photo on the *National* news as she finished closing up her restaurant. It gave her a start. Her old boyfriend looked older—much older—and stooped. As if he were carrying something heavy on his back. She glanced in the mirror and saw her own image there—older, much older, and not just a bit stooped herself. *Damned time,* she thought.

MARTIN ARMISTAAD—INMATE BW212890
LEAVENWORTH PENITENTIARY

Saw the image of Decker and the tiny woman on the wall TV between the beefy shoulders of two bare-chested, tattooed fellow inmates. Then one of them reached up and turned the channel to cartoons or professional wrestling—what was the difference? But Martin had seen enough to know that if the camera had panned in all likelihood Special Agent Yslan Hicks would have come into view. That would have been an unexpected treat. Then he thought of the tall man and the tiny woman—these two . . . *Two whats?* he asked himself. But he knew the answer to his own question before he'd completed it.

Two more of his kind. Two in the clearing—not at the crystal palace but in the clearing, like him.

He smiled and plodded his way back to his cell. He took out his calendar, which he'd already annotated using the pi ratio to find relevant days. The previous one had been the day of the blast at Ancaster College. He flipped the page to May. And there it was, only one day away—May 2, 2011—and it was a quadruple helix day. Something big was going to happen on May 2, 2011.

He checked his stock market tables—nothing there for tomorrow. So it had to be something else in the events of men—something big, something really big.

64

AN OBJECT OUT OF PLACE—AFTER

DECKER'S MARINE OPENED THE BASEMENT DOOR OF THE CHURCH and indicated that Decker was to enter.

Decker hesitated, then stepped through the door with a "Yes, boss, yes" that he didn't complete before the door slammed shut behind him.

It took a moment for his eyes to adjust to the dimness of the place. He found old churches pretty creepy but as he looked around he realised that old church basements were even creepier, and this one's obsessive symmetry—well, was just plain odd.

The wide space was unfurnished and spotless, and like all good Calvinist buildings, perfectly symmetrical. Its walls were nothing more than mortar and raw fieldstone holding back the earth, but the stones were meticulously stacked—and matched the pattern of stonework on the opposite wall.

The floor was mostly compacted soil, although one area dead centre along the north wall did have a cracked cement slab upon which sat a huge rusting oil furnace that was shut off at this time of year. The thing was as big as three Cadillacs stacked one on top of the other. On either side of it were twin cement industrial sinks at which two fingerprint techs were plying their craft on a mop handle.

Over their heads dead centre was the grated entrance to the brushed-metal ductwork that bisected the ceiling. The grating sported the clear markings of recent welding.

Decker walked to the centre of the room and turned slowly to take it all in—the door, the furnace, the sinks, the ductwork, the stairs on the far side leading up to the chapel in perfect balance with the exit door—and immediately sensed that something was out of place, although as he rescanned the area he couldn't say exactly what.

Yslan came down the stairs from the church with two men at her side. One was a square-shaped Slav. The other was dressed like he came out of the film *Men in Black,* so Decker assumed he was a security officer of some sort.

Yslan quickly introduced them to Decker, although she didn't bother introducing Decker to them—which was just fine with Decker.

"Both these men saw Walter Jones in the church before the president spoke." Then turning to the men Yslan said, "Tell me again about the last time you saw Walter Jones."

Decker listened closely, periodically closing his eyes. He only asked one question; "After the gratings on the ducts are welded shut, is there a way to get into them?"

"Nope—or out for that matter. A good weld—and we do the best—is stronger than tempered steel."

Decker nodded and glanced at the duct cover over the sinks and understood what had disturbed his sense of semblant order in the first place. The place was so orderly—everything in its place. Everything complete, balanced, except the welds on the grating over the duct entrance—and the grating itself. There were four screw holes in the grating, but only three screws.

For a moment he stared at the thing and thought, *There's a mass murderer up there. Walter did come to see the funeral.*

The outsider got in.

But now it's his choice how his life ends. If he calls for help someone'll hear his cries and they'll come and get him—and probably execute him. Or if he doesn't call for help . . . Decker wondered how long it would take to starve to death.

The two men completed their accounts and Yslan dismissed them. Once they were gone she turned on Decker. "So?"

"What?"

"Truth, were they speaking the truth?"

"For sure."

She looked more closely at him, then spun quickly and took in the place, the way she'd seen Decker do—the exit door, the sinks, the furnace, the ductwork. She was sensing something amiss and a thought was rising in her mind when one of the fingerprint guys said, "It's his prints on the mop handle."

Yslan thought, *Yeah, that's what happens when you use a mop.*

Then she looked back at the room and Decker, and the thought that was rising . . . had vanished and she was once more bewildered.

When she looked at Decker he was smiling.

"What's the smile about?"

"Nothing, Special Agent Hicks, nothing," he said as he took one last look at the welded seal on the ductwork and the hole without a screw that threw off the place's perfect symmetry.

65

THE LEAVING OF A DREAMER—AFTER

GARRETH PUT ASIDE THE BRUCE HUNTER NOVEL THAT HAD momentarily distracted him. He granted the man's knowledge of firearms and the particularly sordid culture that surrounded them. The book, like so much fiction, was about retribution. Revenge. *Funny how the writers of the religious right missed the idea that revenge belonged to Him—it's pretty clear in the Book,* Garreth thought. He remembered a saying about revenge being best served cold but had never really understood what that meant.

It had been Garreth's experience that unless you were willing to involve yourself in real violence there was no revenge in the world. People can do the most awful things to each other but there is no way of getting back at them unless you are willing to go outside the realm of human morality—something that Garreth had done exactly one time, thanks to meeting Decker Roberts on that cold January day. If he'd never met that kid he'd never have taken that money from those Vietnamese drug dealers—and slid to his own personal hell.

He flicked on CNN and was surprised to see the footage of Decker and the diminutive woman entering the church down the hill from Ancaster College.

For a moment he considered leaving his surveillance of the San Francisco Wellness Dream Clinic and heading to Dundas, New York. But he quickly put aside the idea. The town would be loaded with feds. Besides, he was all set up for a capture here, and he was pretty sure that Roberts would eventually come for his son, since the info he'd gotten from his cop friends on Vancouver Island said that Decker Roberts was out there fourteen months ago and tore the place apart trying to find the boy. He would eventually come after him again—and when he did, Garreth would be waiting for him. For retribution.

He wondered briefly if there could be a connection between Decker in Dundas, New York, and yesterday's early morning departure of the grey-haired freak who ran the dream clinic.

He'd been watching the place for days, and the routine was pretty much standardized. The actors, or whatever they were, arrived between 6:15 and 6:30 in the morning, already in costume—be it orderly, nurse or patient. Three hours later the grey-haired freak, who he now knew was named W. J. Connelly, arrived and stayed until 1:00 or 2:00. Then he got in his fancy car and drove off. The actors left at 10:00 p.m.—like clockwork.

But not yesterday. Yesterday a limo arrived for the grey-haired freak. He was carrying a travel bag and a computer case. And he was clearly angry that the limo was late.

After reaming out the driver he got in the car, and off he went. For a moment this confused Garreth, since he wasn't heading toward the San Francisco Airport. Then he consulted a more detailed map of the Bay Area and saw that the limo had headed in the direction of a private airfield. He made some calls and established that indeed that was where W. J. Connelly was headed—his corporate jet at the ready.

He cracked a new bottle of bourbon and took a long pull.

He tried to remember when he'd had his last drink—and couldn't.

Garreth had seen Decker's kid only twice since he'd set up surveillance on the converted warehouse. There was no sign on the building or any indication what went on inside. But there were barred windows on the second floor through which he'd spotted Seth Roberts—and taken a series of digital photos of the young man with the help of his long zoom lens.

When he first saw him he'd had a shock—the likeness to the five-year-old Decker Roberts, his father, was startling. Granted, this young man was older, but you didn't need fancy aging software to see how that kid back then could grow into this young man. Well not *that* kid into *this* man. He reminded himself that it was this young man's father whom he'd known as a five-year-old kid—a kid who murdered a six-year-old girl—and sent his life spiralling out of control.

The second time Garreth had seen Seth he was at the side of the tall grey-haired freak. He took more photos.

As he watched the two chatting in the window he found his rage on the rise, and before he'd realised it he'd downed a sizable portion of the fifth of bourbon he always carried. And the alcohol fuelled the rage. Weird Stallone-style scenarios whipped through his head, and only a stumble that sent his bourbon bottle crashing to the pavement below sobered him enough to think straight.

It was not this kid who'd sent his life to hell—it was this kid's father. The father was the sinner, not the son. "I'm only here to find the father," he said aloud to the empty tenement room.

Later that day, he watched the broadcast of the president's speech at the memorial service—and wondered what good it did. He doubted the whole concept of closure. He'd certainly had no closure since that cold day in Toronto when he sat in his police car with a very scared five-year-old boy named Decker Roberts.

He watched the Pacific mist roll in and felt it cool down the day.

At ten the actors all left.

He watched, and watched, and finally acted.

Breaking into the place wasn't that difficult, although getting past the locked metal door took some doing. There were no guards, no nurses, and only one patient—Seth Roberts. He unlocked Seth's door and quietly entered the room. The lights were off and the boy was lying on his back, his eyes wide open, but he was clearly asleep. From the rapid eye movement Garreth assumed he was in deep REM sleep, dreaming away.

He took out his camera and took a series of shots. Then he carefully tossed the room. He found nothing of interest except a photo of a dead boy encased in ice in a small river. On the bottom of the photo in Magic Marker were the words: *This is what happens when you get close to people, Dad. Stay away from me.* He was tempted to take the photo but decided instead to photograph it. As he took the third shot he was surprised to hear the young man call out in his sleep, "No. Please. I'm only twenty-one years old."

He slipped out of the room, then out of the warehouse and returned to his tenement perch.

The moon set—and a blackness within the darkness of night entered his heart. Hate.

Three days after the funeral Garreth was running out of patience. He'd been casing the clinic for almost two weeks.

And every day he'd been drinking more and more heavily.

Why? he asked himself. *Maybe after all these years I'm frightened to close this case.*

Maybe Decker Roberts just gave him the excuse he needed to drink.

It was then he saw the first of the moving vans arrive. The actors all seemed to leave at once, some opening pay envelopes as they did. Then the doctor, or whatever the grey-haired freak was, giving orders as to what was to go where. Three hours later the vans were packed and ready to go when the freak wheeled out a gurney with the clinic's sole patient, Seth Roberts, clearly sedated—and manacled hands and feet to the metal sides of the bed.

He took shot after shot until the gurney was inside the van and the van sped away.

A PAUCITY OF GOOD-BYES—AFTER

DECKER AWOKE WITH A START. SOMETHING WAS WRONG. HE leapt out of bed and called out, "One, boss, one." No one answered. He yanked at the door. It opened—no guard.

He threw on his clothes and ran into the hall—no one.

Down the hall and then out onto the campus—everything was different. There were a few students but no army presence, no marines.

He ran to the provost's office and was stopped by an octogenarian secretary he'd never seen before.

"Yes?"

"Who are you?"

"Professor Endicott's secretary. Be polite, young man."

It'd been a long time since he'd been called a young man, but he managed to respond. "Whose secretary?"

"The provost's."

"Ah, yeah, right." He moved past her toward the provost's closed door.

"Do you have an appointment?" she asked brightly. Evidently politeness was compulsory on campus.

He threw open the provost's door. The man looked up from his desk, then changed glasses so he could see his visitor.

"Yes?" he said.

"Where are—"

The provost sighed, then finally said, "Gone. Thank the heavens. Gone. It's time for us all to try to just move on." He was smiling. It bothered Decker.

Decker raced out of the building then up the hill toward the windowless room where they kept Viola Tripping.

There was no one guarding the door.

Decker pushed it open and stepped into the windowless room—and saw no one. He switched on the light and for the first time saw the depth of the room and that it was L shaped. He ran to the far end and found another long room—but it too was empty. He turned and retraced his steps. When he stepped into the front room, the door opened.

Yslan.

"Where is she?" Decker demanded.

"Clearly not here."

"I know that, but—"

"She's gone, Mr. Roberts."

It didn't compute. "Gone?"

She glanced at her watch. "Her plane left a while back."

"Plane? Plane to where?"

"That's for us to know. But believe this—you can search for a very long time and you'll never find her."

All Decker could think to say was, "Why?"

Yslan suddenly felt a sharp pain in her chest and knew it was his anguish affecting her physically. This was completely new and unexpected. "She left this for you." She held out a slender volume.

Decker took it. It was Viola Tripping's copy of Shakespeare's *Pericles*.

He flipped through the pages.

"There are no notes—we checked, Mr. Roberts."

"Of course. Of course you did."

"So why that, Mr. Roberts? Why did she leave that play for you?"

Because Pericles gets redeemed by the love of his daughter, he thought, but what he said was, "That's for me to know."

The pain in her chest subsided and Yslan shrugged.

"So it's finished here?" Decker asked.

"Yeah, we're finished here."

"But what about—"

"We'll catch him. The manhunt is on."

Decker nodded. He was tempted to ask what would happen to Walter Jones when she caught Walter Jones but didn't. What he did ask was, "Can I go? You don't need me here anymore."

He looked around—still no guards.

"Can I?"

Yslan shrugged again.

"Where's my son?"

Yslan stepped toward him. Her face for the first time since he'd been shanghaied from Namibia was relaxed. For a moment Decker thought she was going to hug him or something. But, although her translucent blue eyes were locked on his, he couldn't read anything there.

"If I didn't know better, Special Agent Yslan Hicks, I'd say you were calm."

"Not until we have Walter Jones."

Decker nodded and finally said, "Right."

"What? You don't think we should hunt him down?"

"No. I think he needs to be caught and incarcerated."

"But not executed?"

"Will that bring back any of those who died here?"

Yslan didn't answer.

"Do you really think it will stop anyone from imitating this . . ." He waved his hands in the air, not knowing what word he wanted to use to describe what had happened at Ancaster College.

"No. There's no way to stop a madman."

Decker looked away.

"Now what? You don't think he was a madman?"

Decker shook his head. "Can a madman plan and execute something like this? Can he dupe Professor Frost? Can he manage to escape what I assume is already a massive countrywide search? You don't have to answer any of those questions."

"So how would you go about stopping men like Walter Jones?"

"The hard way."

"What are you talking about?"

Decker took a deep breath and was about to forget it, then de-cided not to. "It's that winner crap again."

"Excuse me!" Yslan said. It wasn't a question. It was a demand for an explanation.

"Winners. We've made a religion out of winning."

"You'd prefer losing?"

"I'd prefer a world where there didn't have to be thousands of los-ers so the few winners can feel that they are special."

"Come again?"

"Think. Our whole system is set up to reward winners. To get people to work themselves to the bone to be winners. To climb over top of one another to win."

Yslan looked at him but said nothing.

"Don't you see?"

"No, I guess I don't."

"If winning is everything, then what do you do with all those who haven't won? How can you make them feel part of all this?"

"Of what?" Yslan was clearly getting exasperated.

"How can there be a civil society—a place that doesn't need gated communities and private police forces—if people don't feel they're part of the same world as the winners?"

"So now you're a communist?"

"No. I worked in Moscow under Brezhnev and directed in Shang-hai before the changeover. Their answer isn't right either. 'I pretend to work and they pretend to pay me.'"

"You've lost me yet again."

"It was the Moscow joke."

"Those wacky Russians—always good for a laugh."

"Not so ha-ha funny when you sat for hours waiting for a server to take your order in a restaurant because he was paid the same if he worked hard or if he didn't work at all. I'm not proposing that."

"Then what are you proposing?"

"A system where somehow we all feel part of what is happening to us. Where we don't use the SUV answer."

"Well, I have to congratulate you, Mr. Roberts, you've lost me

twice in under two minutes." Decker turned away. "No, you're not allowed to do that. The SUV answer? What the fuck's that?"

"Do you know what the thinking was behind the making of
SUVs?"

"There was thinking from Detroit, how novel."

Decker looked at her—she'd spoken almost exactly like him. For a
moment both felt the bizarre connection. Finally Decker said, "Yeah.
There was some thinking from Motor City. The death toll on American highways had hit a new high. The roads were fucking dangerous."

"So?"

"So, rather than dealing with the hard problem—"

"Which was?"

"How to make people more respectful of one another and hence
drive more carefully, Detroit came up with a simpler solution. Make
a car like a truck—which is what an SUV is. Let the winners buy the
safety of a truck and be damned what happens to the losers who
drive small cars."

Yslan thought about that for long moment, then said, "So you
want a world without winners?"

Decker didn't answer.

"Wasn't it you who told me that this university produced an important product—brain power? Surely that's special, about winning.
Surely this kind of brain power will make the majority of these kids
winners. On top of which you said that the brain power that elite institutions like this produce is essential for the good of the country—
fuck, you said for the good of the world."

Decker again didn't answer.

"So what you're saying doesn't really make any sense, does it? Besides your other business, your acting business, deals with stars—not
workaday actors, stars, aka winners. And to completely demolish
your argument, and to get somewhat more personal, you know that
you're not 'one of the people.'" She made air quotes as she said that,
then continued, "You're special, Mr. Roberts, and you know it."

"As are you, *Special* Agent Yslan Hicks."

"I worked hard for that Special title."

"I have no doubt you did. I also assume that unlike your jerk of a boss, you don't hold it over the heads of the people you work with."

"How would you know that?" But the moment the words were out of her mouth, she knew how he knew. He'd been watching her as much as she'd been watching him.

"What's the private name you had for yourself when you were a little girl, Special Agent Yslan Hicks?"

She was stunned by his question. How did he know she had a private name for herself when she was a little girl? A name she told no one. She looked away. She wasn't going to tell him that when she was a little girl she had a secret name for herself—from a card game. She thought of herself as a waif called Solitaire.

She smiled.

"What?"

"Nothing." Then she reached into her pocket and pulled out a piece of paper. She looked at it for a long moment, then handed it to Decker.

He took it, opened it and read: *I've okayed the publishing of your book on acting.*

"You stopped—"

"Turn it over, Mr. Roberts."

He did and read: *Your son, Seth, is in the Wellness Dream Clinic in San Francisco.*

He looked at her. She'd changed a lot since he first met her when she kissed him in the restaurant in Manhattan's Chelsea district.

"Be seeing you around, Mr. Roberts. You can count on that. And, oh yeah, our deal is still in place—you don't leave the country without notifying me."

"Won't you be watching me anyway?"

"What do you think, Mr. Roberts?"

"I think you will.'

"And why would that be, Mr. Roberts?"

"Because I'm an asset."

"No."

"No?"

"No, Mr. Roberts—you're a *valued* asset." Then she winked as she said, "Travel safe," turned and left Decker to his thoughts.

He raced back to his dorm room. Threw his things into his knapsack—contemplated leaving his script of *Love and Pain and the Dwarf in the Garden,* then stuffed it into a side pocket—and after taking a brief moment to look at the church headed to the nearest airport.

67

A SCHEMING OF CRAZY EDDIE—AFTER

EDDIE DIDN'T LIKE LINES, SO HE HAD TO WORK AT KEEPING HIS
feelings in check as he waited to clear security at the Hamilton
International Airport.

He glanced at his watch. He still had lots of time to make his
plane. Then he checked the GPS on his BlackBerry and saw that
Decker's plane was somewhere over Middle America. He rechecked
his watch. Decker's flight was early—too much ahead of him.

He whispered an apology to the gods of flying and punched in a
twenty-digit code. When the prompt came up he typed in "Potential
right engine failure—advise landing in nearest airport for safety check."

Then he looked down at his pant leg. A police dog was there—
and way too interested.

He saw a cop coming toward him with a grim look he'd known
for a very long time—that every pot smoker has known for a long
time. He pulled up his pant leg revealing the old metal gizmo that
lifted his foot so he wouldn't trip on his downturned toes.

The cop stopped and looked at the contraption.

"What—"

"Torn Achilles tendon—long time ago. Football injury."

The dog whined.

"Come on, Copper," the cop said.

Eddie thought, *Fuck, the cop called his dog Copper. More cleverness
from the constabulary,* but decided silence was a better response to
the situation.

"Next!" the immigration guy hollered.

Eddie elaborated his limp as he made his way to the counter. Over his shoulder he heard Copper growl, then bark. *Life's tough then you die,* he thought, then added a second thought: *Eat crap, Copper.* But he had a large smile on his face and said to the immigration officer, "Good morning. How's your day going?"

The officer looked at Eddie, then at his passport. "Where're you off to today?" the man asked—no, demanded.

"Portland, Oregon, then on to San Francisco."

"Ticket."

Eddie produced it and the officer looked at it closely.

"Not a very long stopover in Portland."

"No, just long enough to pick up someone."

The "someone" was waiting for him at the Portland airport. Standing by herself in the midst of the arrivals terminal, she had a small bag in her hand, a torn teddy bear in her arms, and a profoundly lost look in her eyes.

"Marina," Eddie said gently.

The girl turned toward him and for a long moment didn't know who he was. Then a smile creased her frightened face.

"Where's your mom, Marina?"

"She said I was to stay here and that someone would come for me."

Eddie had to control his fury. "She just left you here?"

"She drove me."

"But she just left you here?"

"She said someone'd come for me."

Eddie let out a long breath. "Well, I'm here for you."

"Yes."

"And Marina—"

"What?"

"I'll always be here for you—always. Promise."

The girl reached up and took his hand. She was almost fourteen years old, but clearly she was closer emotionally to a six-year-old. Eddie didn't care.

He had his daughter back.

68

A MEETING OF OLD ACQUAINTANCES—AFTER

IT WAS AFTER SUNSET WHEN DECKER FINALLY HOPPED OUT OF THE cab in front of the warehouse building that matched the address Special Agent Yslan Hicks had given him. There was no indication that this was a doctor's clinic, and when he approached the front door he was surprised that there was no buzzer or bell. No sign that this was the Wellness Clinic—no sign that this was anything but an old warehouse.

He stepped back from the door and noticed the glass pane embedded in the upper panel. *Odd for a warehouse,* he thought. Then he saw the outline of a square in glue residue on the glass. He ran his hand over the ridge.

Something ticked in his head. He'd worked on so many film sets and film sets used stick 'em etchings that adhere to glass with cheap glue—like this. With the right lens and lighting it looked like expensive etched glass rather than a cheap Mylar cut out.

He put his hand on the handle—it turned—and the door opened.

He stepped into what looked like a reception lobby. He flicked on the overhead and quickly he saw that something was wrong. The furniture was clearly rental-quality stuff. The prints on the walls were pretty close to what he'd seen on cheap television sets. He walked behind the empty receptionist's desk and saw it immediately—it was only a façade of a desk.

He turned. The whole thing was like a film set.

He looked at the wall behind the "receptionist's desk" and saw that it had been painted in cheap scene paint, not house paint—it was already beginning to blister and lose its colour.

He approached the only door out of the reception room and was surprised that although it had been painted to look like wood, it was in fact metal. The steel in the door was the only real thing in the whole place—that and the bolting mechanism.

He turned the doorknob, heard the lock click, and to his surprise the thing opened.

He quickly made his way down a corridor and past a nurse's station that fell over when he pushed it. "Seth! Seth!"

He was running—and shouting—no screaming—his son's name.

He threw open the doors to the "patient rooms." One after another—empty, empty, empty.

"Seth! Seth!"

He turned a corner and faced a long dimly lit corridor. A figure was at the far end, leaning against a wall . . . then it was speaking.

"He's not here."

Garreth Senior heard his words slur. He was tempted to reach for the bottle he kept in his coat pocket but resisted the impulse. "In fact, they're all not here."

Decker stepped forward. It took a moment for his eyes to adjust to the gloom of the long, vacant corridor. When they did he saw an older man, maybe sixty maybe sixty-five, with deep lines on his face and the classic sunburst of blood vessels on his cheeks that marked a serious drinker. He had a camera with a big zoom lens on it over his shoulder.

The man took a step forward and stumbled—he almost fell. The camera came off his shoulder and he caught it by the strap and let it dangle there.

"Who's not here? I don't know what you're talking about," Decker said.

"What a lousy liar you are." Again Garreth Senior heard his words slur again. *Shit, of all times not to be able to hold my liquor!* "You were a lousy liar all those years ago, too, Decker Roberts."

Decker resisted asking how this drunk knew his name and what he meant by "all those years ago." Instead he asked, "Where's my son?"

"He went with the dream healer or whatever the fuck he is. The rest of them—the actors or whatever they were—are gone, too." The liquor was in control and it wanted to laugh—so he did. The laughter rolled from him and the camera dropped to the ground. The lens cracked with a sickening crunch.

Decker fought the desire to walk away from this creature and forced himself to ask, "Where did he go?"

"The actors?"

"No, my son."

Garreth Senior spread his arms and lifted his shoulders in the international symbol for "who knows," and moved forward. A goofy smile crossed his face, although he didn't want it to.

"But Seth was here, right?"

"Yep."

"When did he leave?"

"A few hours after sunrise."

California was three hours behind upper New York State, so that would be right around the time when Yslan told him where Seth was. Had she warned Seth he was coming? Maybe. Seth was the strongest card she had to make him work for the NSA. So maybe she did. He wasn't sure. "Who are you and what business is this of yours?"

"Don't recognize me, Decker Roberts?"

Decker really didn't like the way he said his name—knowingly. As if he were talking to a child. "No. I never met you before in my life."

"Not true, lad. Very, very not true," the man said as he continued to move toward Decker.

Decker detected the rising of a Scottish accent in the midst of the drunkenness.

"We've met before."

Decker closed his eyes—cold, metal object and slime between his fingers, three parallel lines across his retinal screen—a truth. He opened his eyes and looked more seriously at this strange gnarled man. Something about him was vaguely familiar, but what? Then he remembered a conversation with Special Agent Yslan Hicks fifteen months ago in a hotel room on Lakeshore Avenue in Toronto:

"Who's this guy, Mr. Roberts?" He'd looked down. There were

photographs: a man outside then inside Leena's restaurant. The same man two tables away from him and Trish at Rancho Relaxo. "This is the same guy you showed me last night who was watching the house I grew up in," he'd said.

She'd nodded.

"Who is he?"

"That's what I want you to tell me."

"Well I can't, because I don't know who he is."

"Think, Mr. Roberts, think."

"I don't fucking know. I don't know him."

"Is that the truth, Mr. Roberts? The truth?"

"Yes. Yes and yes. I don't know who that is."

"You're a lousy liar, Decker."

"Be that as it may, I don't know who the fuck that is. Got it?"

Yslan had nodded.

"But you know who he is, don't you?" Decker had demanded.

"No."

Squiggly lines. Special Agent Yslan Hicks had lied to him.

That man was *this* man—standing in front of him now.

"When did we meet?" Decker demanded.

"Long ways back." The Scottish accent was thickening.

"When?"

"January sixteenth, thirty-four years ago, to be precise."

More parallel lines.

"Where?"

"Two twenty-one Strathern, City of Toronto, County of York, Province of Ontario, the Dominion of Canada."

The man's accent was now a thick brogue—old Toronto talking.

Decker felt himself somehow falling although he was still on his feet—"What!"

"January sixteenth, in the year of our Lord one thousand nine hundred and seventy-three. At your parents' house."

The man stepped forward.

Decker felt something shift inside him.

"It was very cold."

Another step.

Decker felt something metal in his hand.

"And there was a dead little girl."

Another step.

Decker felt blood between his fingers, and cold—terrible cold.

"And you lied to me then, like you're lying to me now."

Another step.

The man's grizzled face was inches from Decker's. His sour breath filled Decker's nostrils.

Fear filled his heart.

"Who are you?"

"Now? No one."

"But then?"

"Detective Garreth—"

And Decker finally knew. Finally knew how it had all begun. Inside the igloo. He and his friend Kristen from next door. They were inside. They'd piled up the wet, heavy snow till it was taller than either of them. Then they'd taken a spade and dug a hole in the bottom. As they pulled out the snow the hole enlarged until it was big enough for both of them to slither in on their stomachs. Once inside they turned over to face the snow ceiling. Then she suggested that they carve out the thing from the inside. She had brought a metal garden trowel with her. Lying on their backs they took turns carving layers off the ceiling, then passing it over their bodies and out of the igloo. At one point he'd said to her, "There's so much snow up there. What if it fell on us?" She'd laughed and called him a baby. So he'd grabbed the trowel and said, "I'll show you who's a baby!" and he'd cut deep into the ceiling of snow. A large chunk fell down on them and they both gasped from the cold. Then they'd managed to shove it down to their feet toward the entrance. But they hadn't pushed it far enough. It covered the exit, blotting out the light.

Then the whole roof fell in.

Weight and cold.

And she had the trowel, the means to dig their way out, but she wouldn't let it go—even though he was nearest the exit.

So he'd grabbed it.

It cut her.

Blood.

So much blood.

And cold.

Then his mother screaming. And an ambulance, and a man—THIS MAN!—asking questions in his Scottish accent.

Decker allowed his eyes to meet Garreth Senior's. And he saw cold hatred there.

"I've done you no harm," he said.

"Not true. Definitely not true."

Decker closed his eyes—two perfect squares floated across his retinal screen. He *had* harmed this man.

He opened his eyes and stared at this man. "What do you want of me?"

Garreth thought, *What the fuck do I want?* Then he snarled, "I want my bloody life back, you filthy heathen." Then he was on Decker, his strong hands tight around the younger man's throat.

Decker staggered under the surprise assault and felt his head smack hard against the wall.

Then he felt the wall give a bit—a faux wall, a set wall.

Then pressure on his larynx.

Blots of colour flew across his eyes, and he felt himself about to pass out. He smashed his elbow into the wall, and it gave enough to turn an inch.

Of course it would—it's a film set wall, made to pivot to allow a camera a better shot.

Another shove and the cheap thing turned.

Without the wall as a support, Garreth lost his balance and staggered back a step.

Decker forced his eyes open and over the drunk's shoulder he saw a blur of motion accompanied by an odd clacking. Then Eddie was there, his arm around Garreth Senior's throat, yanking him off Decker and slowly squeezing the air from him.

The man's knees went weak and his eyes rolled up in his head.

"Eddie, you're killing him."

Eddie stared straight at Decker and said with a remarkable calm, "No, I'm not. I'm just going to put him under for a while." He released his arm and the man slowly slid down. Eddie's injured foot cradled his head so that it didn't bang on the cement.

"Where did you learn—"

"Four years on the streets teaches you a few interesting things." He tapped Garreth Senior's body with his foot, then turned away, evidently satisfied that the man was under.

Decker stared at Eddie, not knowing what to say. Eddie saw it and smiled. "Nice to see you speechless. A rare treat. Let me help you. Perhaps you'd like to know how I found you."

"Okay."

"So ask."

"So how did you find me?"

"You told me that you never throw away a script once you've directed it."

"So?"

"So check your bag."

Decker did and pulled out *Love and Pain and the Dwarf in the Garden*. Holding it out to Eddie, still confused, he asked, "So?"

Eddie pulled out his pocket GPS and turned it to Decker.

Decker saw the map and the flashing figure.

"You put a transponder in the script?"

"A few pages after my suggestion that you look at that YouTube site. Never say I don't give you anything."

"Okay. I promise never to say that." There was a moment of silence between the two, then Decker asked, "Can I say thanks?"

"Sure, gratitude is an undervalued commodity in the world." Eddie reached down and picked up Garreth Senior's digital camera. The long lens fell off and what was left of it made a crackling sound when it hit the ground.

"Why—"

Eddie held up a hand to silence Decker. He turned the camera in his palm, then hit a toggle switch. "Ah," he said. He clicked his way through picture after picture and his face grew very dark.

"What?"

"Prepare yourself, my friend. Come take a look; you need to see these." Decker stood over Eddie's shoulder as photo after photo of the warehouse came up. Then, of a tall grey-haired man, then that man talking to Seth. Then shot after shot of Seth—Seth at a barred window, Seth sleeping with his eyes open, Seth, Seth, Seth. The final one of Seth clearly drugged and manacled to a gurney being shoved into a moving van with the grey-haired man standing there watching.

"Oh, God," Decker said, and he felt his legs go to jelly. Eddie caught him before he fell. But then something even darker crossed Eddie's face. "What?"

Eddie turned the camera so Decker could see the image: the dead boy from Stanstead, locked in ice, and Seth's damning scribble at the bottom: *This is what happens when you get close to people, Dad. Stay away from me.*"

"Daddy!"

A girl's cry!

From the darkness a very thin girl with straggly hair that was probably blond if it were washed stepped slowly forward and held out her arms.

"Don't be frightened, Marina," Eddie said. "Come say hello to my friend Decker Roberts."

The girl stood at Eddie's side—the likeness unmistakable—and said in a tiny voice, "Decker is a funny name."

Decker replied gently, "Yes, it is. But Marina is a very beautiful name." He turned to Eddie. "How did—"

"That unscheduled stop in Nebraska?"

"What about—you did that, didn't you?"

"Yeah, well my timing was a little off—forgot the time zones—so you and your fellow passengers had a slight five-hour layover in the heart of the nation while I went up to Portland. Such is life in the early twenty-first century."

Then there was more movement in the darkness and Eddie pulled Marina behind him to protect her.

It was Mr. T and Ted Knight. "Well, this is a fine mess you've gotten us into, Mr. Roberts," the large black man said, clearly not knowing he came close to quoting Oliver Hardy. He pointed at Garreth Senior on the ground. Mr. T knelt down and put a huge index finger to the man's jugular. Nodded. "I think it's time for you to disappear again, Mr. Roberts. This man was a cop. He's not dead, but he won't be out for much longer."

"Did Yslan—"

"You're a valued asset, Mr. Roberts; I believe she mentioned that." He waited for Decker to nod an acknowledgement. He finally did and Mr. T continued, "And we keep our valued assets safe."

Eddie held Marina's hand as they left the warehouse and shivered in the night fog. Decker could see the girl's eyes wandering, unable to find purchase. He looked at his friend.

"She's just on a different path, Decker—a different path."

Decker didn't say anything.

"Decker." He'd never heard Eddie's voice so centred, so strong—so angry.

"Okay. I buy that."

"Good. Now it's time for you to disappear as your rather large African-American friend suggested," Eddie said.

"I will. But one question?"

"Shoot."

"How'd you—"

"Get Marina back? Once I told my ex that Charendoff was soon going to be out of the picture she had no reason to resist."

"Why's that?"

"Charendoff was paying her to keep Marina. Without the assurance of his money . . . well, it was easy from there."

Eddie stepped out into the street and flagged down a cab. Holding open the back door, he motioned to Decker to climb in. Eddie slammed the door.

"Aren't you coming?"

"No. Decker—as I said, time for you to disappear, remember? So give it to me."

"What?"

"Love and Pain and the Dwarf in the Garden."

Decker took the script from his bag and handed it over to Eddie, who tore out a page and then handed it back to Decker, saying, "Time for you to be truly on your own, Decker. Remember, change cabs at least three times before you go wherever you're going." A moment, then, "Travel safe." Then he turned and Marina ran into his waiting arms.

In the back of the cab, Decker looked down at the camera in his hands and at the image of Seth asleep with his eyes open, then told the cab to drive to the famous skateboard spot by the water—Pier 7, where he had taken Seth when he was a boy, when the boy still loved skateboarding, when the boy still called him Daddy.

69

A STIFLE OF MR. IRA CHARENDOFF—AFTER

A LAWYER IS PARTICULARLY SURPRISED WHEN COPS BREAK INTO his home at five in the morning. Yslan thought it best to embarrass him in front of his wife, so she led a team of six NSA officers who demanded and got access to Ira Charendoff's $2 million plus home in Westchester County—on a formerly peaceful Sunday morning.

The man was so flabbergasted that it took him a full twenty minutes before he demanded a lawyer.

"For what?" his wife whispered.

"Shut up, Lissa," he barked.

"Do you use the PROMPTOR protocol?"

"I don't need to answer that question."

"Are you the programmer of the PROMPTOR protocol?"

He turned to his wife and said, "Don't say a word to these people."

"A word about what?" she whimpered.

But before Charendoff could say "a word about *anything*" Yslan held up the photo of the dead Stanstead boy encased in the icy river and said, "We have PROMPTOR anonymity protocols taken from your office computer that may contravene the Patriot Act and also imply that the protocol was used to cover up your involvement in the murder of Robert Irwin of Stanstead, Quebec."

Her eyes wide, his plump wife finally found her voice. "Who the fuck's Robert Irwin and what the fuck's the PROMPTOR protocol?"

Yslan held up her part of the bargain. Ira Charendoff was frog-marched to the police car in handcuffs and shackles. The car just happened to have left its siren blaring—just so the neighbours got to know that they had a felon in their midst.

Shortly thereafter, Yslan leaked details to Fox News, and Ira Charendoff's name and image quickly became synonymous with the word "traitor."

And then there were the indictments and Mr. Charendoff's being turfed from his Patchin Place law firm, then disbarred, then the mortgaging of his house to pay for his defence team. All the while dealing with his wife's divorce suit, which her lawyer informed her she should get on with "while there was still something to get" from the hide of one Ira Charendoff, late of Patchin Place, New York City, late of the legal profession—and still years away from a trial for conspiracy in the death of a seventeen-year-old boy in Stanstead, Quebec, and his involvement with the PROMPTOR protocol.

70

A MOTHER OF MANHUNTS—AFTER

THE MANHUNT FOR WALTER JONES WAS THE LARGEST EVER staged in the United States. Every television station showed his photo at the beginning of every newscast. Every newspaper had his face on the front page.

Distant relatives, some of whom had never met Walter, were rousted from their beds. The entire town of Stoney River was brought in to be interrogated—but nothing. Walter was an outsider to them, too. No one seemed to know anything substantial about him.

Finally a headwaiter from a fish restaurant three towns over called the police and said he remembered this Walter Jones person—and he had had a girl with him.

It took a day to figure out who the girl was and then two hours to track her down to her mother's house in Shaker Heights outside of Cleveland.

When they knocked on the door her mother was shocked, but Marcia Lavin was not. She calmly sat on the expensive chaise in the well-appointed living room. She wore a tank top that left her bra straps exposed and sweatpants that had the college's name stamped across her athletically trim butt.

"Do you know why we're here?" Yslan asked.

"The guy in the paper. The bomb guy."

"Right. Walter Jones."

Marcia giggled.

"Did I say something funny?" Yslan demanded.

"No," Marcia answered, "it's that it just occurred to me that when I went out with him I didn't even know his name."

"Tell us about going out with him."

"Sure." And she did. Meeting him outside the gym. Thinking he was working his way through school. Going to "that goofy restaurant." Pink champagne. Discovering he wasn't a student. The silent ride back to her dorm. "Finding the creep in my room and complaining to the college. Which did nothing."

"Who did you complain to?"

"My RA, who sent me to the student Complaints committee."

Yslan checked her notes and shook her head slowly.

"What?" Marcia asked.

"Professor Neil Frost chaired that committee, didn't he?"

"Another creep."

Marcia then began a rambling exegesis about male creeps, but Yslan wasn't listening. *So that's how Frost and Jones met,* she thought. *At least that question's answered. And if that's how they met, it's unlikely there's a third or fourth or fifth conspirator—let alone a cadre, whatever the fuck that is.*

Interpol chimed in. France claimed they'd captured him, but didn't have the right guy. Al-Qaeda websites claimed him as a sleeper operative, but this was quickly dismissed. Iran named a street in Tehran after him. But the weeks passed, and Walter Jones finally fell from the centre of public concern.

71

A REVERIE OF MR. WALTER JONES—AFTER

WALTER HAD GIVEN UP KICKING AT THE GRATING A LONG TIME ago. Maybe days ago—he couldn't remember. A long time after his pants had dried, anyways—and now even the smell of his pee was gone. And he hadn't taken a dump since that day near the beginning—way far from where he was now, looking down on the church like a god. And besides, now he was too tired to do much moving. It'd taken a lot of energy to get himself back up to the highest point of the tight ductwork. And now his face had been pressed against the grille work for—well, for he couldn't guess how long.

He only vaguely remembered seeing the president and all those people coming to praise his fine work. He'd hoped Marcia would be in the church, to tell her he was sorry about the pink champagne—really sorry.

But somehow, recently, Marcia Lavin had gotten into the duct-work. Funny how she could get in but he couldn't kick his way out. Funny that.

But he guessed it was just one of those things—things he knew other people understood but that he'd never be able to figure out.

But that was okay—yes it was. It didn't matter anymore that other people got things that he didn't.

He brought the perfume bottle to his nose and breathed deeply.

Cause now Marcia was with him all the time. Right here at his side, telling him that he was her guy and would always be her guy.

And he was surrounded by her—and even as he took his last rasping breath—he was the happiest he'd been in his whole life.

* * *

For several days after the president's eulogy, parishioners claimed they could smell perfume in the church. One went so far as to identify it as a very expensive brand.

But no one could figure out where the perfume smell came from, and after a few days it was gone.

And so the church proceeded in its business. The pastor gave sermons and the parishioners did their best not to look at their watches as he droned on, until one day months later in the depth of the summer heat, when the church's powerful air-conditioning system failed.

For three days a sour smell pervaded the space—and then, of course, there were all those flies.

Thousands and thousands and thousands of fat black flies that seemed to come out of the grating of the ductwork high up in the north ceiling of the sanctuary.

72

A SOLITAIRE OF MS. YSLAN HICKS—AFTER

AS SHE SAT IN THE DARKNESS OF THE WINDOWLESS ROOM IN which she had kept Viola Tripping on the Ancaster College campus, Yslan kept thinking of the video of the speaker for the dead talking to Decker Roberts.

"Are you of the clearing or not?" she heard Viola ask Decker. "Or are you of the enemy?"

An enemy of the clearing?

She clicked her BlackBerry on —it was the only light in the darkened room. On it she watched Decker Roberts' profile come into view. He was on a plane watching something on the monitor on the seat back in front of him.

Four computer commands later and she saw what he was watching—the Rayna YouTube video of her playing with Paul Simon. She watched closely, trying to understand why Decker was watching it over and over again.

She heard Viola Tripping ask, "Are you of the clearing?" then wondered if this Rayna was of the clearing. Was the Rothko Chapel in Houston of the clearing?

She sat back against the wall and clicked off her BlackBerry. The room was in absolute blackness as Viola Tripping had requested. For a moment she felt the weight of the girl/woman curling up on her lap, then she sensed herself slipping—to an interrogation room in Leavenworth Penitentiary where another one of her gifted synaesthetes sat scratching his arm, acting as if he'd just stuck his tongue in her mouth.

Evil fuck, she thought.

Then she thought back to Decker's comment about that Swedish film *Fanny and Alexander.* She grabbed her BlackBerry and called Mr. T's number.

"Boss?"

"Get me a Bergman film called *Fanny and Alexander.*"

"That's a bit chichi for you, isn't it?"

"Just get me the damned film!"

She heard Mr. T chuckle.

"What?" she demanded.

"It's downloading even as we speak. Should be on your Black-Berry in . . . two and a half minutes."

It wasn't until the end of the film that Yslan understood what Decker was talking about—that art doesn't come when there's just understanding and kindness, art demands the cruelty and stricture of the pastor in the film.

She immediately switched to the YouTube video of Rayna singing with Paul Simon and watched it again. There it was—Rayna's wildness only made art by the strict demands of the mathematics of the music. Black smashed up against white; cold attacking heat; salt and sugar together. Without the salt you can't taste the sugar. Cold is only the opposite of heat. White only exists as the diametric opposition of black. Without the opposite there is no there, there.

But was art, the profound mixing of good and evil, what Decker Roberts was about? Was that what being in the clearing meant?

No.

But it was the dangerous path through the woods to the clearing. Of that she was somehow sure. A perilous path that she was pretty sure she had to follow.

She flicked off her BlackBerry and sat in the darkness for a long time. Then she began to shiver. There was a way not to take the path. Sure there was. There was no turning back, but there was a way off the path. Or was it just another path—the anchorite's path.

Stories of anchorites had terrified her as a little girl, and she hadn't thought of them for years. But here in the darkness it occurred to her that perhaps an anchorite's willingness to utterly retreat from the world—to allow herself to be walled into a windowless, doorless room in the side of a church—was her path to safety. A way that they didn't have to take the path in the woods. To leave being bewildered behind. To sidestep the world.

She held up her BlackBerry and turned it on. The screen cast a dim tent of light on the cement floor. She slid her other hand into the light—pale skin, slender tapering fingers, a hand alone.

Alone. Like she was as a little girl. A girl who called herself Solitaire.

She leaned back against the cold wall and heard the buzz of the locusts from so long ago.

She felt like crying. So, for the first time in a very long time—Solitaire did.

73

A WAKENING OF A LEAVENWORTH CONVICT: YSLAN'S THIRD GIFTED SYNAESTHETE—AFTER

MARTIN ARMISTAAD WOKE WITH A START. HE'D SENSED THE SHIFT for several days, but now it was pronounced. Things were in motion. Alignments were being switched and worlds were attempting to refind their balance.

He smiled. Oh yes, this was worth smiling about.

He had no idea what the time was, but it had to be late—only coarse snores broke the unusual silence.

Prisons are noisy places—all metal and cement, all anger and fear.

He walked to the bars of his cell and wrapped his fingers around them, then slowly moved his hands up and down—up and down— and with the worlds trying to realign he was able to feel the molecular structure of the metal, atoms attached to atoms, linked electrons intertwined and keeping steel, steel.

He bent his head back and allowed his mind to touch dreaming as his fingers continued to move—and feel.

And there it was. He gave a quick jerk and the bonds that held the atoms together sundered, and Martin Armistaad, convicted felon, one of Special Agent Yslan Hick's gifted synaesthetes, was at large—and heading toward the clearing.

74

A SPINNING OF MS. VIOLA TRIPPING—AFTER

VIOLA SENSED IT TOO.

As she stared out the window of her small room in the heart of Iowa farm country, she shivered. The moon was just beginning its growth, but there was something wrong—maybe not wrong, but different, and she felt it.

She pulled a shawl around her shoulders and stepped outside. The corn was already growing and the wind made the tassels sing to her—like her mother had done so very long ago.

She moved her right hand, the one she'd held Decker's hand with, and brought it to her nose. She smelled him on her skin—her father, on her skin.

A star shot across the cloudless sky, and she wondered if it was . . . well, if it was a message from her to Decker to be careful. That there are dangers in the clearing—so many dangers. But only if you are in the clearing can you find the crystal house.

The wind suddenly stopped.

A dense quiet fell upon the land, and Viola shivered.

Was it coming?

Was it?

And could she defeat it this time, or would it take her from the clearing, through the portal, to the scaffold—like those young boys.

75

A CONSPIRACY OF MR. LEONARD HARRISON—AFTER

LEONARD HARRISON SAT IN HIS OFFICE IN WASHINGTON AND twirled an expensive fountain pen back and forth through his fingers as he watched the world outside his window, knowing that the world he saw was not the only world there was.

He'd known it for years. It was why he'd insisted on the gifted synaesthetes program and arranged for Yslan Hicks to run it.

But now things were moving too quickly.

Decker in flight, Viola in hiding, Martin Armistaad on the loose— and Special Agent Yslan Hicks suspecting that there are more things in this world than are dreamt of in any philosophy.

He lit a filterless Camel, breathed deeply and pondered his next move.

76

A DREAM OF SETH ROBERTS—BENEATH

HE WAS DEEP IN HIS DREAM—DEEPER THAN HE'D EVER BEEN.

Hours ago he'd "awakened" in his dream and did his usual test. He willed his hand up into his line of dream vision—and there it was. He waggled his fingers at himself and felt himself smiling. Then, he willed his hand upward and his vision rose. And he'd traveled—traveled farther than he'd ever traveled. Through a great wood. Through a clearing broad and sun filled.

Then he saw it—and moved toward it.

This was new, very new.

Then he jumped in his dream and was in a Renaissance building of some sort, a circular building leading to a high dome. He willed his hand to circle and his vision circled with it—a perfectly cylindrical building.

Then he saw the slash of light across the floor and followed it to a small open door.

He turned his hand, and he moved toward it.

Emerging from the door, he momentarily couldn't see—the sun was so bright and bouncing off something, something large.

He averted his eyes—and saw it.

A huge glass building. A diamond of a building shimmering in the sun, like a huge Victorian greenhouse—a house of glass. A simple thought popped into his head: *A diamond.*

He willed his hand forward and he followed, through the glass door into the heart of the diamond. And as he stepped there he heard music, single notes that cascaded down from the ceiling in full chords.

He turned and realised the single notes were coming from his mouth and the chords coming back down from the ceiling were enwrapping him, lifting him, and he was almost weightless.

Then he bent his knees and leapt, and he was looking at himself from outside the clear glass building and he was spinning slowly, arms outstretched. Then his breath was taken from him as he inverted and spun slowly—head down, arms out—as a beautiful diamond inside the diamond of his dream.

Then he heard the old woman's voice, a voice that although he knew he'd never heard it before was as familiar as the sound of the waves against the pebbles on a Vancouver Island beach:

For fear of nightmares, humanity is abandoning dreaming. You have been chosen, Seth—chosen to maintain dreaming in a world that shortly will dream no more.

And over and over he heard the voice—and round and round he turned, upside down, arms spread wide, in the midst of the diamond—and finally knew the path that was chosen for him.

You have been chosen, Seth, to maintain dreaming in a world that shortly will dream no more.

Shortly will dream no more.

Dream no more.

Dream no more.

Dream no more.

Now, Seth, dream the dream of the future—of that which you will bring into being.

A SOLITUDE OF MR. DECKER ROBERTS—BEYOND

DECKER LOOKED DESPERATELY FOR SOLACE. FOR A MOMENT OF peace in a world gone crazy. A son in the clutches of a madman, his own life—now that he knew what had happened in that igloo all those years ago—spiralling violently out of control. And now him in flight yet again, but this time running—to hide, to find a moment of relief, to . . . he didn't know what.

On the endless plane ride he purchased Internet access and went to the YouTube video Eddie had noted in his script of *Love and Pain and the Dwarf in the Garden* in what seemed like years ago, back in their hotel room in Las Vegas.

Paul Simon was playing a concert in Toronto and someone called out "Play *Duncan*" and then a woman shouted, "I learned how to play the guitar to that song." And Paul Simon said, "You learned how to play the guitar to this song?" She answered yes, and Paul Simon said, "Well then, come up."

And she did.

A T-shirted woman in her middle thirties named Rayna stumbled up to the stage, her hands openly trembling, fingers all atwitch—but when Simon handed her a guitar she put the strap over her shoulder, fingered her long lank hair behind her ears, and a delight bloomed on her face as she fell into a deep present tense.

At first there was only awe on her face, but it was quickly re-placed by glory when she realised that she was going to actually play with Paul Simon.

And although she flubbed an opening chord change she

persevered and joy—sheer joy, wild joy, ecstatic joy, God's wind filling her—pulled her head up into the pure air of the jet stream, and
she sang, and flew.

And when she came to the fourth verse where she took him to the
woods, she sang the line:

Here comes something and it feels so good

and she screamed in ecstasy, a garden of gifts around her, the
profound opening of music in her.

Decker played it over and over again—marvelled, cried and
laughed at the same time and hoped that at some time in his life he'd
feel the freedom of flight she felt. Although on the Boeing 747 he felt
a captive as it plunged through the night, an unwieldy falcon carrying him back to Windhoek, Namibia—and an uncertain future.

Like Tom Hanks at the end of *Cast Away,* Decker allowed the rented
Jeep to lead him. Of course in Namibia there weren't that many
choices.

He followed Highway 1 for days, sleeping in his vehicle with the
Southern Cross above him and Scorpio rising. In the morning the
Hindi people's oddly magical mannequins appeared from somewhere beside his car. Each morning with the pale moon on the horizon he left money in the pouches of the statues then got back in his
car, and drove.

Just past nightfall on the fifth day he approached the junction of
Highways 1 and 6, where there was a rest spot—a petrol station, a
gift shop, and a bakery that smelled of fresh-cooked apple pies.

As he got out of the Jeep he saw a large white man blowing the
Namibian dust off his hands with an air compressor used for filling
tires.

The man looked up and saw Decker, and his large round face
turned dark and stern. Then words came from his mouth. "Welcome
to Solitaire, Mr. Roberts. I've waited a long time for your coming. I'm
glad you finally found your path."

ACKNOWLEDGMENTS

I'd like to thank my valued friend, talented director at the University of Cape Town and tour guide extraordinaire, Geoffrey Hyland, for insisting that I see Namibia. There are places of real magic in the world—Namibia is one of them—and I would never have discovered it without Geoff's help. I'd also like to thank the teachers of Pro Actors Lab—Rae Ellen, Glen, Marvin, John and Bruce—who worked overtime at the studio while I banged away on my computer keyboard. As well the many talented acting students that it has been my privilege to teach over these now twenty-plus years. Finally, my attorney/agent Michael Levine who has been in my corner for a very long time; Alison Clarke from Simon & Schuster Canada whose tireless work on the manuscript helped me wrestle this one to the page; and Kevin Hanson of Simon & Schuster Canada whose belief in my writing has been so important to me.

DAVID ROTENBERG has published five Zhong Fong novels, police procedurals set in modern day Shanghai (*Hua Shan Hospital Murders* was short-listed for best Canadian mystery); an historical novel *Shanghai, the Ivory Compact* (that reached the best seller list); and the first of the novels in the Junction Chronicles series, *The Placebo Effect,* which received rave reviews. He has directed on Broadway, for regional theatres, and for television. He has run a major American regional theatre and adapted several famous novels for the stage— the latest an adaptation of *The Great Gatsby* that opened a new theatre in downtown Toronto. He has been a master acting teacher for more than twenty years. He is the founder and artistic director of Pro Actors Lab, which draws actors from all over the world; the list of his students reads like a who's who of North American stars. He lives in Toronto with his wife, Susan Santiago.